"[An] engrossing legal thriller. . . . Gripping court-room scenes, crisp details of the legal system, vividly realized local color, and a nuanced portrait of the close-knit community, including Marty's personal life, all add up to a satisfying, often poignant debut novel. Recommend Connors to fans of Perri O'Shaughnessy and Lisa Scottoline."

—*Booklist*

"Gripping . . . Connors writes with an immediate, photographic intensity, and the characters will stay with you. A truly unique talent."

—Deborah Crombie, author of *A Finer End*

"There are many twists here and the climax is harrowing and truly surprising."

—*Romantic Times*

BOOKS BY ROSE CONNORS

Absolute Certainty
Temporary Sanity

Available from POCKET BOOKS

ROSE CONNORS

TEMPORARY SANITY

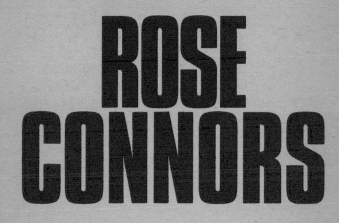

POCKET BOOKS
New York   London   Toronto   Sydney

This book is a work of fiction. Names, characters, places and incidents are products of the author's imagination or are used fictitiously. Any resemblance to actual events or locales or persons, living or dead, is entirely coincidental.

 POCKET BOOKS, a division of Simon & Schuster, Inc. 1230 Avenue of the Americas, New York, NY 10020

Copyright © 2003 by Rose Connors

Previously published in hardcover in 2003 by Scribner

All rights reserved, including the right to reproduce this book or portions thereof in any form whatsoever. For information address Scribner, 1230 Avenue of the Americas, New York, NY 10020

ISBN: 0-7434-4882-0

First Pocket Books printing July 2004

10 9 8 7 6 5 4 3 2 1

POCKET and colophon are registered trademarks of Simon & Schuster, Inc.

Cover design by Jae Song

Manufactured in the United States of America

For information regarding special discounts for bulk purchases, please contact Simon & Schuster Special Sales at 1-800-456-6798 or business@simonandschuster.com

For my son, Dave,
who shouldered this difficult year
with quiet courage and uncommon resolve.

ACKNOWLEDGMENTS

It really does take a village.

Heartfelt thanks to: Garland Alcock, M.D., for extraordinary insight into the human mind and body; the Chatham Writers' Guild, for meticulous critiques and rowdy lunches; the first-class staff of the Barnstable Law Library—Martha Elkins, Janet Banks, and Mareda Flood—for endless professional and moral support; Sara Young—you know what you did.

Humble thanks to Susanne Kirk, the mystery world's premiere editor, and to Nancy Yost, the finest literary agent an author could hope to find.

And to my family, of course, thanks for everything.

TEMPORARY SANITY

1879. I asked Janet, the law librarian, where I might find a thorough discussion of the temporary insanity plea, and she referred me to a case decided in January of 1879.

"That's too old," I told her. "I'm looking for a more recent decision, one that explains why we preserve the defense, one that addresses the current philosophy supporting it."

Janet climbed the ladder, then, to the top shelf, and pulled out a book so decrepit that portions of its dark brown binding fell in flakes to the library floor as she descended. She opened the yellowed pages to a case already flagged with a sheet of folded notepad paper. Apparently, she'd been asked this question before.

She flipped through the first portion of the decision, then pointed to the center of a page and handed the fragile book to me. "Mr. Justice Paxson gave it a lot of thought," she said. "Read." And so I did.

> We are obliged by the force of authority to say to you that there is such a disease known to the law as homicidal insanity.
>
> What it is, or in what it consists, no lawyer or judge has ever yet been able to explain with precision.

1

Janet was heading back to her desk when I looked up, but she paused to cast a meaningful glance over her shoulder. I got the message. A hundred and twenty-five years have passed. And nothing's changed.

Chapter I

⫼

Monday, December 20

"Your client is a vigilante, Martha. He blew a man away on live television, for Christ's sake. We'll get murder one at trial; the jury won't have any choice. Murder two is a gift. I can't do any better than that."

Geraldine Schilling points a finger-gun at me and fires. She's the newly elected District Attorney in Barnstable County, a jurisdiction that includes all the towns on Cape Cod. She's our first female DA, and she won the election by a landslide with her "tough on crime" campaign. She plans to improve her margin the next time around. And she thinks this case will help her do it.

Technically, Geraldine is still the First Assistant to the incumbent District Attorney, Rob Mendell. His term won't expire until the end of this month. Geraldine's been the First Assistant for eighteen years now, and I worked with her for ten of them, until about six months ago. This is the first time I've looked at Geraldine from the opposite side of the table. She's formidable.

Some prosecutors—maybe even Rob Mendell—would go easy on my client. This is no ordinary case. But not Geraldine. And the fact that she's not yet sworn in as top dog is of little consequence. Geraldine Schilling is in charge around here. She always has been.

"Then why did you call me, Geraldine? What is there to discuss?"

She's been on her feet throughout our meeting; Geraldine almost never sits down. She stares at me from behind her imposing oak desk, perhaps considering my question, more likely trying to decide if I'm bluffing. She drags hard on her cigarette, stubs it out in a crowded ashtray on the desktop, and folds her thin arms across her tailored jacket. She doesn't answer, though. She tilts her blond head to one side and half-smiles. Her pale green eyes dart over my shoulder as she blows a steady stream of smoke my way.

I don't have to turn around to know that Geraldine's new sidekick, the soon-to-be First Assistant, is about to join us. J. Stanley Edgarton III always clears his throat before he speaks. It's an annoying practice designed to alert all of us that his words are coming, lest we miss one of them.

"Reality, Attorney Nickerson," he drones at my back. "Perhaps we should discuss reality."

Geraldine hired Stanley a month ago—stole him,

actually, from the New Bedford office—to replace me. A meticulous, prissy sort of man, he leaves behind an enviable track record. Stanley tried a dozen homicide cases during his eight-year career in New Bedford. He won them all. He doesn't intend to lose this one.

"You do have some grasp on reality, don't you, Attorney Nickerson?"

Geraldine's office is spacious, but Stanley positions himself so that the tips of his tasseled shoes almost touch my boots. He does it on purpose. He's always too close, always making me feel there isn't enough oxygen in the room for both of us.

I move away from him and head for the door. "If that's the best you can do, Geraldine, we're going to trial."

Stanley inserts himself in my path. "And your client's defense, Attorney Nickerson, what might that be?"

My silent glare doesn't deter him. He sidles toward me, eliminating the space I had put between us, and picks up a videotape from the edge of Geraldine's orderly desk. He holds it in front of my face for a moment—as if I might not otherwise notice—before he moves toward the VCR.

"Perhaps it's . . . *Gee, I didn't mean to gun him down in front of so many people.* That's a good defense."

Stanley pops the tape into the slot and watches intently, a savage glee in his eyes, as the television screen lights up. He's seen this tape before, of course. We all have.

"Or maybe it's . . . *Oops, I just meant to stand there holding the weapon.* That might work."

Stanley sports a vicious smile as an olive green military chopper appears on the small screen, descending to the only runway at Chatham Municipal Airport. When it lands, Stanley turns away from the TV and watches me instead.

A half dozen squad cars, and at least as many press vans, greet the chopper. Its door opens and Hector Monteros emerges, hands cuffed behind his back. He begins his descent to the floodlit runway, an armed guard on the steps ahead of him, another right behind. All three men lean forward, into the wind. The first hint of dawn is on the horizon.

In the lower-right corner of the screen, behind the wall of police cruisers and press vans, Buck Hammond steps from the hangar's shadow. He's my client. He stands perfectly still until Monteros and his escorts reach the runway. Then he raises a hunting rifle and fires. Monteros drops like a felled tree.

Stanley's still smiling. "Or maybe it's . . . *Darn, I didn't realize those TV cameras were rolling.* Now, there's a defense. One of my favorites."

Stanley is shorter than I am—he's shorter than most people, for that matter—and I examine the top of his bulbous head before I respond. Sparse, almost colorless hair parts just above his right ear, long strands of it combed over his pink scalp, the wispy ends just touching the top of his left ear. Beneath his vast forehead sit muddy brown eyes, too small for the head that holds them, too dark for the pasty skin that surrounds them.

6

He smiles up at me, apparently delighted by his own humor, revealing tiny, discolored teeth. "You people . . . ," he says, shaking his head, a thick vein pulsing across his forehead. I've noticed that vein before; it turns blue when he's mad. And J. Stanley Edgarton III seems to get mad a lot.

Stanley has been calling us "you people" since he got here. New Bedford is only about thirty miles away, just on the other side of the bridge, but Stanley seems to regard Cape Codders—some of us, anyway—as an alien species. He turns his back to me, flicks off the TV, and wipes his hands together. I'm dismissed.

Members of the New Bedford defense bar warned us about Stanley. He's an odd one, to put it mildly. He takes pride in being the first person in the courtroom each day, they report. He greets all trial participants upon their arrival, thereby establishing himself as the man in charge. For lay witnesses, people unfamiliar with courtroom procedure, Stanley even assigns seats. He is, in his own mind, one powerful fellow.

It's going to be a long week.

"See you tomorrow," I tell him.

Stanley faces me again, still shaking his large skull, his expression suggesting he pities my inability to see the light. "Looking forward to it." His forehead vein throbs steadily.

I head for the office door, hoping I've dropped no hint of how worried I am. Buck Hammond had his reasons. And Monteros got precisely what he deserved. But that videotape is damning.

Geraldine leans across her desk toward Stanley as I

head for her office door. I catch her words just before the heavy wooden door slams shut behind me. "Don't underestimate her," she says. I can't help but smile. Coming from Geraldine Schilling, that's high praise indeed.

CHAPTER 2

Harry Madigan's last day with the Barnstable County Public Defender's office was November 1. He planned to take a month off before opening his private practice. After twenty years, he said, it was time for a real vacation. Real or not, it lasted all of four days. And he never got off-Cape.

Barnstable County's troubled residents—those who live on the edge when they're not confined to county facilities—know Harry well. Some have been with him his entire career. They trust him. They filled his office, and his file cabinets, before he hung out his shingle.

Joining him was like throwing a life ring to a drowning man. No thought required. I wasn't eager to return to practice after my years with the DA's office, and

Harry knew that. But when he approached me about Buck Hammond's case, I had no choice. Harry knew that, too.

Sometimes I think Harry knows me better than I do. He knew I'd fight Buck's battle, knew I'd view Buck's act as justifiable homicide. We have a problem, though. Our criminal justice system doesn't see it that way.

The system hasn't yet acknowledged certain basic human truths. One of them explains the single shot Buck Hammond fired at the Chatham Municipal Airport. Our only hope is that a jury of Buck's peers will rise to the occasion—set the rules aside, if necessary— to reach a just result. Juries do that sometimes.

Hector Monteros raped and murdered Buck Hammond's seven-year-old son. Monteros was in police custody, charged with the crimes, when Buck fired the now infamous shot that took Monteros down. And he did it while two dozen people looked on, half of them police officers.

Evening news anchors and editorial columnists have been asking since: "How could this have happened?" My question is different. I wonder why it doesn't happen every day, every time a child is victimized.

It shouldn't have happened, of course. Buck Hammond shouldn't have taken matters into his own hands. He should have let the system work, should have allowed Monteros to stand trial for his crimes.

Monteros would have been convicted. The DNA evidence against him was conclusive. He'd have spent the rest of his miserable days in a cell at Walpole, the Commonwealth's maximum security penitentiary.

10

And perhaps that would have been a more just result. Generally speaking, inmates don't take kindly to child murderers.

That's what should have happened. That's the way our society should function. But I'm not prepared to condemn Buck Hammond for what he did. It wasn't my son in the morgue.

Buck's defense is an uphill battle, of course, and it isn't made any easier by the fact that he shot Monteros while three television cameras were rolling. All cases have problems, but Buck's has more than its share.

Harry was appointed to defend Buck Hammond on the day of the shooting. Buck was assigned a new lawyer when Harry announced his resignation from the Public Defender's office, but neither Buck nor his family was happy about it. They wanted Harry back; no one else would do.

The relatives raised enough money to pay the initial retainer and asked Harry to meet with them. Harry said yes, of course; he's never been able to say no to an underdog. They met at his new, not yet opened law office on the Friday of his first week of vacation. By the end of the meeting, Harry's long-anticipated vacation was over.

After more than an hour of discussion with the extended family, Harry agreed to refile his appearance and resume Buck Hammond's defense. Lucky for Buck. Geraldine Schilling made Buck the poster boy for lawless behavior during her campaign, calling him the Vigilante at every press conference. She put his case on a fast track; trial was six weeks away.

When Harry emerged from his office with Buck's relatives that Friday, he found a dozen people in the waiting room. And he knew most of them. He'd parked his old Jeep Wrangler in the front driveway, visible from Main Street. His regular clients pulled in and parked too. And they brought a few friends.

He called later than usual that night. He couldn't do it, he said. No one could. In one day, he'd opened more files than any solo practitioner could handle. He would have to call Buck Hammond's relatives and reverse his decision. He couldn't possibly carry this workload and be ready to try a murder-one case in six weeks. Unless, of course, he had a partner.

Even at the time, I knew Harry was playing a trump card. He'd been hounding me for weeks about joining the practice. I wasn't ready, I kept telling him. I didn't think I'd be any good at defense work. I didn't want to be pressured into a decision. In Buck Hammond's case, though, there was no decision to make. Harry knew that. I showed up for work the next day, and it happened to be Saturday.

Within the week, we lured Kevin Kydd away from the District Attorney's office. Geraldine is still sore about it; she hasn't replaced him yet. That means she's stuck in the courtroom more often than she'd like. It means she isn't available, at times, for the important things. Political rallies. Press conferences. Fundraisers.

Geraldine has every right to be sore about losing her associate. The Kydd, as we call him, is a year and a half out of law school and probably the hardest-working young lawyer in Massachusetts. Any firm in the Commonwealth would hire him in a heartbeat. But Harry and I made him an offer he couldn't refuse: long hours, longer headaches, and a salary with no way to go but up.

The Kydd gave Geraldine notice and joined us two weeks later. He went straight to work on the misdemeanors. Harry focused on the felonies. And I took on Buck Hammond.

Harry and I will try Buck's case together—the relatives wanted him, after all—but I will take the laboring oar. Harry is swamped with other matters, and I have devoted my time exclusively to Buck. Now, the day before trial, Buck is as ready as he's ever going to be to face the first-degree murder charge against him. So am I. I head back to the office anyway, though, to think it all through again, and again after that.

Harry is holed up in his office with Theodore Chase when I arrive. Steady Teddy, as he's known on the streets, is charged with trafficking cocaine in a school zone. This is his third drug offense, and, if convicted, he faces a hefty jail term. Steady's pretrial conference is scheduled for this afternoon and Harry, I'm certain, is trying to persuade him at least to consider a plea bargain. Harry and I both worry about this one. Steady Teddy isn't a guy most Barnstable County jurors will like.

The Kydd has two clients seated in folding chairs in the front office, waiting to see him, but he's fielding phone calls when I arrive. The cash flow won't support a secretary yet—generally speaking, our clients aren't high rollers—so the attorneys here answer their own phones, type their own pleadings, and open their own mail. It's a no-frills operation. "Lean and mean," Harry calls it.

Lean and mean though it may be, our practice is housed in a charming building, an antique farmhouse on Main Street in South Chatham. Harry chose that location, he said, so I would have the world's easiest commute. I told him to forget it. I wouldn't rush back into practice, I said, not even if he set up shop in my backyard. He bought the old farmhouse anyway.

And it suits him. South Chatham is a gem of a village, a seaside community of quaint shingled cottages and owner-occupied small businesses. Harry's farmhouse was built in 1840 and it wears all the charm of that era; its original wide-pine floors are still in place, uneven and sloping through every room. Our clients are comfortable here in a way they would not be in the wealthier areas of Chatham. Their tired pickup trucks and work vans aren't so glaringly misplaced here.

Harry and the Kydd both have offices on the first floor, on either side of our only conference room, a space with a large brick fireplace and built-in ovens. It served as the keeping room when the house was used as a residence. I work in a small, pine-paneled office on the west end of the second floor, a rustic, airy room with a view over the treetops to Taylor's Pond, and beyond that to Nantucket Sound. Harry lives in the rest of the second-floor space. Turns out he's the one with the world's easiest commute.

I'm barely seated when the Kydd clambers up the steep staircase. I know it's the Kydd because he always takes the steps two at a time, and my middle-aged partner doesn't.

The Kydd bursts into the room with his usual air of urgency. "Can't stay," he warns, both hands in the air. "People waiting. But I have to know. What'd ol' Geraldine have to offer?" His grin expands when he mentions his former boss.

The Kydd's speech drops no hint that he ever left Georgia. He's slender and tall, but his posture is poor; his shoulders are stooped. "Stand up straight," I always tell him, but he never does. Instead, he routinely gives me his slow, Southern grin and says, "Gert." Gert, he finally admitted last week, is his great-aunt, the nag. I haven't told him to stand up straight since.

"Murder two," I tell him now.

"What does Buck say?"

"Buck says no."

He grins again, pointing his pen at me. "What do you say?"

The Kydd is a quick study. He assumes more and more responsibility each day, it seems, taking on clients Harry and I would otherwise have to turn away. He learned the basics from me, in the DA's office. Now he's learning from Harry how to blend that competence with a tough compassion. Our clients are, for the most part, people battered by life and baffled by the system. Handling them is something of an art form, and Harry has it mastered.

I take off my glasses and consider the Kydd's question. "I don't know," I tell him honestly. "My crystal ball is cloudy this week."

"Well, are you ready?" he asks, already turning back toward the staircase.

"Nobody's ever ready for trial, Kydd, you know that. But I'm as close as I'm going to get."

The Kydd rolls out his Southern grin from the top step. "You're ready," he tells me. "My crystal ball says Stanley's about to meet his match."

I start to thank him for his vote of confidence, but the look on his face stops me. His eyes dart from me to the first floor and back to me again. He utters one word before he disappears. "Trouble."

CHAPTER 3

The Kydd takes the entire staircase in three strides. I follow as fast as I can. The door to the front office is wide open, a raw northeast wind blowing snow inside, papers flying everywhere. A stack of files on the edge of the Kydd's desk slides to the floor.

The waiting clients are on their feet, easing a tall, wafer-thin woman into the Kydd's high-backed leather desk chair. She's coatless and it's freezing. Her face is swollen and bruised. Her white blouse is blood-spattered and open in front, the top buttons torn off. Her lower lip bleeds profusely, a dark red stream running down her neck and pooling at her collar.

The men part to let me through, and I see at once that her right arm is broken. It hangs from her shoulder at a tortured angle, the wrist taking a brutal bend.

17

I take off my suit jacket and cover her chest, press my handkerchief against her lips.

"Who did this to you?" My own hands suddenly tremble.

Her eyes meet mine, but she doesn't answer.

The Kydd reappears with a makeshift ice pack in a kitchen towel and an old blanket from the hallway closet. I replace my saturated handkerchief with the ice pack and cover the thin woman up to her neck with the worn blanket.

"Who did this to you?" I ask again, holding the ice pack away from her mouth so she can answer.

Her eyes dart around the room before she speaks. "My husband," she whispers finally, "but he didn't mean it. It was the drink. He didn't mean it."

Swell. That's great. This scenario had walked into the DA's office more than once during the years I worked there. She defends the bastard even before she's sewn up. By sunset, she remembers falling down a flight of stairs.

"How did you get here?" I ask, pressing the ice to her lips. She points behind me with her good hand, the left one, and I turn to see a skinny teenage girl wearing silver hoop earrings and a faded denim outfit, gnawing a thumbnail. She can't possibly be old enough to drive—not legally, anyway. I decide not to inquire, the hallmark of a good defense lawyer, Harry says.

"Your father did this?" I ask instead.

The skinny girl gives up her thumbnail reluctantly. "He's not my father." She shakes her head. "And he's not her husband either. She just says that. Like he's some kind of prize."

18

Harry rushes into the front office, Steady Teddy following at a slower, almost leisurely, pace. Steady's light gray suit, a fine Italian cut, probably cost more than all of Harry's suits put together. Steady has a narrow build, and he's about four inches shorter than Harry's six-foot frame, but he wears enough gold around his neck to stoop a much larger man. He stays behind Harry, adjusting his shiny watchband, looking away from the injured woman in the chair.

Imagine that. Steady Teddy doesn't want to get involved.

Harry, though, moves to the woman's side without a word and takes her pulse, one of those skills career criminal defense lawyers master somehow. "She's not in shock," he says, his eyes moving from the wall clock to the ice compress on the woman's bleeding lip. "But she's got to get to a hospital."

Harry looks to the Kydd. "I'm due in court in an hour. Can you take her?"

The Kydd's eyes widen and he gestures helplessly to the two men who've been waiting to see him since I got here. Harry's eyes move to mine, but he doesn't ask. He knows how anxious I am about tomorrow's trial.

"I'll call the rescue squad," he says.

The woman pushes the kitchen-towel compress away and tries to get out of the chair, but she falls back against it almost at once. "No," she cries. "No ambulance. No rescue squad. I won't go with them."

"She won't go in an ambulance," the teenage daughter confirms, her eyes rolling to the ceiling. She shakes her head again and sighs. "Never mind," she says. "Forget it. I'll take her."

The mother sobs now, leaning to one side in the chair, her good arm over her eyes. "He didn't mean it," she repeats. "He didn't. He had too much to drink, that's all. He loses his temper when he drinks that much. He didn't mean to hurt anybody. He probably won't even remember."

Harry lifts the telephone receiver, but I press my hand over the keypad before he can punch in the numbers. "I'll take her," I tell him. "I'll take her to Cape Cod Hospital. But that's all, Harry. I can't do any more than that. You can't either. Not with Buck's trial starting tomorrow."

Harry presses the receiver against the front of his suit jacket, looking like a schoolboy about to pledge allegiance to the flag. "Okay," he says. "I'll call and tell them you're coming."

The Kydd and his two clients struggle to raise the thin woman from the chair without hurting her arm. My suit jacket falls to the floor, but she manages to hold on to the blanket and the ice compress. The men wrap the blanket carefully around her shoulders before guiding her out to the porch, down the front steps, and across the snow-covered lawn toward my ancient Thunderbird.

The teenage daughter follows without a word, her thin denim jacket wide open in the winter wind. She looks back at me from the bottom step and when our eyes meet, it hits me. Something is wrong with this picture.

The young girl brought her bleeding mother to a law office. Not a hospital; not even a doctor's office. A law office.

Somewhere in the depths of my stomach I register a once familiar tightness. A few seconds pass before I can name it: it's the onset of dread.

I hurry up the old staircase, grab my parka from the hook at the top, and head back down. I'm almost out the door when Harry catches up to me. "Marty," he says.

I pause in the doorway. Harry's rugged features are worried. He feels it too. Something isn't right here. There's a reason this skinny teenage girl brought her battered mother to us.

He cups the side of my face in his big hand the way he always does now. "Be careful" is all he says.

CHAPTER 4

The Kydd and his helpers install the long woman in a prone position on the backseat of the Thunderbird, leaving her sullen daughter with no choice but to ride shotgun. When I get behind the wheel, she moves to the far edge of her seat and stares out the side window. I look to the rear, where the mother has her eyes closed, her left arm once again slung over her face. The blanket lies across her chest, the cold compress against her mouth.

I look out my own window at the Kydd as I start the car and turn both the heat and the defrost on high. He shrugs his stooped shoulders at me and grins. "Good luck," he says.

If we don't hit traffic, we'll reach Cape Cod Hospital in little more than half an hour. For the first ten minutes, the teenager beside me doesn't utter a word. She keeps her face turned away, her thumbnail back between her teeth. Her limp, dirty-blond hair hangs forward, almost covering the fine features of her profile.

"I'm Marty Nickerson," I finally say to her. "What's your name?"

She turns toward me, looking surprised to see me here, as if she assumed the car had been driving itself to the hospital. "I know who you are," she says, so quietly I can barely hear. "I saw you on the news all weekend."

The news. Stanley and I argued pretrial motions in Buck Hammond's case on Friday. The press was all over us. They were even worse with Buck's wife. One group of reporters essentially held her hostage in the courthouse hallway; I had to elbow my way in for the rescue.

My head aches all over again as I remember the mobbed courtroom, the microphones outstretched to receive Stanley's caustic comments, the camera lights blinding all of us. Buck's trial promises to be nothing short of a circus.

I look back at my soft-spoken passenger, still turned toward me. Her eyes aren't quite focused, like those of someone under hypnosis. "I'm Maggie," she says after a pause, and it occurs to me that Harry should have checked her pulse as well. "Maggie Baker," she adds.

She turns toward the rear seat, then looks back at me. "That's my mother, Sonia Baker. Don't even think about calling her Sonny. She hates it when people do."

"Okay." I'm grateful for even this tidbit of volunteered information.

Maggie turns away again, so I check on her mother in the rearview mirror. Sonia Baker appears to be asleep—eyes closed, breathing deep and regular—though it's hard for me to believe that's possible under the circumstances.

I'd like to ask Maggie why she brought her injured mother to our law office, but something tells me to wait, to move slowly here. This young girl, nothing but tough and surly until just moments ago, now seems vulnerable, fragile even.

"Where do you and your mom live?" I'm hoping to stay on neutral territory a little longer.

Maggie twirls one long strand of fine hair around her right index finger; she's distracted. "On Bayview Road," she says after a while. "You know where it is."

I nod, aware that Maggie's response was a statement, not a question.

Bayview Road intersects with the east end of Forest Beach Road, just a stone's throw from Buck Hammond's cottage. I've been there at least a dozen times during the past six weeks, visiting Buck's wife, Patty, eliciting the awful, necessary details. Preparing her—to the extent possible—for Buck's trial, for the ordeal she will have to endure on the witness stand, the nightmare she will have to relive, this time in public.

The entire Forest Beach area is a magnet for summer tourists. Its beaches are wild and pristine, vast stretches of white sand punctuated by rugged black jetties, year-round favorite sunning spots for hundreds of harbor seals. The cottages in the Forest Beach neighborhood are quaint, but small; most aren't winterized. The year-round residents are few and far between.

"You must know Buck Hammond, then," I say to Maggie. "You're practically neighbors."

"We know Buck. Mom and I both know Patty and Buck. He's in big trouble, isn't he?"

"Yes, he is."

She shakes her head. "It's not fair," she says, her small voice growing strong for the first time. "After what that creep did to their little boy."

I agree, of course, but say nothing.

Minutes pass before I summon the courage to broach the matter at hand. "Maggie," I ask, "the man who did this to your mother, what's his name?"

"Howard," she says to the dashboard. "Howard Davis."

I catch my breath before I can stop myself, but Maggie doesn't seem to notice. She looks back at her mother, then closes her eyes and shakes her head again, letting out a short, bitter laugh. "Mom calls him Howie, if you can believe that."

I know Howard Davis; he's been a Barnstable County parole officer for two decades. He's an enormous hulk—he hardly seems human—with a booming voice and an intimidating stance. He routinely handles the most dangerous of the county's parolees; he's the only employee on staff with any chance of keeping them in line. The first time I saw Howard Davis, in the courthouse hallway with one of his clients, I was at a complete loss. There was no way to tell which one was the ex-con.

Sonia Baker is lucky she's breathing. And Howard Davis is going to jail, parole officer or not. I don't say either of those things to Maggie, though. She doesn't need any more drama at the moment.

"Does Howard Davis live on Bayview Road with you?" I ask instead.

Maggie stares at me without speaking for a minute, tears pooling in her eyes, but not falling anymore. "Yes," she whispers.

"Has he done this before?"

Maggie opens her mouth, but no sound comes out. She nods her head up and down, though, hard enough to dislodge her tears from their pools, hard enough to tell me that the answer is a resounding yes. "When he drinks," she says at last. "And he drinks a lot. He was drinking again before we left."

She's had enough. I had planned to explain to her some of what lies ahead—the reporting requirement imposed on the hospital; the police interviews; the arrest; the necessary restraining order—but Maggie Baker has had about all she can handle for the moment. We're just minutes from the hospital anyway; the shingled cottages we're passing now have all been converted to doctors' offices, pharmacies, and medical supply stores. The process will unfold soon enough.

"Maggie," I ask, "how old are you?"

She squirms a little at this, and I'm charmed by her innocence. Under the circumstances, even Geraldine Schilling wouldn't press charges against Maggie for driving without a license.

"Are you asking as my lawyer?"

I laugh. "Do you think you need one?"

Maggie's thumbnail goes back to her teeth and she speaks to the dashboard again. "Maybe."

"Okay then," I tell her. "I'm asking as your lawyer."

"Fourteen."

"When did you learn to drive?"

"Today."

She really has had enough. I pull to the curb in front of the emergency entrance and an orderly pushes a wheelchair up to the backseat almost immediately. Harry called ahead as promised. Sonia Baker lifts herself from the car with a modest amount of help from the orderly, still pressing the blanket to her chest and clutching the bloody kitchen towel at her mouth. The orderly slams the back door and whisks her away.

"Maggie, go ahead in with your mother. I'll park the car, then come and find you."

Maggie does as she's told, but her eyes are like pinwheels. Her hands tremble when she reaches out to close the car door, and a wave of guilt rushes through me. I had to send her ahead with her mother; I need a few minutes alone to make a phone call. But I should have given her some idea of what to expect. The unknown is a terrifying thing.

CHAPTER 5

Cape Cod Hospital's parking lot is just about full. It takes ten minutes to find a vacant spot, and even that one is partially blocked by a drift from yesterday's snowfall. I maneuver the Thunderbird into it anyway, cut the engine, and dial the District Attorney's office on my cell phone. I need to alert them.

One of the ADAs will have to be available, when we're through here, to appear before a District Court judge with Sonia Baker and secure a restraining order against Howard Davis. Given the extent of Sonia's injuries, we're likely to be here for a while.

Geraldine can't take my call; she's in a meeting. Stanley, though, is available. He picks up at once. "Attorney Nickerson, so good to hear from you. May I assume you've come to your senses?"

Stanley is probably about thirty-five. I wonder how many times he's been decked.

"No," I tell him, "you may not assume any such thing. I'm still daft."

The line is silent. He's apparently not surprised.

"Listen, Stanley, one of you needs to be in the office at the end of the day. I'm at the hospital right now with a woman who's been roughed up big time by her live-in. And her live-in happens to be Howard Davis, the parole officer."

"Jesus Christ," Stanley mutters.

"Yeah. Sounds like he drank himself stupid and then lost it."

"Jesus Christ," Stanley repeats.

"She can't go home with him there; he was drinking again when she left. I'll bring her straight to the courthouse from here, but it might be a while. She's in rough shape."

"Not a problem. We'll be here."

Those might be the kindest words J. Stanley Edgarton III has ever said to me. I thank him and cut the connection, not wanting to press my luck.

The car door smashes into frozen snow when I squeeze out. I hurry back toward the emergency room, my hood useless against the unrelenting wind. It's about two-thirty. This morning's sunshine is gone, blanketed by a thick bank of darkening clouds. More snow is headed our way.

The hospital's automatic doors open as I approach, and I run through them, hoping to join Maggie and her mother before too much happens. Signs in English and Portuguese are posted every three feet or so on the white plaster walls. Some direct patients to have their insurance cards ready. Others inform us that seriously injured patients will be given priority. Still others warn that public cell phone use may interfere with the functioning of diagnostic equipment. I reach into my jacket pocket and shut down my phone.

Two different television sets are on in the crowded waiting area, each tuned to a different channel, making their own small contribution to the general chaos in the room. Sonia Baker must have qualified as seriously injured; there's no sign of her or Maggie among those waiting for medical attention.

"Sonia Baker?" I ask the young nurse at the desk.

She's a striking blonde who looks as if she's been on duty too long. Her pale blue smock is stained and she's obviously harried, but she checks her list of names, then looks up at me and smiles. "We took her straight back for stitches," she says. "She needs to go to X ray, but the lip's got to be sewn first. Her daughter went with her. You're free to join them." She points down the brightly lit corridor behind the desk. "The young girl seems upset."

"Thanks," I call back to her, already heading down the hallway, a seemingly endless tube of fluorescent light. I hear Sonia even before I reach her small curtained cubicle. "He didn't mean it," she's repeating, this time to a young surgeon who's pleading with her to be still. "He didn't. He'll feel awful about it. I know he will."

I wish she'd stop that.

Maggie sits alone in the area outside the cubicle, her tears gone. She hugs herself with her skinny arms and rocks back and forth on her plastic chair, shaking her head each time her mother speaks on Howard Davis's behalf. I can't say I blame her; Sonia Baker should give it a rest.

"Maggie, there are a few things that have to happen now. I want you to know what to expect."

She stops rocking and stares at me, panic in her eyes. "What do you mean?"

"I mean certain steps have to be taken. The hospital has obligations under the law. All hospitals do."

"Like what?" she whispers, her panic up a notch.

"Like the police have to be called."

"No," she insists. "No cops." Maggie jumps to her feet and speaks with a force I wouldn't have guessed she had.

I sink into an orange plastic chair across from hers and tell myself to answer calmly. "You don't have a choice, Maggie. No one involved has a choice. The hospital has to report this to the police. It's the law. Someone here has probably called them already."

Maggie drops back into her own chair and says nothing, but her tears begin again.

"Maggie, you shouldn't be afraid to talk to the police. You didn't do anything wrong. Neither did your mom. Howard Davis is the only one in trouble here."

A look of disbelief seizes her wet face and she gets up again. She rubs both eyes with her fists, leaving a dark half-moon of mascara under each. "Is that what you think? That Howard is the one in trouble?"

"Maggie, he beat your mother. He's done it before. But this time she's injured badly. He broke her arm,

31

for God's sake. We can't let him get away with that."

She shakes her head at me, streams of dark water running down her cheeks. "You don't get it, do you?" Her small voice is desperate. "I thought maybe you could help, but you don't even get it."

"Get what, Maggie? Get what?"

She leans over me. "He knows them," she whispers in my face. "He knows all of them. He tells us that all the time. He knows every cop in the county. And every cop in the county knows him."

"That's probably true. He's been a parole officer for twenty years. But that doesn't mean he gets away with beating your Mom."

"They won't touch him."

"But they will, Maggie. They have to. They're probably on their way to your house as we speak, because of the hospital's report."

"Oh, sure, they might pick him up. They'll have to now, I guess. But he'll be out in no time. The cops are his friends."

"The cops have nothing to say about it. A judge will decide."

Maggie straightens up and dries her face with the heels of her palms, leaving small patches of water on her cheeks. "But he'll get out on bail first. He'll be out before any judge decides anything. And you know what will happen then?"

Maggie points backward toward her mother's now incomprehensible words. "Do you?"

I shake my head. I want to hear it from her.

"He'll kill her," she spits. "He'll just plain kill her." She turns away and buries her face in her hands.

32

The waiting area suddenly falls silent. Even Sonia Baker is abruptly quiet.

I lower my voice to a whisper. "Maggie, did Howard Davis say that? Did he say he would kill your mother if she turned him in?"

She stares at me, her eyes red, her cheeks stained, and says nothing.

I leave my chair, cross the small space between us, and take hold of her bony shoulders. "Maggie, you have to tell me. Did Howard Davis threaten to kill your mother?"

She looks away and talks to the floor. "Yeah," she whispers, "he says he'll break her neck with his bare hands. Right after she watches him break mine."

CHAPTER 6

Cape Cod Hospital's parking lot is emptying, the seven-to-three nurses and technicians just off their shifts. The snow is falling in sheets, the afternoon sky a nighttime gray. I pull my hood tight around my face and insert myself and my cell phone into a crevice where the granite wall takes a jog, in a futile attempt to escape the gale-force winds and the driven snow. I take one glove off just long enough to punch in my office number.

Sonia Baker needs more than a restraining order. She needs more help than the District Attorney's office can give her. She needs a lawyer of her own—to walk her through the process of swearing out a criminal complaint; to convince the District Attorney's office to charge Howard Davis not only with domestic violence but with threatening to commit double homicide as well; to persuade a Barnstable County judge to put one of his own parole officers behind bars—and keep him there.

I can't do it; I've already taken too much time from Buck Hammond's case. Harry can't either, of course. He's in court on a suppression hearing right now, and he's got Steady Teddy's pretrial conference at the end of the day. Sonia Baker needs help today, not tomorrow. The Kydd will have to do it. It's a serious matter—he's never handled one of these before—but I know the Kydd. He's up to it.

He answers the phone on the first ring and starts talking as soon as he hears my voice. "Marty, where the hell have you been?"

This is not the greeting I expected. "Do you think I dropped them off and went shopping, Kydd? I'm at the hospital, for God's sake."

"I've been trying to reach you for half an hour. Your cell phone's been shut down."

"I know that, Kydd. What's going on?"

"Where is she?"

"Where's who?"

"Sonia Baker."

A shiver runs down my spine, and it has nothing to do with the weather. The Kydd knows Sonia Baker's name now. He didn't when we left the office. "She's on her way to X ray," I tell him. "Why?"

He takes a deep breath before he answers. "Chatham police are headed your way."

"Good. They can take her statement, then pick up the murderous boyfriend."

"Marty . . ."

"The boyfriend is Howard Davis. You know, that giant parole officer. Can you believe that?"

"Marty . . ."

"Sonia Baker is lucky she's alive. Howard Davis is big enough to break her in two. And he's threatened to do just that—to her and the girl."

"Marty!" The Kydd screams so loudly I almost drop the phone in the snow.

"What, Kydd? For God's sake, what?"

He takes another deep breath. The wind whips the hood from my head and hurls heavy wet flakes into my eyes.

"Howard Davis is dead."

My vision blurs and I press my free hand against the granite wall for balance.

"Dead?"

"Stabbed to death with a steak knife," the Kydd says. "One from a set in Sonia Baker's kitchen."

CHAPTER 7

Chatham's Chief of Police pulls into the hospital parking lot just as I snap my cell phone shut. I race across the slippery lot to the Thunderbird, grab my camera and a fresh roll of film from the glove compartment, then head back to the ER. I hurry through the automatic doors again, maneuver around the crowded waiting area, and run down the long tube of fluorescent light. I can't get there fast enough.

Sonia Baker is reciting her litany all over again, this time to the X-ray technician. Her voice has grown hoarse, though, and she's lost some volume—a small improvement. I wish I had a muzzle.

I find Maggie in the waiting area first and pull her to her feet. "Forget everything I said about talking to the police," I tell her. "Don't answer any questions.

37

Not for the cops. Not for anybody else. Do you understand me?"

Maggie nods her head yes, but her terrified eyes say no. Of course she doesn't understand me.

"Maggie," I tell her, "give them your name. If they ask who you are, answer. But that's it. Nothing else. Tell them those are my instructions."

She nods again, but says nothing.

I rush into the X-ray suite and lean over Sonia while the technician scolds me from his booth. "Hey," he yells out, "what are you doing? You can't be in here. Where the hell did you come from?"

I ignore him.

"Sonia." My hand moves above her stitched lips to stop her recital. "Be quiet. I mean it. Don't say another word."

Sonia stares at me while I load my camera, her expression suggesting she's never seen me before. "I provoked him," she mutters, the word sounding through her damaged lips as if it has a *b* in the middle. "He wouldn't have done it if I hadn't proboked him."

"Shut up," I tell her. "For God's sake, shut up."

"Sonia Baker?"

The sound echoes through the hallway, a voice I know well. It's Tommy Fitzpatrick, Chatham's Chief of Police. The dead man was an insider; the Chief's handling this one personally. Two uniformed Chatham detectives are with him, but only Tommy Fitzpatrick speaks. "Sonia Baker?" he repeats.

"This is Sonia Baker," I tell him. "She doesn't want to answer any questions. She doesn't want to talk to you."

The Chief gives me a friendly nod with his full head of strawberry blond hair. He's more comfortable with my new job than I am. "Okay," he says, "but she needs to listen."

I know what's coming. I wish I'd warned her.

"Sonia Baker," the Chief recites, towering over her on the X-ray table, "you're under arrest for the murder of one Howard Andrew Davis."

Sonia gasps and raises her upper body from the table. She looks at me, shaking her head back and forth, disbelief creeping into her eyes. I nod at her. She pulls herself to a seated position, holding the hem of her hospital johnny with her good hand.

"You have the right to remain silent," the Chief continues. "Anything you say can and will be used against you in a court of law."

Maggie Baker leans through the doorway, dwarfed behind the uniforms, her eyes as big as their badges. She stares first at her mother, then at the Chief's back.

"You have the right to talk to a lawyer and have that lawyer present with you while you're being questioned."

I drop my hand to my side and wave Maggie out of the room. She hesitates for just an instant and then disappears before the Chief wraps it up.

"If you can't afford to hire a lawyer, one will be appointed to represent you before you're asked any questions."

Sonia shakes her head at the Chief, her mouth open.

I hope no one noticed Maggie. We've had enough casualties for one day. No need to add her to the list.

The X-ray room is full of hospital personnel; white coats are everywhere. And not just technicians. Nurses and doctors came to see the show too.

"We'll get out of your way," the Chief tells them. He takes a closer look at Sonia. "We know you've got work to do." He gestures toward the two uniformed detectives. "But when you're finished, she's to be released into police custody."

He turns his attention to me and points toward my camera. "You on this one?"

"I guess I am."

"When she leaves here, she goes straight to lockup. Arraignment's tomorrow morning. Judge Gould says eight o'clock sharp, before the regular docket."

"No waiver," I tell him. "Don't even ask her what time it is unless I'm with her."

"Don't worry." The hint of a smile flickers in his Irish eyes. "We know better."

Sonia leans forward and stares at me while I photograph her face, focusing first on her stitched lip, then on her swollen right eye. "Howie's dead?" she whispers.

"Be quiet," I instruct her, refocusing on her contorted arm.

Her eyes fill and I regret my tone at once. "I'm sorry, Sonia," I tell her, lowering the camera. And I mean it. The anguish in her eyes now is far worse than anything I saw when her pain was just physical. During my years with the District Attorney's office, I saw enough of these cases to know she probably loved him. No matter what he did to her—no matter what she did to him—she probably loved him.

One of the uniformed detectives returns to the small room with a blue surgical scrub suit and hands it to me.

"We'll need to take her clothes," he says.

I take the scrub suit and hand him the plastic bag containing Sonia Baker's clothes. The cops expect to find more than one person's blood on her stained white blouse.

"There's a child," the Chief says, sorting out his paperwork on the bedside tray. "A young girl. She'll need to go to the Service for a while."

I scan the room, relieved to see no sign of Maggie Baker. No child should be entrusted to the Massachusetts Department of Social Services. A child from Chatham would be safer on the streets.

"I don't know where she is," I tell the Chief. "But I'll find her, and she can stay with me. No need to involve the Service."

"You a relative?" the Chief asks, not looking at me.

"Yes. A second cousin."

The Chief snorts at his paperwork. "Sure you are. And my cousin's the Queen of England." But he balls up the Department of Social Services referral form and tosses it into the wastebasket. He and the uniform leave the X-ray suite without another word.

I'm relieved and grateful. It's good to know that on some issues, at least, Chief Tommy Fitzpatrick and I are still on the same side.

CHAPTER 8

Defense attorneys don't show up at crime scenes. They're not welcome. Now that I've crossed the aisle, I'm not expected to appear at the site of Howard Davis's murder. Police officers and prosecutors enjoy exclusive control over every newly discovered suspicious death. It's one of the perks of working for the Commonwealth.

Old habits die hard, though.

During my years as an assistant district attorney, I attended dozens of crime scenes. Almost always, important facts can be gleaned from the physical details of the site—the position of the body or the location of the weapon. Sometimes, the significance of what's there, or not there, isn't apparent until months later, when the evidence is being pieced together for trial.

Once the scene is dismantled and sanitized, much of that information is gone for good.

I figure it's worth a shot. I leave Maggie Baker at the office with Harry and the Kydd and drive the short distance to Bayview Road. Sergeants Terry and Reid are on duty, stationed outside Sonia Baker's modest cottage as if it houses the crown jewels. Even through the winter darkness, I see the two men exchange nervous glances when they recognize my pale blue Thunderbird.

Not all cops are the good guys they're cracked up to be, but these two are. I've known them both for years, and I can feel their anxiety levels rising as I approach. They're used to seeing me at crime scenes. But they know I wear a different hat now; they didn't expect to see me at this one. And they're not quite sure how to get rid of me.

Sergeant Terry must have drawn the short straw. He steps out to the small, snow-covered lawn as I slam the car door and cross the road.

"Counselor," he calls, his breath leaving a single white cloud in the air, "how goes it?"

"Can't complain," I tell him, though it occurs to me I could do so at length given the right opportunity.

"How's the new job?" He ducks under the yellow tape that surrounds the perimeter of the small property.

Nicely done. Remind me at once that I have a new job; I don't belong here.

"Not all that different from the old one."

He chuckles and looks down at the grass, then gestures toward the moonlit sky, gloved palms up, and looks back at me. He's about to tell me he's sorry—he doesn't make the rules, after all—but I can't have access.

"Come in, Martha," I hear instead.

Sergeant Terry is as startled as I am. Geraldine Schilling is standing on Sonia Baker's miniature front porch, waving at us. "By all means, do come in."

The sergeant turns his wide eyes back to me, shrugs his shoulders, and lifts the yellow tape so I can pass. "She's the boss," he says.

I smile at him.

"Guess I didn't need to tell you that," he adds.

Geraldine moves inside, still waving for me to follow, as if she just bought the place and is anxious to show me around. She's here, I realize, covering for Stanley, a fact that hits me like a hammer. Stanley is busy doing what I should be doing—walking through Buck Hammond's case one more time.

I hurry up the cottage steps and shut the front door tight against the winter wind, wondering what motivates Geraldine's hospitality. There are two possible explanations. She may think my viewing the scene—particularly if it's grisly—will make me reconsider my move to the defense bar. When I left the DA's office, she predicted I'd be back, her tone that of a preacher telling a sinner he'll eventually reconcile with his maker.

More likely, though, Geraldine plans to gloat.

She stops in the center of the tiny living room and gestures toward the couch like a Tupperware hostess unveiling the latest in snap-top containers. "You're on for the lady of the house, I hear."

44

She takes a drag on her cigarette and watches me digest the scene. It's grisly all right.

"It was a girlfriend of hers who called," she says. "Stopped by to see if your client was okay."

Geraldine blows a stream of smoke from the side of her mouth when I look up. "Touching," she adds.

The crime scene photographer was delayed—at his wife's office Christmas party, he says—and he's just getting started. Nothing has been moved. Howard Davis is sprawled on his back on the couch, bloody from the neck down. His eyes are closed, his expression that of someone in peaceful slumber.

The dead man's arm hangs from the couch, his fingers resting on the threadbare carpet. Next to them is a bloodstained serrated knife, a tape measure already aligned with its blade for the photo shoot. Nine inches, it reads. On the other side of the knife is an empty bottle. Johnnie Walker Red.

A large maroon pool over Howard Davis's left breast suggests that the single incision beneath would have done the job. It didn't have to, though. It's one of multiple stab wounds, too many to count through the patches of almost dried blood. His flannel shirt is sliced open in at least a half dozen places. His heavy work boots are stained red. Even the couch cushions are saturated.

There is little blood elsewhere. A few drops in the bathroom sink, Geraldine points out, and a smear on a hallway light switch, but the rest is confined to Howard Davis's body and the living-room couch.

The cottage is not otherwise disturbed. We walk quickly through each of the small rooms, ending up in the kitchen. There's no evidence of forced entry, no sign of a struggle.

"What have you got on Sonia Baker?" I ask.

She laughs. "What haven't we got? Motive, opportunity, motive, fury, motive, the weapon. Did I mention motive?"

"For Christ's sake, Geraldine, the man was a parole officer. He handled the most violent cretins the system spit out. He's probably got as many enemies as you do."

Geraldine rolls her green eyes to the ceiling, flicks her cigarette ashes in the sink, and shakes her head like a parent trying to reason with a misguided teenager. "Martha, Martha, what's become of you? Surely you're not serious."

"You bet I'm serious. This guy's been a parole officer most of his adult life. You've got to investigate the payback angle." The confidence in my voice astounds me.

She takes a long drag and answers as she exhales. "Only if the evidence warrants it."

She's right, of course. They'll dust the house and the weapon for prints, type and cross the bloodstains, take DNA samples. If the only matches are the people who live here, they won't look any further.

It's one of many prejudices built into our system. If a murder victim lived alone, the search for his killer begins with the analysis of evidence. If the deceased had a spouse or a live-in lover, that person is assumed to have crossed the narrow line between love and hate. The significant other is automatically identified as the prime suspect, before any analysis is conducted.

This is not something I can fix—at least not tonight.

"When do you expect the reports, Geraldine?"

The Commonwealth is required to turn over the results of its fingerprint and blood analyses to the defense. If that evidence discloses the presence of an outsider in Sonia Baker's cottage on the day of the murder, Geraldine is obligated to tell us so.

She looks up at the ceiling to calculate. "Monday night," she says. "It'll all go out in the morning. Should have blood work back late Wednesday. Prints sometime Thursday."

"I'll wait to hear from you then."

"Oh, you'll hear from me," she says, blowing smoke through her half-smile.

I head for the door.

"But Martha . . ."

I turn back to face her.

"Don't get your hopes up."

CHAPTER 9

The female violent offenders unit of the Barnstable County House of Correction is an austere, forbidding place. Nonstop gray cinder blocks serve as walls. Cement slabs—the same dull gray—make up the ceiling. The narrow hallway is poorly lit by yellow bulbs protruding overhead, protected by wire cages. The concrete floor dips every six feet or so to accommodate built-in drains, testaments to the need for occasional hose-downs.

My escort is a well-endowed, gum-chewing matron with wide hips bulging under a heavy holster. She's annoyed. Evening meetings with inmates disrupt the all-important prison routine. Generally speaking, visits outside the established schedule are prohibited. But when an inmate newly placed in lockup asks to speak with her attorney, she's entitled to do so. To hell with the schedule.

My escort doesn't seem to share that view.

It makes matters worse, of course, when my obligatory trip through the metal detector produces a series of high-pitched shrieks. The noise doesn't surprise either one of us, even though I turned in all coins and keys at the front desk along with my handgun. The metal detectors in the Barnstable County Complex scream for no reason all the time. Technicians are called in weekly, it seems, but the machines are never calibrated properly.

Miss Congeniality is obligated, because of the shrieks, to conduct a manual search, first with a handheld electronic scanner, then with her bare paws—an old-fashioned pat-down. Both are mandated by her job description, not by any real concern on her part. The rhythm of her gum chewing is unchanged. No weapon manufactured could make me a threat to her.

Apparently satisfied that my snow-sodden clothes hide only my underwear, she directs me toward the hallway with a toss of her head and a smack of her gum.

"Must be the dental work," I tell her.

She walks past, wearing no sign that she heard, and continues down the hallway in front of me with neither a word nor a backward glance. Charm school didn't work out, I guess.

She stops in front of a white metal door on our right and selects a key from dozens on her large oval ring. She shoves the door open with one hand and, with yet another toss of her head, directs me inside as she checks her watch.

Her glance at the watch prompts me to check my own. It's after nine. "I won't be long," I promise, a futile attempt on my part to mollify her.

"Knock yourself out," she says, the gum momentarily socked in her cheek. She assumes the pose of a sentinel as the heavy door slams shut between us.

The space has all the comforts of a telephone booth. Sonia Baker is already here, seated on the other side of a plastered partition, staring at me through a pane of bulletproof glass. She's dressed in the standard prison-issued jumpsuit, a one-piece, bright orange version of the surgical scrub outfit she wore earlier.

I sit down in the solitary plastic chair that faces hers and pick up the black telephone on my side. She winces when she lifts her receiver, the movement apparently exacerbating some ache or pain. Neither one of us says anything at first. I'm wet, cold, and tired. Sonia Baker looks like she barely survived a train wreck.

The cast starts just below her shoulder, bends at the elbow, and extends to her wrist, with a narrow loop of plaster between her thumb and index finger. It's the kind normally accompanied by a sling, but Sonia doesn't have one. No such device is allowed in lockup; too many potential alternative uses. She supports the cast instead with her other arm, the phone cradled between her neck and head.

Her lips look somewhat better than they did earlier, but her right eye is much worse. We never iced it, I realize. It's turned a deep purple, swollen completely

50

shut. Her shoulder-length, bleached hair is tangled and matted on one side. It occurs to me that if I could slip her anything right now, it would be a hairbrush.

"What happened?" Her voice is brittle.

"I'm not sure."

That's a lie, of course. I have a pretty clear picture of what happened. But I want Sonia to do the talking.

"He's really dead?"

The image of Howard Davis sprawled on the couch is fixed in my mind's eye. He's really dead.

"Yes, he is," I report.

Her eyes fill. She lowers her head and hugs her cast tighter, but says nothing.

"Sonia, we need to start at the beginning. You need to tell me what happened to you."

"To me?"

"Yes, to you."

"What difference does that make?" She shakes her head. "Howard's dead. I'm not."

"It matters," I tell her. "You've got to trust me on this."

It's too late and I'm too weary to delve into the legal and psychological complexities of battered woman's syndrome.

"Please, Sonia, tell me what happened before you came to my office."

She stares at her cast, apparently unsure where to start. "Sunday-night poker," she says.

"What?"

"That's what happened. Howie plays poker on Sunday nights. Every week it's the same thing. He stays out too late, drinks too much, wakes up hung-over." She lowers her eyes to her lap. "Mondays are always bad."

"But this one was worse than usual," I venture. Good God, I hope I'm right.

"Yes." She looks up at me, tears streaming down both cheeks. "This time he did it up big."

I wait in silence.

"He was out all night. It was after five when he came crashing through the door. And he's supposed to be at work at eight. He passed out on the couch, didn't even make it to the bedroom."

I nod.

"I tried to wake him at seven. I really did. I tried five or six times to get him up for work."

It seems important to Sonia that I believe this particular piece of information. "I'm sure you did," I tell her.

"When he wouldn't get up, I called in for him. Told them he was sick. Lots of people get sick this time of year; I think they believed me."

I nod again.

"That doesn't usually happen. Howie almost never misses work."

A man with a work ethic. What a catch.

Sonia rests her cast on the counter and wipes her face with her sleeve. "He woke up around noon, really mad. It was my fault he missed work, he said. It was my fault because I didn't get him up. I told him I tried. I swore I tried, but he didn't believe me."

Sonia shakes her head, her expression bewildered, and lowers her eyes again. "When I told him I called in for him, called in sick, he got even madder."

I stare hard at her. She doesn't recognize the insanity in what she's describing.

"He started drinking again," she continues, still staring into her lap. "The day was wasted anyway, he said. He was storming around the living room; he was so mad his eyes were bulging. I went into the kitchen to get away from him, but he came in and grabbed me and slammed me against the refrigerator. He kept slamming me; I thought the damn thing was gonna fall over. When he let go, my knees wouldn't work and I fell."

She looks up at me. "He kicked me then."

"Where?"

She points to her swollen, purple eye.

Howard Davis's thick work boots appear before me.

"I thought he was finished," she says. "Maggie was already outside and . . ."

Sonia catches her breath and interrupts herself. "Maggie," she breathes, her good eye wide with panic. "What about Maggie? Where is she?"

"She's fine. She's at my office. She can stay with me until things get sorted out."

Sonia sits back and takes a deep breath. "Thank you," she whispers.

"It's no problem. But Sonia, today's Monday. Why wasn't Maggie in school this morning?"

She drops her head onto her cast and I wait.

After a while, she looks up at me, embarrassed. "Maggie misses a lot of Mondays," she says.

Of course. Mondays are always bad. She told me that.

"Okay, Sonia, so you thought he was finished."

"Yeah. Usually it's just one fit, you know what I mean? Usually once he takes a break, it's over."

"But not this time."

"No, not this time. I tried to get to the kitchen door. Maggie left it open and was calling for me to come out. She'd started the car."

Sonia almost smiles, her tears still falling. "I didn't even know she knew how."

I do my best to smile back at her. "So you ran for the kitchen door."

"Yeah. But Howie grabbed me from behind. He threw his arm around my neck, really tight. I couldn't breathe. When I tried to pull away he grabbed my arm with his other hand." She pats her cast. "He bent my arm back, and he kept bending it."

I close my eyes, picturing the physical disparity between Howard Davis and Sonia Baker.

"He wouldn't stop." She cries harder with the memory. "I heard a bone snap. He heard it too. He had to. But he wouldn't stop."

I remind myself to breathe.

"When he let go, I tried to get out again. Maggie was screaming outside. But I wasn't fast enough. He smacked me in the face with the back of his hand."

"That's when your lip split."

"I think so. Anyway, I fell into the kitchen table. I remember the salt and pepper shakers rolling onto the floor." Sonia shakes her head and almost smiles again. "It's funny I remember that, don't you think? With everything else going on?"

I nod, encouraging her to continue, but she falls

silent. We're just getting to the hard part, I realize. "Then what, Sonia?"

"Then what?"

"What happened next?"

"Nothing happened next. He was done. He let me go. I got into the car with Maggie and she drove to your office. She said it was time to put an end to this and that you could help. She'd seen you visiting Patty Hammond, she said. And she'd seen you on the news. I wasn't in any shape to argue."

I stare at her. She's composed now.

"Maggie driving," she says. "I still can't get over it. She did all right, too."

I lean forward and look into her only open eye. "Listen, Sonia, I'm your lawyer. You need to tell me what happened."

"I just did."

"That's everything?"

"Isn't that enough?" She's incredulous.

I'm not asking the right questions, and I'm not surprised. I knew I'd make a lousy defense lawyer. I was a prosecutor for too many years. "Sonia," I lean forward and try again, "what happened to Howard?"

She stares at me and shakes her head. "I don't know. I thought maybe you'd tell me. That's why I asked to see you."

If she's lying, she's damn good at it.

"Do you know where he was when you ran from the cottage?"

"Of course I do. I didn't dare take my eyes off him. He was headed back to the living room. Back to his couch and his bottle."

The bottle.

"Sonia, what was Howard drinking this morning?"

She lets out a long sigh. "Same thing he always drinks. Johnnie Walker Red."

"Did you see it?"

"See what?"

"The bottle."

"Of course I saw the bottle. He was pouring from it when I went into the kitchen."

"How much booze was in it?"

She tilts her head to one side. "About half."

"Are you sure?"

She nods and looks off into space. "Yeah, I'm sure. I watched him pour. I remember thinking it was going to be a long day." She hangs her head and looks up at me again. "I didn't know it would be this long."

She's used up.

"Sonia, at the arraignment tomorrow, we're going to raise all possible defenses. If it turns out we don't need some of them, we'll drop them, okay?"

"Sure." She shrugs one shoulder.

"I'm going to ask the court for funding to have you evaluated by a psychiatrist, okay?"

"Okay."

The look on Sonia's face tells me it's not okay, though. She's starting to wonder about me.

"I'm going to say some things you don't want to hear. I want you to be prepared for that. I'm going to raise a legal issue known as battered woman's syndrome. I'm also going to raise a self-defense claim."

Sonia stares at me, but says nothing.

"Try to sleep," I tell her. I start to hang up my phone, but she raises a hand to stop me.

"You think I killed him," she says.

"The Commonwealth thinks you killed him, Sonia. And until we know how much evidence the prosecutor has to back that up, we can't leave any stone unturned."

"I didn't."

"Okay."

"Can you tell me—are you allowed to tell me—how he died?"

I look hard into her open eye and see only the question. "He was stabbed."

No words. Just a sharp intake of breath.

"Sonia."

She looks up at me, her eyes running like faucets.

"Maggie wanted me to tell you she loves you."

Sonia smiles through her tears and hangs up the phone.

I fudged a little. That wasn't exactly what Maggie wanted me to tell her mother. She wanted me to tell her that we'll straighten out this mess, that everything will be okay. I just couldn't bring myself to say that.

CHAPTER 10

When we got the footage of Buck Hammond from the local news station, Harry moved his television and VCR out of his apartment and into the conference room. The next day, the Kydd stocked us with video games. That wasn't what Harry had in mind, of course. But we made space on a library shelf anyway.

The Kydd and Maggie are engrossed in animated warfare when I get back to the office at ten-thirty. Their eyes are glued to the TV screen, where flashing multicolored lights erupt in the center of the darkened conference room.

Harry is slumped in a chair behind them, watching the action, feet up on the pine conference table and hands behind his head. His baffled expression suggests he might as well be reading hieroglyphics.

"One of you needs to surrender," I tell them. "Maggie and I have to go."

The Kydd looks up from his controller, but Maggie doesn't. "Hah!" she shouts as the sounds of explosions fill the room. "You're dead!"

"Hey, no fair," the Kydd whines, his Southern drawl thicker than usual. He stares first at Maggie, then at me. He looks like an eight-year-old who wants his mom to intervene.

"War is an ugly thing," I tell him.

Maggie dons her little denim jacket, pats the Kydd on the shoulder, and heads out into the winter night. "Rematch tomorrow," she calls from the doorway, "if you're not too scared."

The Kydd frowns at her and shuts down the machine. I head out behind Maggie, Harry on my heels.

"How'd it go?" he asks.

"She says she didn't do it."

"Maybe she didn't."

"Maybe. I can't think about it anymore tonight. I need some sleep. Arraignment's tomorrow morning, before Buck's trial."

Harry stops in the shadows on the porch and pulls me toward him, his big arms pressing me close. "Okay," he says, "I'll see you tomorrow."

His kiss is soft and long. I'm warmer than I've been all day and I'd just as soon not move, but I pull myself away. "My houseguest is waiting."

Harry laughs. "Good luck with that one," he says.

She's already seated in the Thunderbird, her eyes and hoop earrings reflecting the glow from the streetlamp. "What should I call you?" she asks as soon as I join her. I realize she hasn't called me anything all day.

"Marty."

"Okay. Thanks for doing this, Marty."

"No problem."

"I know what would happen if you didn't."

"What do you mean?"

"Social Services," she says. "If you didn't let me stay with you, I'd have to go to Social Services."

She's a worldly little thing. "How do you know about Social Services?"

"Howard," she says. "He's always threatening to call Social Services, have them come get me."

She leans toward me, poised to share a secret. "And he tells me about all the terrible things that happen to teenage girls at Social Services."

Someone should have slapped Howard Davis before he died.

"He's a real bully, that Howard," Maggie adds.

Her use of the present tense concerns me. "Maggie, you realize Howard's dead, don't you?"

She sits back again, stares at the glove compartment. "Yeah," she says, "I got that."

"And you understand your mom is charged with killing him?"

"Yeah," she repeats. "I got that, too. But she didn't. I was there. He beat her up, but all she did was run away. She didn't do anything to him."

The darkness swallows Maggie's features as we leave the driveway. "You'll get her out, won't you?" she whispers.

"I'll do everything I can, Maggie, but your mom's

not coming home anytime soon. You need to know that."

She's silent.

"It's been a hard day, Maggie. Tomorrow we'll talk about the details. For now, just be aware that this process will take months, at best. And it's not going to be easy. You and your mom are in for some tough times."

"That's not how I see it," she says.

"What?" Maybe I misunderstood. I come to a stop at Main Street's only traffic light and turn toward her. She meets my eyes with a steady gaze, her tears on the verge of spilling.

"Howard Davis beat my mom whenever he felt like it," she spits. "On Mondays we knew it was coming. If he didn't get her before work, he'd get her after."

Streams of water pour down her face. "Other times it would happen if he had a lousy day in court, or if traffic was bad, or if dinner wasn't ready when he wanted it."

She wipes her face with her denim sleeve. "My mom's in jail and that's awful. But Howard won't ever hit her again. So the way I see it, the toughest times are over."

The light's green. I face front again but it takes a few moments for my boot to find the gas pedal. I wonder if this young girl is happy about the murder; happy that her mother's abuser is dead.

Like a mind reader, she answers my unvoiced question. "I'm sorry Howard got killed," she says. "But I'm not sorry that we'll never see him again."

Janet is one law librarian who loves to bend the rules. When I headed toward the library's copying machine with Mr. Justice Paxson's lengthy decision, she hurried across the room to stop me. "Take it home," she said, pointing to the dilapidated book in my hands.

"Are you sure?" I asked. Casebooks aren't normally available to take home, and that particular casebook looked like it might not survive the trip.

"Yes," she insisted. "You should read from the old parchment, not a sanitized copy on cheap paper."

She was right, of course. I pulled the book from my briefcase late that night and centered it in the small circle of light on the desk in my bedroom. The deterioration of the volume lent authority—wisdom, even—to the words within it. And I was desperate for wisdom, desperate to understand, and believe in, the only viable defense the law allows to Buck Hammond.

When I opened to Janet's bookmark, my eyes fell at once—as if beckoned—on a question posed in the text. It was followed by what would prove to be the first of many attempts by Mr. Justice Paxson to answer it.

What, then is that form of disease, denominated homicidal mania, which will excuse one for having committed a murder?

Chief Justice Gibson calls it that unseen ligament pressing on the mind and drawing it to consequences which it sees but cannot avoid, and placing it under a coercion which, while its results are clearly perceived, is incapable of resistance—an irresistible inclination to kill.

An irresistible inclination to kill. I found this answer inadequate, unsettling even, and I was disappointed. Because the question, penned more than a century ago by a man long dead and buried, was precisely mine.

CHAPTER 11

≣

Tuesday, December 21

Maggie Baker is a freshman at Chatham High School. My son, Luke, is a senior and a starting member of the varsity basketball team. When Maggie and I got to the cottage it was close to eleven o'clock, and Luke apparently had abandoned all hope of his mother coming home to make dinner. He was outside paying the pizza delivery boy.

Maggie all but fainted. "That's your son?" She looked stunned.

"That's him."

"Your son is Luke Ellis?"

"Last time I checked."

"Why didn't you tell me?" she snapped, fixing her hair in the rearview mirror. When she tore her eyes from the mirror, she fired an exasperated glance in my

TEMPORARY SANITY

direction. She was genuinely annoyed. I tried not to laugh.

The next hour was comical. Luke was his usual affable self. He didn't ask why Maggie was with us; he acted as if we'd been expecting her. He shared his pepperoni pizza as well as his senior-year wisdom. He filled Maggie in on precious details about the upperclassmen in general, the basketball players in particular. She hung on every word.

Heavy winds kept the cottage chilly in spite of a blazing fire in the woodstove. I gave Maggie a pair of baggy flannel pajamas and an old fisherman's knit sweater. She looked at me as if I'd lost my mind. I made a mental note to arrange to pick up her clothes from Bayview Road.

At midnight, Luke set up the sofa bed for Maggie and dug two heavy quilts out of our old cedar chest. I came out to the living room to say good night, then, and Luke headed upstairs with Danny Boy, our elderly Irish setter, on his heels. Maggie Baker had stars in her eyes.

I dropped them at the high school at seven-fifteen, both of them griping about these last two days of school—full days, no less—before the Christmas break. Three times during the five-minute ride, Maggie mentioned that she'll turn fifteen in just a few weeks. Each time, Luke wished her a happy birthday. My son doesn't get it.

The roads are plowed and sanded, but the radio weatherman says we'll see another foot of snow by day's end. Traffic is thin—it's too early in the day for holiday shoppers—and I reach the County Complex in just half an hour. The parking lot is almost full, even though most county offices don't open—and most courthouse proceedings don't begin—until nine. The combination of Sonia Baker's arraignment and Buck Hammond's trial has drawn a crowd, winter storm warning or not.

The District Courtroom is packed. All of the dark brown benches are filled. Those members of the public who were too late to get seats lean against the walls. A dozen court officers stand guard in the back of the room, guns on their hips, prepared to eject any onlooker who might disrupt the proceedings. The building's ancient steam radiators hiss persistently and the air is heavy with the smell of damp winter clothes.

A half dozen benches in front are roped off and reserved for the press. It's not nearly enough space to accommodate their numbers. Photographers and reporters roam the vast room, their bright lights and microphones in search of targets. Sonia Baker's defense lawyer seems to be just what they had in mind; I'm blinded as I approach the bar.

My vision clears when I turn my back on the gallery and, for the first time in my career, take a seat at the defense table. Geraldine is oblivious to the occasion. She's focused on paperwork on the opposite side of the room, the details of Howard Davis's demise, no doubt. Once again, she's covering for Stanley. He's not a multitask employee, it seems.

Stanley, I'm certain, is already stationed in Superior Court, the first to arrive for Buck Hammond's trial. Positioned, no doubt, to greet all witnesses. Prepared to assign seats, if possible.

I'm tired already.

Just before eight, Sonia Baker enters the courtroom through its side door, her ankles shackled, her good wrist cuffed to one of the two armed matrons escorting her. Her purple eye is still swollen shut. She keeps the other one focused on the floor, even as reporters hurl questions at her. They jockey for position and call her by name, but she doesn't look at any of them, doesn't let on that she hears.

The orange jumpsuit is far too big for her; I didn't realize that last night when she was seated. The blouse billows around her thin frame. The tired elastic waistband hangs down on her narrow hips. The frayed hems of the pants drag on the old wooden floor.

A matron removes Sonia's solitary cuff but leaves the shackles in place. Sonia drops into the seat next to mine. It's obvious she hasn't slept much, if at all. Her open eye is bloodshot. Except for the bruises, her face is a ghastly white. She doesn't look at me.

The bailiff shouts "Court!" and we all rise. Judge Richard Gould emerges from chambers and strides to the bench, ignoring the bright lights and flashbulbs trained on him. When the judge sits, the rest of us do too, all but Dottie Bearse, District Court's veteran clerk.

Dottie stays on her feet, holding a copy of the criminal complaint, and waits for quiet like a patient grandmother. Only when the room falls silent does she recite the docket number and announce: *"The Commonwealth of Massachusetts versus Sonia Louise Baker."* Geraldine is on.

"Your Honor, the defendant is charged with the

first-degree murder of one Howard Andrew Davis."

Geraldine hands me a thick document with multiple tabbed attachments—the medical examiner's preliminary report, no doubt—before delivering the identical package to Judge Gould. She remains close to the bench, facing the judge.

"The deceased was found yesterday on his living-room couch, Your Honor . . ."

Geraldine pauses and turns a cold stare on Sonia.

". . . in what can only be described as a blood-bath."

I'm on my feet. This is arraignment, for God's sake. Geraldine is acting as if we're in trial. She's performing for the press, of course. The next election is just four years away. Never too early to kick off the campaign.

Judge Gould is way ahead of me. He bangs his gavel just once, hard. "Attorney Schilling, please. No need for drama. Stick to the facts."

I sink back to my chair.

Geraldine gives me the slightest of smiles before facing the judge again. "Of course, Your Honor. I'll be happy to."

The packed courtroom grows still and silent. The facts are what everyone came to hear, after all. The gory details of Howard Davis's death are what drew this crowd to the courthouse. And I don't need the medical examiner's report to tell me they aren't pretty.

"Howard Andrew Davis was stabbed eleven times."

Sonia's gasp is the only sound in the room. She raises her head for the first time today and gapes at

Geraldine, horrified. The photographers are busy behind us; they can't see her expression. But I can.

I don't know much about criminal defense work. But I've met more than a few criminal defendants over the years. I've seen more than a few emotions—real and contrived—displayed on their faces. And I know one thing for sure at this moment. Sonia Baker didn't kill Howard Davis.

"Five of the lacerations were to major organs, Your Honor," Geraldine continues, "not to mention a fatal puncture wound that reached the aorta."

She crosses the room to our table. "There's no question there was a physical altercation between the deceased and the defendant, Your Honor."

Geraldine gestures toward Sonia as if she's Exhibit A. "Howard Davis lost the fight."

Once again I get to my feet, but I hold my tongue. Judge Gould isn't looking at Geraldine. He's not looking at me, either. He's reading the medical examiner's report, his expression troubled.

The room grows quiet once more, the only sounds Sonia Baker's small sobs, until the judge looks up. "I remember Mr. Davis, Ms. Schilling. He was an unusually large man." Judge Gould removes his glasses and taps them on the medical examiner's report. "Six feet four; two hundred sixty pounds." The judge looks over at Sonia and shakes his head. "It doesn't seem physically possible."

I sink to my chair again. Never argue with opposing counsel if the judge will do it for you: one of the earliest lessons I learned from Geraldine Schilling.

Geraldine nods at Judge Gould, apparently having

expected his reaction. "Your Honor, if you'll turn to page four of the report, you'll see that the victim's blood alcohol content at the time of death was point three-three. The medical examiner tells us this level indicates he'd had twelve to fourteen drinks during the four hours immediately prior to his demise."

Geraldine pauses to stare at Sonia again. "He would have been just about comatose when he was stabbed, Your Honor."

Judge Gould's gaze falls on me while he absorbs this information in silence. "Attorney Nickerson," he says at last, "how does your client plead?"

I'm up again. "Not guilty, Your Honor."

I hand my written request first to Geraldine, then to the judge. Neither one of them is surprised. "The defense moves for a psychiatric workup pursuant to Massachusetts General Laws chapter 123, section 15(a)."

Judge Gould puts his glasses back on and peers first at my motion, then at me, through thick lenses. "Battered woman's syndrome," he says.

I head back to the defense table and stand next to Sonia. She's quiet now, her head bowed, both eyes closed. "No doubt about it," I tell him. "There's no doubt in my mind that Sonia Baker meets all the requirements."

Sonia doesn't look up when I rest one hand on her shoulder.

"And we reserve the right to raise that defense if necessary. But there's also no doubt in my mind that she's innocent. Sonia Baker didn't kill Howard Davis."

Geraldine swivels her chair around and looks at me as if I just announced that the earth is flat after all. The judge stares at me too, but says nothing. There are defense attorneys who routinely proclaim their clients' innocence, whether they believe it or not. Geraldine looks as if she thinks I might have joined their ranks. Judge Gould's expression suggests he's wondering too.

The judge turns his attention back to Geraldine. "Any objection from the Commonwealth?"

An objection from the Commonwealth at this point would be futile. Geraldine knows that. She raises her hands in the air as if she couldn't care less. "None."

"All right, then." Judge Gould reads from my written motion as he rules. "The defendant's request for a court-appointed expert under General Laws chapter 123, section 15(a) is granted. The defendant, Sonia Louise Baker, will be examined by a mental health professional—at the expense of the Commonwealth—to determine whether or not she suffers from battered woman's syndrome. If she does, the expert should discern whether she is capable of assisting her attorney with her defense, and whether she has a rational and factual understanding of the proceedings against her."

The judge looks out at the crowded gallery and flashbulbs begin popping again. "We're adjourned until the assessment is complete."

He escapes from the bench as the bailiff instructs us to rise. By the time we get to our feet, Judge Richard Gould has already disappeared into chambers.

The matrons appear at Sonia's side in a flash.

"Give us a minute," I tell them.

They do, reluctantly. One looks at her watch as if she plans to time us.

"I don't want that battered woman thing," Sonia says, looking at me for the first time today.

"I know you don't."

"Howard's dead. Now you want me to trash him?"

"No, Sonia. It's not about that."

She stares at me, daring me to tell her what it is about.

"Look, we don't need to decide anything right now. But we had to keep our options open. I'll arrange to see you at the end of the day. We can talk then."

The matrons hover.

"Try to get some sleep between now and then."

Sonia gets to her feet and faces me, surrendering her wrist to the metal cuff attached to a matron. "Thank you," she says.

"For what?"

"For telling the judge I didn't do it."

I nod.

"I know you probably don't believe me, but I didn't."

Sonia turns away, crosses the room, and disappears with the matrons through the side door.

I'll tell her tonight, I guess. She should know. For whatever small comfort it might bring, Sonia Baker should know that I believe her.

The District Courtroom is empty when I leave, the nine-o'clock cast of characters not in place yet, still milling around in the lobby. I see through the courthouse doors that the snow is already falling steadily. I pull my hood up and head out into the frigid morning, steeling myself for the day ahead. In ten minutes, jury selection for *Commonwealth versus Hammond* will begin in Superior Court, Judge Leon Long presiding.

The Barnstable County Complex looks almost festive in its new white blanket, an appearance that belies the grim business conducted here. Small, heavy flakes drift down as I cross the parking lot. It occurs to me, as I reach the back door of the Superior Courthouse, that my new career is off to a rather humble beginning. I have two clients, and neither one is much interested in being defended.

CHAPTER 12

Judge Leon Long is the only black judge ever to sit in Barnstable County. He has been on the Superior Court bench for more than eighteen years. A liberal Democrat who began his legal training during the turbulent sixties, Judge Long is the favorite draw among criminal defense lawyers. He is immensely popular with the courthouse staff and the bane of Geraldine Schilling's existence.

I met Judge Long more than a decade ago, on Christmas Eve of my first year as an assistant district attorney. I handled only the small matters that year. Geraldine tried the serious cases, as she had for eight years before I was hired. Because of that arrangement, I knew all of the magistrates and judges in the District Court but almost no one from the Superior Court bench.

That Christmas Eve, though, the magistrate assigned to hear traffic offenses in District Court was down with the flu, and Judge Leon Long from Superior Court volunteered to fill in. Insisted on it, the bailiff reported. A civil trial in progress before Judge Long had settled on the courthouse steps that morning, the judge explained, freeing him to step in for his ailing colleague.

It was odd, I thought, for a Superior Court judge to seize the reins so eagerly in traffic court, especially on a Thursday morning, the slot set aside in Barnstable County for contested parking tickets. Every Thursday morning, the county's aggrieved citizens packed into District Court to argue about how far their cars were, or were not, from the hydrant or the neighbor's driveway. Not exactly the stuff that great judicial opinions are made of.

There he was, though, a portly man of average height who somehow filled the entire courtroom the moment he walked through the door. He wore his robe, but he didn't take the bench. Instead, Judge Leon Long strode the length of the cavernous room, took my hands in his as if we were old friends, and flashed a dazzling smile. "Judge Leon Long," he said. "Leon when it's just us."

Leon's smile disappeared before I could answer. His eyes moved to the courtroom's side door, and I turned to follow his gaze. There she was, glaring at the judge, just three feet away. Geraldine.

"Sit down, Martha," she said.

I did, thinking that an odd situation had just taken a turn toward the bizarre. A Superior Court judge appeared more than eager to review parking tickets. And the First Assistant District Attorney, buried up to her eyeballs in violent crime, apparently intended to prosecute traffic infractions instead. I half expected F. Lee Bailey to show up at the defense table.

Judge Long retrieved his radiant smile for Geraldine. "Attorney Schilling," he said, beaming at her. "Always a pleasure."

In her spike heels, Geraldine was almost as tall as the judge. She planted herself squarely in front of him, crossed her arms over her tailored jacket, and cocked her blond head to one side. "Go ahead," she said to Judge Leon Long, "get it over with."

The judge turned to the crowded gallery, his arms in the air like a televangelist addressing the living-room masses. "Brothers and sisters," he bellowed, "how many of you are . . ."

I swear I thought he was going to say "without sin."

". . . here because you have been accused of a parking violation?"

I felt sorry for him then. I thought he didn't realize they were all accused of parking violations.

They raised their hands. Every person in the jam-packed room put a hand in the air, but not one of them made a sound. Their eyes were glued to the judge.

"Brothers and sisters," Judge Leon Long repeated, his bellow louder now, his drawl thicker, "I can't hear you. Tell me. I want to know. How many of you stand accused of parking your automobile where it did not belong?"

"I am." "Me." "Me too," came from the gallery, the voices hesitant and low.

"And brothers and sisters," Judge Long boomed, "how many of you stand wrongly accused? How many of you know in the depths of your soul that you had the right to park your automobile exactly where you did?"

Geraldine glowered at him as the answers began.

"I'm wrongly accused," ventured one brave soul. "I am, too," said another. "Me, too." "Nothing wrong with where I parked."

They all started talking at the judge then, a chorus of voices growing to a full crescendo in about ten seconds.

"Just as I thought," the judge announced, his booming Baptist minister's baritone silencing the room once more. "We are here today, brothers and sisters, to right the wrong that has been done to each and every one of you."

At this point I thought I had seen it all. But I was wrong. Judge Leon Long turned his back to the crowd and, for the first time, ascended to the bench. He took a small figure from the pocket of his robe and wound the key in its back, set it on the edge of the raised judge's bench, released his grip on it, and music began. Judge Long stepped back to enjoy the show, his smile enormous.

Santa Claus. An instrumental version of "We Wish You a Merry Christmas" lilted through the courtroom as the small mechanical Santa Claus marched the length of the judge's bench, turned around, and marched back.

The judge's arms were in the air again, this time brandishing a blank parking ticket. "Brothers and sisters," he implored, "dispose of these false allegations."

With that, the judge ripped his parking ticket in half, in half again, and again, until he held nothing but tiny squares of white confetti. After just a moment of stunned silence, those in the gallery began shredding their own tickets, hooting and hollering in the process.

I left my seat and joined Geraldine, who hadn't moved a muscle. "He does it every goddamned year," she said, her face like stone.

"Every year?"

"It's his little Christmas gift to the citizens of Barnstable County," she told me, her voice barely audible above the ruckus from the gallery.

"But the magistrate," I questioned, "the flu?"

"No flu. Just a day off."

"But the settlement—on the courthouse steps?"

"No settlement," she said, "just a brief recess."

Judge Leon Long threw his handful of confetti in the air then, and everyone in the room followed suit. Tiny squares of white paper snowed down on us as Judge Long left the bench and joined the crowd in the gallery, shaking hands, clapping shoulders, and exchanging wishes for happy holidays. Santa Claus continued his march and the music played on.

Even then, even as a prosecutor, I liked everything about Judge Leon Long. Now that I'm defending Buck Hammond, I view Judge Long as a godsend. In Judge Long's courtroom, the presumption of innocence is more than a constitutional protection. It's a sacred guarantee. And that means Buck Hammond has a fighting chance.

Judge Leon Long flashes his radiant smile when he takes the bench for jury selection, and I laugh out loud. I can't help it. I still remember Geraldine's final words that day, as she headed for the courtroom door. "Proceed, Martha," she called over her shoulder. "Convict the bastards. I just stopped by to make sure you and the good judge were properly introduced."

CHAPTER 13

In some courtrooms, jury selection in a case like Buck Hammond's would take days. In Judge Leon Long's courtroom, we'll wrap it up before lunch. I know this from experience. "People are fundamentally decent," Judge Long is fond of announcing. "No need to search for skeletons in the average citizen's closet. Oh, you'd find plenty. But old bones won't tell you anything about a person's ability to be fair and impartial."

During my decade as a prosecutor, I tried at least a dozen cases before Judge Long. I am used to his rapid-fire approach to jury impanelment. And to tell the truth, I tend to agree with his assessment of the average person's ability to judge fairly. J. Stanley Edgarton III, though, does not. The scowl he wears this morning makes that abundantly clear.

We all agreed there was no need to interrogate the potential jurors about what they've seen on television or read in the newspapers. They've all seen the footage dozens of times. They've all read the reports and the editorials for weeks on end, first when it all happened, again as the trial date approached. We'd have to go to Mars to find a juror who hasn't been saturated with media opinion about the now infamous shooting on live TV. The tabloids are calling it a modern-day public execution.

Instead, Judge Leon Long asks the first prospective juror if he can disregard what he has heard from the press, and base his verdict solely on the evidence presented in this courtroom. Of course he can, the juror claims. The entire panel nods in agreement.

Judge Long asks the next candidate in the box if she understands that Buck Hammond is presumed to be innocent as he sits here in the courtroom today. She is dumbfounded. "But he isn't," she blurts out. "We all saw him do it."

Buck stiffens between Harry and me. Stanley gets to his feet, but Judge Leon Long doesn't acknowledge him. "Thank you, Mrs. Holway," the judge says. "Thank you for your candor. You are excused with the sincere thanks of the court."

Mrs. Holway appears to take offense at her dismissal.

Stanley intervenes on her behalf. "Your Honor," he says, his voice rising in pitch, "perhaps I should voir dire this juror?"

Stanley is hoping to rehabilitate Mrs. Holway, get her to say that of course she has an open mind, of course she won't make a decision until all of the evidence is in. Mrs. Holway is a juror J. Stanley Edgarton III wants to keep. He likes the way she thinks.

Harry and I agreed that I will handle jury selection and he will deliver the opening statement. That way the jurors will hear from both of us on day one. Ordinarily, I'd be on my feet by now to oppose Stanley's request for voir dire, to state my opposition on the record before the judge has a chance to rule. But Judge Leon Long is shaking his head at Stanley—losing patience, if I'm reading him correctly—so I stay put. Never argue with opposing counsel if the judge will do it for you. I have to remember to thank Geraldine.

"Mrs. Holway is not a juror, Mr. Edgarton," the judge says. "I just excused her."

"But Your Honor . . ."

"That's all, Mr. Edgarton."

Stanley has the good sense to sit down, and Mrs. Holway leaves the courtroom in a huff.

Judge Long's courtroom clerk, Wanda Morgan, selects a new name from the glass bowl on her desk. The new potential juror comes from the gallery to the box to replace Mrs. Holway. His juror résumé identifies him as a fifty-six-year-old restaurant owner. More important, he is the father of three adult sons.

We will select fourteen jurors this morning, including two who will be told—only at the close of the case—that they are alternates. Judge Long addresses the panel first. "Ladies and gentlemen," he says, smiling at them, "let me tell you at the outset that the lawyers handling this case have assured me that this trial will take three days, no longer."

The judge points at Stanley, then at Harry and me, and we all nod our acquiescence.

"That means," the judge continues, "that they'll finish not later than Thursday afternoon, at which time the case will be turned over to you. Now, no one can predict how long your deliberations may take. But I believe it's safe to assume we'll all be home for Christmas on Saturday morning."

Stanley leans over his table and stares at Buck, his expression suggesting that Buck shouldn't include himself in the judge's assumption. Buck doesn't look back at him.

Next, the judge conducts a general inquiry into matters such as the presumption of innocence, the burden of proof, and reasonable doubt, then asks each potential juror a series of more specific, and more personal, questions. Only then do Stanley and I get our turns.

Each of us is allowed just two follow-up questions per juror. Judge Long is clear about the two-question limit, but Stanley doesn't seem to believe it. No such cap exists, apparently, in any New Bedford courtroom. Stanley begins a third question with every candidate, and the judge cuts him off every time. Stanley whines like a thirsty dog each time it happens, but the judge shuts him down anyway, always with that dazzling smile.

After our questions are asked and answered, the judge calls upon Stanley and me to state our challenges for cause. I have none. Stanley has just one. Juror number nine should be excused, he says, because she has a seven-year-old son.

"Denied." Judge Long shakes his head and rules while Stanley is still talking.

"But Your Honor," Stanley protests, "I'm not finished."

"But Mr. Edgarton," the judge replies, his smile enormous, "you most certainly are."

The jurors laugh at this exchange, and Stanley glares at Judge Long. No prosecutor wants a panel laughing at any point during a murder trial.

"But Judge," Stanley persists.

"Mr. Edgarton, let me be perfectly clear about this. No juror will be removed from this panel—or from any panel, in my courtroom—because she is a parent."

"But that's not it, Judge. That's not it at all. It's not that juror number nine is a parent. It's that her child happens to be a seven-year-old boy."

"Denied, Mr. Edgarton."

"But Judge . . ."

My gut tells me Stanley just uttered one "But Judge" too many. Judge Leon Long dons his half glasses, lifts Stanley's trial brief from the bench, and pretends to examine the signature line. Judge Long has done this before, more than once. Harry and I both know what's coming.

"Oh, pardon me," the judge bellows, his voice thick with sarcasm. "I must be using the wrong name, sir. You don't seem to understand that I'm talking to you. Mr. J. Stanley Ed-gar-ton the Third," the judge roars, "your challenge for cause is dee-nied."

If he is true to past pattern, the judge will call Stanley "Mr. Ed-gar-ton the Third" for the rest of the trial.

I put my hand over my mouth and swallow a laugh. Buck Hammond watches me, his eyes saying he doesn't know what to make of this. Harry, of course, looks like the Cheshire cat.

In the end, Stanley gets rid of juror number nine by using one of his three peremptory strikes, challenges each side may exercise without cause, without explanation. The new juror number nine is a young construction worker who does not have a seven-year-old son. But he does have a three-year-old daughter.

Stanley's concerns about the first juror number nine tell me that Harry and I are on the right track. We agreed weeks ago to keep as many parents as we could on the panel, more men than women, if possible. We use all of our peremptory challenges to oust three of the four candidates who don't have children of their own. The one we opt to keep is an elderly woman who never married. She did, though, teach English literature at a private girls' school for thirty-eight years.

We impanel nine men and five women. We have twelve parents, the retired schoolteacher, and a young male pharmacist engaged to be married, planning a family. These fourteen people will be outraged by what happened to Buck's son, by Hector Monteros's crimes. But they are law-abiding citizens; they'll be outraged by Buck's crime as well. And his is the only one they will watch played out in living color.

We're not elated with our panel, but we're satisfied. No criminal defense lawyer can ask for more. We explain all of this to Buck Hammond before the guards lead him away for the one-o'clock lunch break, but he doesn't seem to care.

CHAPTER 14

I was gone only ten minutes—fifteen tops. I filled a paper cup at the watercooler and downed it, then stood on the courthouse steps for thirty seconds of fresh air. Between the subfreezing temperature and the wind-whipped snow, that was about all I could stand. But now that I'm back in Judge Leon Long's courtroom, it's clear that I've missed something.

Court's in recess, of course. The room is quiet and the lights are dim. The judge, the press, and the curious onlookers are gone. But Harry, who normally mows down anything in his path to get to lunch, is seated in the front row of the gallery, not going anywhere, surrounded by Buck Hammond's family.

Buck's wife, his parents, two of his three brothers, even his in-laws are here. They all look up at me expectantly, then turn their eyes to Harry. He's supposed to do the talking, it seems.

"You have to open," he says.

"What?"

Harry arches his eyebrows. He knows I heard him.

"I can't open," I tell the family members. "I'm not prepared to open. Harry's ready. He'll open."

Harry stands and stretches, loosening his tie. "They think you should open," he says. "And I think they're right."

"But you're wrong," I tell them. "Harry will do a fine job. He's ready."

Patty Hammond steps forward and puts a hand on my arm. "We don't doubt that," she says. "We don't doubt that at all. We know Harry would do a great job."

She looks to her relatives. They nod at her, and she turns back to me. "But this judge," she says, "he likes you."

Murmurs of agreement come from the family members. "And the jurors like this judge," a brother adds. "Every one of them. They hang on his every word."

They're right about that, of course. Jurors love Judge Leon Long. Almost all of them do. That's one of the things about Judge Long that drives Geraldine crazy.

Harry takes over again. "Marty," he says, pacing the front of the courtroom, "think about it. Judge Long has always liked you. Jurors have always liked Judge Long. And let's face it, we need every point we can score in this trial." He raises his eyebrows again.

The relatives move closer to me as Harry continues,

still pacing. "Besides"—he laughs—"I come with baggage, remember? Twenty years' worth. I'm the creep they all know from TV news, the fast-talking public defender who's always arguing some technicality, always trying to get some no-good hood off the hook."

Harry is a lot of things, but a fast-talking creep he's not. He stops moving and winks at me. "You're still known as the law-and-order lady," he says. "They might listen to you."

I roll my eyes at Harry, but the Hammond relatives, it seems, are serious. Buck's mother steps forward, a petite, gray-haired woman wearing her Sunday best in spite of the snowstorm. She has tears in her eyes. "Please," she says, taking Patty's hand in hers, "it might make a difference."

The pendulum clock on the wall behind the jury box says it's almost one-thirty. I have half an hour to prepare the opening statement for the most difficult trial I've ever faced.

"Okay. I'll open. That means I'd better get to work."

The small herd of family members heads for the courtroom doors, but I stop Patty as she passes. "I'm going to need some help from you," I tell her.

"From me?"

"Yes. Get back here a few minutes early and I'll explain."

"Okay," she says. Nothing surprises Patty Hammond anymore. She's stopped asking questions.

Patty and her sad family head down the aisle and I set up at the defense table. Harry waits until the last of the relatives is gone, then leans over and brushes his lips against the back of my neck.

The tingle down my spine isn't going to do anything good for my opening statement.

"Get lost, Harry." I swat at him. "I have work to do."

"Okay." He laughs. "Lucky for you this old dog needs food. What can I bring you?"

"Coffee."

"Is that all?"

"Yup."

"Nothing to eat?"

I turn around to face him and his expression makes me laugh. Not eating when offered the opportunity is a concept Harry can't grasp.

"Oh, I get it," he says, headed for the courtroom doors. "You don't fool me. You're every bit as hungry as I am." He smiles at me over his shoulder, then narrows his eyes. "But it's the hungry lioness who kills."

CHAPTER 15

Jury nullification. I knew the day it happened that Buck Hammond's defense attorney would ask the jury to nullify the law, to acquit Buck Hammond even though the facts that prove his guilt are uncontroverted. I felt sorry, that day, for the poor lawyer who would end up in that unfortunate position. I would have felt sorrier if I'd known I was that lawyer.

That's not our stated defense, of course. Officially, we're relying on a temporary insanity plea. These jurors may conclude, if they so choose, that Buck Hammond was insane when he pulled the trigger. We'll present expert testimony to that effect. The jurors might find that Buck was unable, during that isolated time span, to distinguish right from wrong, to conform his behavior to the requirements of the law.

But generally speaking, jurors don't like the temporary insanity defense. Neither do I. It's too convenient,
too tidy. More important, Buck Hammond doesn't
like it. He won't cooperate with that portion of our
defense, he says. He'll tell the jurors he knew exactly
what he was doing. He'll say he knew he was break-
ing the law, he did it anyway, and given the opportunity, he'd do it again tomorrow. Further evidence of
insanity, I might have to argue.

Not now, though. Now it's my job to paint with
broad strokes, to give these jurors the gut-wrenching
facts they should bear in mind as they listen to the
prosecution's witnesses. It's my job to invite each one
of them to stand in Buck Hammond's shoes as they
evaluate the testimony against him. It's my job to help
them reach a conclusion they almost certainly won't
want to accept: Put in Buck's circumstances, any one
of us is capable of pulling the trigger.

Stanley ended his opening statement with the television footage of the predawn shooting. The panel sat
in sober silence as they watched the chopper land at
Chatham Municipal Airport amid squad cars, canine
units, and television crews. The jurors were motionless as Hector Monteros emerged, cuffed, flanked by
U.S. marshals, their weapons drawn. The panel held
its collective breath when Monteros descended to the
floodlit runway and Buck Hammond stepped from
the shadows of the airport's only hangar, six feet
away.

Not one juror blinked when Buck Hammond raised
his hunting rifle and took careful aim. They flinched,
though, and some of them raised closed fists to their

mouths, when Buck fired and the bullet found Hector Monteros's temple. Not one of them breathed, it seemed, as Monteros bled to death—in vivid color—on the airport runway.

Stanley would have shown that videotape a hundred times if he could have. The judge limited him to two runs during the course of the trial. Stanley used the first one today, and my bet is he'll wrap up his closing argument with the second. J. Stanley Edgarton III knows what he's doing.

When Stanley sits down, I leave my seat and roll the television table away from the jury box. I station myself in front of the panel, but I don't speak. Not until the silence grows uncomfortable. Not until a few of the jurors start to squirm.

"Seven-year-old Billy Hammond lived near the beach his entire short life," I tell them quietly. "He loved to fish."

Twenty-eight eyes are glued to mine just as they were glued to Stanley's moments ago. These eyes remind me why I once loved the practice of law, why I once believed there was no higher calling. Even now, jaded as I am, I stand in awe of this particular piece of the puzzle that is our criminal justice system. Whatever failings the system may have—and they are legion—the jury is its jewel. These fourteen conscientious people will struggle with every fiber of their beings to do the right thing.

"On June nineteenth," I tell them, "just six months ago, seven-year-old Billy Hammond went into the kitchen with his fishing pole and bait bucket. He told his mom he was headed to the beach."

I gesture toward Patty Hammond, who is seated in the front row, directly behind her husband. The jurors all look in her direction, and she is ready.

Patty nods to the panel, making eye contact with one juror at a time, just as we planned. She's a striking woman, with classic cheekbones and thick brown hair cropped close in a boyish cut. But at the edges of her eyes and the corners of her mouth, the ravages of grief are evident. She is much older than her twenty-nine years, much older than she was on June 18.

"You'll hear from Patty Hammond during this trial," I tell the panel. One by one, their gazes leave Patty—reluctantly, it seems—and return to me. "She'll tell you she gave little Billy a Popsicle and a kiss that morning."

I pause and look at each of them. "She never saw him again. And she never will."

The creak of Stanley's chair tells me he's getting to his feet even before he clears his throat. "Your Honor," he whines, "I hate to interrupt my Sister Counsel's opening statement. Really I do. But we're getting off-track, I'm afraid, heading awfully far afield."

Stanley's objection is bogus. Having raised a temporary insanity defense, we're entitled to discuss almost everything that had an impact on Buck Hammond's state of mind during the days leading up to the shooting. The fact that I'd like the jurors to use this evidence to nullify the law is beside the point. But the objection makes me wonder if Stanley is more worried about the possibility of nullification than I thought.

Judge Long knows I'm within proper limits; he

doesn't need me to tell him. I'd rather the jurors hear it from him anyway. I face the bench and stare at him, but say nothing.

Judge Long leans on his elbows and rests his chin on his fingertips, white cuffs and gold cufflinks sandwiched between the black of his robe and the nearblack of his hands. "I'll allow it," he says. "It goes to the defendant's state of mind, an issue that's paramount in this trial."

Score. Most of the jurors look eagerly at me when I face them again. The wise judge says the defendant's state of mind is paramount. They want to hear more about it.

Stanley remains on his feet, looking as if he has more to say, but I resume my opening statement anyway. I never uttered a word in response to his objection, never even looked in his direction. My ignoring him sent a message to the jurors, I hope. J. Stanley Edgarton III doesn't matter, people. Listen to the wise judge. And then listen to me.

"There's a reason Patty Hammond will never see her little boy again," I tell them. "There's a reason Billy Hammond will never go fishing again."

I cross the room and position myself behind Buck's chair, careful that the jurors can still see both him and Patty.

"There's a reason Billy Hammond will never celebrate his eighth birthday."

Patty lets out a single sob and Stanley jumps to his feet, looking personally wounded. Patty covers her mouth and raises one hand toward Judge Long, nodding her head and pumping the air as if calling a time-out. She's okay, she's signaling, and she's sorry; she won't make another sound.

"Sit down, Mr. Ed-gar-ton the Third," the judge says.

Stanley does so with a thud, shaking his oversized head at the jurors, and their eyes move from Patty to him. I had wanted to let their gazes linger on Patty a little longer, but Stanley's theatrics are effective; he's in the spotlight again.

I walk toward them slowly and wait until their attention shifts to me. "Hector Monteros is that reason."

Stanley jumps up again. "Your Honor, once more I apologize for interrupting. But my Sister Counsel is assuming facts that won't ever be in evidence."

"Not so, Judge," I tell him. "Not so."

Harry knew the day it happened that Buck Hammond's defense would necessitate a postmortem attack on Hector Monteros. He ordered complete DNA testing on both Monteros and the boy before either one was interred. Stanley knows that. So does the judge. Buck Hammond won't necessarily walk if we prove Monteros's guilt, but he doesn't stand a chance if we don't.

Judge Long raises his hands to silence Stanley and me, then turns to the jurors. Instantly, he has their undivided attention. "Ladies and gentlemen," he says, "it seems I should explain to you what an opening statement is. But first"—he flashes his smile at them—"I'm going to tell you what it isn't."

I slip into my seat beside Buck and pour a glass of water. When Judge Leon Long has the stage, there are no costars. Stanley, though, seems to expect a supporting role. He remains on his feet.

"Opening statement is not an argument," the judge says, glancing first at Stanley, then at me. "Though you wouldn't know that from what you've heard so far."

The jurors laugh and Judge Long leans back in his leather chair, relaxed and smiling. "Opening statement isn't evidence, either. It's nothing more than each lawyer's opportunity to talk to you." The judge leans toward them in a conspiratorial pose and lowers his voice, as if he doesn't want Stanley and me to hear. "And we all know how lawyers love to talk."

The panel laughs again, a good-natured chuckle, and so does the judge. Stanley, though, shifts on his feet and runs a nervous hand across his sizable scalp. A long wisp of lifeless hair from his comb-over separates and falls to the right side of his head, forming a single pageboy loop. The end of it just touches the collar of his starched white shirt.

I'm pretty sure it's not the lawyer joke that bothers Stanley; it's the laughter. This is a murder trial. There shouldn't be any laughter.

"Opening statement is not the same as closing argument," Judge Long continues. "Closing argument is a fight." He glances over his shoulder at me, then at Stanley, before turning back to the jurors. "And believe me, in this case it's going to be a real one."

The jurors chuckle again. They look from me to Stanley and back to the judge. He continues his monologue.

Harry leans forward on the defense table, in front of Buck, to whisper. "Defer."

96

"Defer?" I stare at him.

His return gaze is steady. He's serious.

No defendant—civil or criminal—has to give his opening statement at the beginning of the trial. He can defer until the close of the plaintiff's—or prosecutor's—case. In criminal cases especially, there are distinct advantages to waiting. It leaves the prosecutor in the dark, unsure of the defense strategy until after the Commonwealth rests its case. More important, it allows the defendant to hammer twice on the weaknesses in the evidence against him—after the prosecutor rests and again at the end, in closing argument.

But rarely does a criminal defendant opt to defer. The stakes are too high. If he waits that long to give the jurors a glimpse of his side of the story, it may be too late. The prosecutor may have been too persuasive. Too many jurors may have already made up their minds. Harry knows that at least as well as I do.

"Why defer?"

"You can't do any more."

Harry leans closer and Buck lowers his head between us to listen. "You told them enough about Monteros to whet their appetites. The judge told them that Buck's mental state is the key issue in this trial. What else can you accomplish at this point?"

The answer, of course, is nothing. Harry's right.

"But we can't defer now, even if we want to. We've already started. It's too late."

Harry shakes his head. "I don't think so. Stanley hasn't let you finish a thought without objecting. Tell the judge you've been interrupted enough for one day. Tell him at this point, you'd just as soon defer."

Buck shrugs when I look at him for an opinion.

Judge Long isn't talking to the jurors anymore. He's facing our table, waiting semipatiently for our whispering session to end. "Attorney Nickerson," he says when I look up, "we're ready when you are."

I steal a final glance at Harry. "It's worth a shot," he says.

Stanley drops into his seat as I get out of mine. I pause to set my glasses on the defense table. "With all due respect to the Court, Your Honor, the defense opts to defer its opening statement."

The judge wasn't expecting this. He drops his chin to his chest and stares at me over the flat rims of his half glasses.

Stanley jumps up so fast his chair topples backward. "Defer? She can't defer. She's already started her opening statement."

The judge's eyes move to Stanley, then back to me, his brows arched high.

"Barely," I tell him. "I tried twice, and twice I was silenced." I gesture toward Buck to suggest that this is his idea. "We're not up for strike three. We'll defer."

I turn toward Stanley but my attention is on the jury box behind him. They're listening intently to this exchange, some eyes on the judge, others on me. Their expressions are impossible to read.

I face the judge's bench again. "Maybe Mr. Edgarton will calm down a bit—and allow me to open properly—after he rests his case."

"Don't believe her," Stanley sputters. "Don't believe her for a minute." He points his pen at me, then at the judge, and finally at the jurors. His forehead vein turns blue. "I didn't silence her. The National Guard couldn't silence her."

I'm flattered.

Judge Long continues to peer at me over his glasses. "Attorney Nickerson," he says, "this *is* unusual."

"It is, Judge. I can't remember another case when I was shut down twice without getting a single fact in front of the jury."

That wasn't what he meant, of course. But he folds his arms on the bench and nods, conceding the point.

"We haven't been able to start, Judge. Not in any meaningful way. And now we opt to defer."

The judge nods again. "All right," he says.

Stanley runs up to the bench. He's so close to it the judge has to lean forward to see him.

"You can't be serious." Stanley points at me again. "You're not going to let her get away with this."

"Nobody's getting away with anything, Mr. Ed-gar-ton the Third. The defendant has the right to defer. It's in the Rules of Criminal Procedure."

"Not now he doesn't. Not after his lawyer has already addressed the jury."

"I've ruled, Mr. Ed-gar-ton."

"But Your Honor, don't you see?" Stanley is on tip-toes, his eyes barely clearing the judge's bench. "She wants an extra bite of the apple."

Judge Long leans forward even farther and stares down at him. "Apple?"

Stanley grabs the edge of the bench with both hands and his knuckles turn white. "She wants to have her cake and eat it too."

Judge Long's eyes meet mine, then move quickly back to Stanley. The judge looks as if he's about to laugh. "Cake?"

I shrug and take my seat. "I'm no match for this legal argument, Judge."

A few of the jurors snicker and Harry laughs out loud. Judge Long fires a cautionary stare in our direction.

"I don't even cook."

"Enough, Ms. Nickerson."

Judge Leon Long doesn't fool me. He's on the verge of laughing too.

"Mr. Ed-gar-ton," he says, so softly it's almost a whisper. "Sit down, sir."

Stanley returns to his table and rights his chair. He shakes his head and mutters a barely audible "you people" before he sits.

Silence. For a moment, it seems no one knows what to do next. Even the cameras are still. Finally Judge Long breaks the quiet. "Mr. Ed-gar-ton the Third," he says, "call your first witness."

CHAPTER 16

"Our first witness is Chief Fitzpatrick, Your Honor, of the Chatham Police Department." Stanley looks uneasy. He glances quickly around the room, then stares at the floor as if he just dropped something precious.

"Bring him in, then."

"I can't, Your Honor."

"You can't?"

"He's not here."

"He's not here?" The judge glares at Stanley. "He's not in the building?"

"He's not in the building."

Harry leans in front of Buck. "Is there an echo in this room?"

"Your lead-off witness in this first-degree murder trial is not here, Mr. Ed-gar-ton the Third?" Judge

Long looks as if he thinks Stanley might be joking. One look at Stanley tells me he's not.

"I didn't think we'd need him today, Your Honor. I never dreamed we'd finish both jury selection and opening statements before the end of the first day."

"You never dreamed?" The judge's eyes are protruding. "You never dreamed?"

Stanley isn't dreaming now, either; he's having a nightmare.

Once again, I cover my mouth and swallow a laugh. Once again, Buck Hammond looks confused. I don't dare look at Harry.

Stanley's assumption wasn't unreasonable. We didn't begin the afternoon session until after two, and Judge Long always adjourns promptly at four, reserving the last hour of his courtroom day for pending cases. Of course Stanley didn't think he'd need a witness today.

He did his part. He talked at the jurors for a full hour, and apparently assumed I'd do likewise. But my aborted opening took just twenty minutes, even with Stanley's tiresome objections. We have forty minutes of trial time left, and Judge Leon Long doesn't waste trial time. "It's the taxpayers' nickel," he always says. "It's not ours to squander."

Stanley's expression brightens, and he raises an index finger in the air. "Perhaps the defense could call one of its witnesses, Your Honor. Several of the defense witnesses are here in the courtroom. We can take one out of order." Stanley looks from the judge to me, pleased with his proposal, happy to have solved the problem.

Harry jumps up like a man who's just heard gun-fire. "No way, Judge."

Judge Long laughs and removes his half glasses, leaning forward on the bench. "Mr. Madigan, how well do you know Mr. Ed-gar-ton the Third?"

Harry doesn't miss a beat. "We're pretty close, Judge. He's Mr. Third to me."

The jurors chuckle yet again, and Stanley reddens. The judge continues to address Harry. "Then you must know he's joking. He can't possibly mean what he just said."

Harry sits, but he's perched on the edge of the chair, neck muscles taut and fists on the table. He's ready to shoot up again in an instant. The seasoned defense lawyer's instincts, I realize, are fueled by adrenaline. I don't know that I'll ever acquire them.

Judge Leon Long turns back to Stanley. "Mr. Ed-gar-ton the Third," he says, chin down, half glasses back on the edge of his nose, "surely you don't mean to suggest that Mr. Hammond should begin defending himself before the Commonwealth has offered a shred of evidence against him."

"Well, Your Honor . . ." Stanley gestures toward the TV as if it's his star witness, and it's already testi-fied.

Harry stands again, but says nothing.

The judge's composure is slipping. He takes a red bandanna from the pocket of his robe and mops his brow. "Mr. Ed-gar-ton the Third, opening statement is not evidence. Were you not listening when I instructed the jurors?"

The blue vein erupts across Stanley's forehead. He

lifts his hands in the air, palms up, helpless. He's out of ideas. The crowd in the gallery grows noisy. The judge is about to lose it.

"Chief Thomas Fitzpatrick is here, Your Honor. He's ready to be sworn in."

Judge Long bolts upright. Everyone else in the courtroom wheels around. It's Geraldine, with the Chief in full uniform at her side, hurrying up the center aisle.

J. Stanley Edgarton the Third looks like a man newly delivered from the fires of hell.

Harry leans down toward Buck and me. "She saved his sorry ass."

"What's that, Mr. Madigan?" the judge asks.

"He got here awfully fast, Your Honor, awfully fast." Harry gives the judge a meaningful nod, as if he's genuinely impressed with the Chief's velocity.

Geraldine whispers to Stanley, then takes a seat beside him as Tommy Fitzpatrick strides to the front of the room. An ordinary witness might be rattled by this abrupt call to the stand, but not Tommy. He has participated in more trials than most lawyers. He's composed and confident. And he's the consummate straight shooter.

Wanda Morgan, the courtroom clerk, approaches the witness box and holds a Bible in front of the Chief. He smiles at her, sets his hat on the box's railing, then stands at attention. He puts his left hand on the Good Book, raises his right in the air.

"Do you swear that the testimony you are about to give in this court will be the truth, the whole truth, and nothing but the truth, so help you God?"

"I do."

"You may be seated," Judge Long tells him.

The Chief settles into the witness box, hat on his lap, and faces the jurors.

Stanley is up. "Would you state your full name for the record, please."

"Thomas Francis Fitzpatrick."

"And your occupation?"

"Chief of Police, Chatham, Massachusetts."

"Were you on duty in that capacity during the early-morning hours of September twenty-first?"

Stanley isn't wasting time with preliminaries. There's little more than half an hour left in the trial day. He wants to end day one with Tommy Fitzpatrick's most damning testimony. Let those words echo in the jurors' minds throughout the night.

"I was," the Chief says.

"Tell us, if you would, sir, where you were at approximately four o'clock that morning."

"At the Chatham Municipal Airport."

"Were you alone at the airport, sir?"

"I was not."

"Who was with you?"

"A half dozen of my own officers and four from the state barracks; two more from a neighboring town, canine handlers."

"Anyone else?"

"Just the press. I'm not sure how many reporters and photographers were there."

"More than ten?"

"Yes."

"More than twenty?"

The Chief shakes his head. "Probably not."

"Why was it, sir, that so many law enforcement officers converged on the Chatham Municipal Airport that morning?"

"We were there to receive Hector Monteros. He was coming in on a military chopper. He'd been picked up at the North Carolina border just before midnight. Federal authorities were escorting him back to Chatham at our request."

"And why did you make that request, sir?"

Stanley pivots and looks at me. He wants to be sure I realize he's raising the issue first—diffusing, to some extent, the impact of this testimony.

"Hector Monteros was the chief suspect in the disappearance of Billy Hammond, a seven-year-old boy from South Chatham."

"The boy was the son of the defendant, is that correct, sir?"

The Chief looks across the room at Buck before he answers. There is, I think, genuine sympathy in his eyes.

"Yes."

"And you wanted Monteros for questioning?"

"Well, yes, and initially, we were hoping he'd lead us to the boy—or at least, to his remains."

Again, a sympathetic glance in Buck's direction.

"Did you ever get a chance to question Hector Monteros, sir?"

"No."

"Why not?"

"He was shot as soon as he deplaned. He died on the runway."

"Who shot him?"

The Chief looks toward Buck, not unkindly. "Mr. Hammond."

"Are you certain?"

He nods. "Yes."

Stanley pauses to make eye contact with the jurors. They're with him.

"Were you aware, sir, prior to the shooting, that the defendant was present at the airport that morning?"

"No."

"He was hiding, then."

The Chief says nothing.

"Was he hiding, sir?"

"I didn't know he was there."

That's Tommy Fitzpatrick. Just the facts.

"What happened, sir, after Mr. Hammond murdered Mr. Monteros?"

I'm up. "Your Honor . . ."

"Sustained. Mr. Ed-gar-ton the Third, you know better."

Stanley offers the judge an apologetic smile. "A slip of the tongue, Your Honor."

The judge glares at him.

"What happened, Chief Fitzpatrick, after Mr. Hammond shot Mr. Monteros?"

"We cornered him. Some of the officers tried to help Monteros, but four of us backed Mr. Hammond up against the hangar with our weapons drawn, to prevent him from fleeing the scene."

"And?"

"It wasn't necessary. Mr. Hammond wasn't going anywhere."

"What did he do?"

"He bent down, laid his rifle on the tarmac, then stood up straight and put his hands in the air."

"What happened next?" Stanley walks closer to the jury box, moving in for the kill.

"One of my men seized the weapon. Another cuffed him. He didn't resist. I read him his rights."

"Did he tell you he understood his rights, sir?"

"Yes."

"Did he seem at all disoriented?"

"No."

"Did he seem to understand what was going on?"

"Yes."

"Did he seem to know where he was?"

"Yes."

"Did he seem to know who you were?"

"Yes."

Stanley pauses and stares at the panel again. He wants them to understand that these one-word responses are important. He'll ask them to recall these answers at the end of the trial, when they evaluate our defense in general, our temporary insanity claim in particular.

"Did the defendant seem to understand why you were placing him under arrest?"

"Yes."

"Did he say anything to you, sir, after you read him his rights?"

Again, the Chief looks at Buck before answering. "Yes."

Stanley clasps his hands together and rests his chin on them, facing the jurors. "What did he say?"

The Chief takes a deep breath and stares at the hat in his lap. "Well, first he jutted his chin out toward Mr. Monteros's body."

"And he said?"

The Chief raises his eyes from the hat and looks at the panel. "'I wish he'd get up, so I could kill him again.'"

CHAPTER 17

An armed matron leads Sonia Baker into the small cubicle facing mine. The guard cups Sonia's elbow with one hand and rests the other on her weapon, as if she fears her prisoner might make a break for it. It's pretty clear to me that the matron has nothing to worry about; Sonia looks like she's sleepwalking. Her orange jumpsuit is twisted and wrinkled. It looks damp. She presses her cast against her stomach as she sits.

The matron waits until Sonia's settled, then hands her the telephone, nods at me through the glass, and leaves us without a word.

Sonia rubs one hand across her eyes. "I took a nap," she says into the receiver.

It must have been a long one. She looks drugged. Her lips are better, though, not so swollen. Her right eye has gone down some too, and it's beginning to open.

"This won't take long, Sonia. I just want you to be prepared for tomorrow morning."

"Tomorrow morning?"

"Dr. Nelson will be here first thing."

"Who's he?"

"She. Prudence Nelson. She's a forensic psychiatrist, a specialist in domestic violence."

"A lady shrink?"

"That's right." Prudence Nelson has been called worse.

Sonia shakes her head and frowns. "You think I'm nuts."

"No. I don't."

"Then you think I killed Howard."

"I don't think that either. You say you didn't. And I believe you."

Sonia doesn't believe me, though. She stares at the cinder-block wall behind me and shakes her head again. "Then why the shrink?"

Time for my "this is war" speech. Sonia Baker isn't going to like what I have to say. And she might not like me after I say it. Too bad.

"Because you're charged with first-degree murder, that's why. Because a person charged with first-degree murder doesn't have the luxury of tossing a viable defense out the window—even if she doesn't like the sound of it, even if it wounds her pride."

Sonia avoids looking at me. Her eyes roam around the room, then settle on the small, empty counter in front of her. She sets her jaw.

"Because the Commonwealth of Massachusetts intends to convict you of first-degree murder. And sometimes the Commonwealth convicts innocent people. Not on purpose. But it happens. Trust me. I know."

Sonia's lips part, but she says nothing. Her eyes stay fixed on the counter.

"Because in the Commonwealth of Massachusetts, women convicted of first-degree murder—guilty or not—go to MCI Framingham, a place that makes this joint look like a spa. And they don't leave. Ever."

Sonia lowers her eyes to her lap. "Okay," she says. "Okay. I get it."

I wait until she raises her head, but she still doesn't look at me. She stares at the wall again.

"I hope you do. You need to cooperate with Dr. Nelson tomorrow morning. Tell her everything."

"Everything about Howard?"

"About Howard. About you. And about anything else she brings up. She can't help us if you don't."

Sonia nods, but says nothing.

"Howard's life is over, Sonia. There's nothing you can do about that. But if you don't come clean about him, yours may as well be over too."

She runs a hand through her bleached hair, then tilts her head back and studies the ceiling.

"Maggie needs you. She needs you more than Howard Davis ever did."

She closes her eyes, head still tilted, and takes a deep breath. "How is she? Maggie. Is she okay?"

"She's fine. But she won't be, down the road, if you don't beat this charge. And tomorrow's assessment is step one. Take it seriously. It matters."

Finally, Sonia tears her eyes from the ceiling and looks at me. "What is it? The battered woman thing—what's it all about?"

The million-dollar question.

"It's a syndrome—described by the experts as a subclass of posttraumatic stress disorder. It's not classified as an illness; it's not even a diagnosis. It's a pattern of emotions and behaviors common among women who've been battered by their partners."

"Like what?"

"Depression. Shame. Self-reproach. Repeatedly leaving—and then going back to—the abuse. The medical community sums it all up as 'learned helplessness.'"

Sonia's gaze returns to the ceiling. "So what? Why does any of that matter?"

"It goes to intent. A woman in the throes of the syndrome lives in constant dread of imminent aggression."

Sonia looks at me, raises her eyebrows. "Translation?"

"She knows she might get hurt—badly—any minute of the day, every day."

Sonia nods.

"The battered woman has a heightened perception of threat. She's on constant alert. Expert testimony on that issue can bolster a self-defense claim."

"I didn't kill him."

"There have been cases where the women didn't remember."

"Didn't remember what?"

"Killing their abusers."

Sonia stares at me, mouth open.

"I'm not kidding. The psychiatrists call it 'dissociative amnesia.' The woman does in her batterer—in one case, she bludgeoned him with a baseball bat—then doesn't remember anything about it."

Sonia knits her eyebrows and shakes her head, slowly. She doesn't buy it. "I've never hurt anyone," she says. "Not on purpose." Her voice is little more than a whisper. "If I killed somebody—anybody—it wouldn't slip my mind."

She falls silent, still staring at me. Her expression says I'm the one who needs a shrink. Our dissociative amnesia discussion is over.

"Okay, Sonia. But I want you to understand the syndrome. So you'll know the kind of information you need to share with Dr. Nelson."

She shrugs.

"The experts all agree it's cyclical. The cycle has three stages. The initial stage is mostly verbal, a lot of yelling. There's some physical abuse too, but it's minor."

"People fight," she says. "What's the big deal?"

"In stage two, the verbal abuse escalates. The yelling gets louder, more threatening. Then there's a single explosion. The woman gets physically beaten up—once."

Sonia nods, says nothing.

"That's followed by a respite, a break. No abuse at all. Until stage three."

She lowers her eyes to her lap again.

"Stage three is essentially a repetition of the first two stages—on fast-forward. The time between beatings gets shorter and shorter."

For a full minute, the telephone line between us is

quiet. Sonia takes a deep breath and looks up at me. "Okay," she says. "I get it."

"You should know," I tell her, "that the law doesn't recognize a woman as battered unless she's gone through the complete cycle—all three stages, and with the same man—at least twice."

Sonia lets out a soft laugh and stares at her lap again, hugging her cast. "Twice?" Her eyes are brimming when she looks back at me. "No problem."

She's had it.

"Are we done?"

"Yes."

She hangs up her phone, stands, and turns away.

I hang up too, and press the buzzer. The matron opens the door behind Sonia in a millisecond. She must have been leaning on it.

It occurs to me, as I pack up my briefcase, that I'm two for two. First in Buck Hammond's case, and now in this one, I'm arguing that the dead guy deserved it. I've barely begun my career with the defense bar, but I seem to be developing a niche.

CHAPTER 18

The moon is almost full tonight. Beams of light shimmer on the salt water at the end of Bayview Road. They light up the beach and the narrow lane, reflecting off the newly fallen foot of snow. The weatherman was right on.

Sonia Baker's cottage, crime scene tape and all, is bathed in a soft yellow glow. Geraldine's Buick is parked at the curb, empty. She's already gone inside.

Every light in the place is on. Soft lamplight peeks out from behind ivory lace curtains. If it weren't wrapped in that black-lettered tape, the small shingled house would look cozy and inviting on this frigid night. It occurs to me, for the first time, that Maggie Baker will probably get good and homesick long before all this is over.

Geraldine agreed to meet me here at seven, but I'm a half hour late. I was only a few minutes behind schedule when I left the Barnstable County House of Correction, then I got stuck behind a sander on the single-lane portion of the Mid-Cape Highway. This isn't good. Geraldine doesn't like to be kept waiting.

The front door is unlocked. I let myself in, tapping on the inlaid glass to announce my arrival. Sonia's living room looks altogether different than it did twenty-four hours ago. Howard Davis's body is gone, of course; so is the blood-drenched sofa, the serrated knife, and the Johnnie Walker Red bottle.

A white, powdery film covers every surface in the room—the remaining furniture, the doorknobs, even the windowsills. It's residue from the print search. Patches of the living-room rug—close to where the couch and body were—have been excised. A scuffed wooden floor shows through the holes.

"In here, Martha."

I follow Geraldine's voice to Maggie's back bedroom, a room we surveyed quickly on last night's brisk tour. It holds only a single bed, an oval braided rug, and an old pine bureau. The lamp on the bureau—a ceramic ballerina with a chipped tutu and a frilly pink shade—is on. Maggie's hairbrush sits beside it.

The room's walls are covered with the predictable tattered posters of movie stars and rock singers, but otherwise the space is surprisingly neat for a teenager's. My stomach registers a small surge of hope; maybe a touch of Maggie's tidiness will rub off on Luke.

Geraldine doesn't look up when I join her. She's busy filling two shopping bags she's positioned on Maggie's bed. I wouldn't have a clue about packing for a teenage girl, but Geraldine selects items from the bureau's open drawers without hesitation, as if she's been Maggie Baker's personal shopper for years.

"How do you know what to choose, Geraldine?"

She gives me that look, the one she perfected during the ten years we worked together. "Martha, get a brain," it says. Then she gestures toward the bureau's open drawers; they're just about empty. No choosing necessary.

"Divine inspiration." Geraldine raises her hands to the heavens, as if even she can't comprehend the extent of her God-given talents. She empties the last few items from the bureau and shuts the drawers. She drops the hairbrush in with the clothes, hands both shopping bags to me, and turns off the ballerina lamp. She pauses to light a cigarette, and heads for the bedroom door.

"Funny," she says, walking in front of me down the short hallway to the kitchen, "you never struck me as the foster parent type."

"It's temporary, Geraldine."

"Temporary?" She throws a skeptical look over her shoulder at me. "As in until-her-mother-serves-a-life-sentence temporary?"

"No." I don't particularly like talking to Geraldine's back, but I seem to do it a lot. "As in until-we-figure-out-who-the-hell-killed–Howard Davis temporary."

She leans against the kitchen sink, her cigarette

118

poised in midair, and shakes her blond bangs at me. Long ago, Geraldine diagnosed me as chronically naive. Now I've convinced her the case is critical.

"Your client killed Howard Davis, Martha. We both know that."

"I don't think so, Geraldine."

"He had it coming. I won't fight you there." She flicks her ashes into the sink. "You'll probably score with the psychiatric workup. If any woman's been battered, she has. And if old Prudence comes through for you, we'll plead it out. But your client's doing time, Martha. Real time."

Suddenly I'm exhausted. I rest the shopping bags on the floor, pull a chair out from the kitchen table, and drop into it. I can't help wondering why it is that Geraldine is always certain of her position and I—no matter which side of the aisle I find myself on—am not.

She can read my mind, of course; she always could. She blows a stream of smoke into the center of the kitchen before explaining it all to me. "Martha, you feel sorry for her. Your emotions are clouding your judgment. And who doesn't feel sorry for her? We all see she's been to hell and back. But stabbing him eleven times wasn't the answer."

I raise my eyebrows. No need to waste my breath; she knows what I'm thinking.

"Yes, they do work," she says. "Restraining orders work in most cases."

Actually, they work in all cases—one way or another. Sometimes the bully is afraid enough of the Big House to stay away from his favorite whipping post for a while. Other times he doesn't give a damn and

119

needs to be sure she knows that. So he shows up and beats her again—often within hours of being served.

In a select few cases, the restraining order is a trigger. The document itself induces a new level of rage. The abuse reaches new heights—or depths—and the woman who sought protection from the system ends up in the county morgue.

Geraldine knows all of this at least as well as I do. No need to argue about it now. I force myself to my feet and lift the two shopping bags. "Thanks for these," I tell her.

I'm almost out of the kitchen when I remember. I stop in the doorway and put the bags down again.

"What?" Geraldine's cigarette freezes and she eyes me guardedly. "What now?"

"I just want to check something."

I go back to the kitchen table and walk around it, my eyes on the wide-pine floor. There they are. Two glass lighthouses, one cracked. They're side by side against the trim on the floorboard, small black and white grains spilled out from their silver caps.

The salt and pepper shakers.

Geraldine crosses the room and stands beside me, cigarette at her cheek, her green eyes following my gaze. "So what?" she says.

"It's just something Sonia Baker told me, a small detail. One that turns out to be true."

She inhales and shakes her head again. I'm apparently a lost cause.

I retrieve the shopping bags, head for the front door, and call back over my shoulder. "I know, Geraldine. I know. It doesn't mean a thing."

CHAPTER 19

If Luke ever discovers the taste of a home-cooked meal, I'm doomed. How he grew to be six feet two is anyone's guess. Good mothers prepare meals for their children, I've heard, but I'm not one of them. I do, of course, arrange for takeout. I'm a mediocre mother, anyhow.

It's almost nine by the time I get to our Windmill Lane cottage. I stopped at the office after I left Geraldine, to ask the Kydd to do some background work for Sonia while Harry and I are in trial. The Kydd was way ahead of me. He filed a written request this morning, he said, for copies of Howard Davis's active files. We should receive the first batch by midday tomorrow. Round one of eligible suspects.

Luke always has the woodstove blazing by the time I get home on winter nights, and tonight is no exception. The sweet smell of burning bark envelops me in the driveway, a warm welcome home. I trudge through the packed snow toward the back of our cottage. The pounding surf of the Atlantic is just beyond the dunes, a few yards away, and I have to brace myself against salty gusts of wet winter wind.

I climb the wooden stairs to the back deck and the kitchen door. During the winter months, our front door is permanently sealed. I'm happy to be home at last. And I'm fully prepared to spring for Chinese food. Any mediocre mother would be.

The windows look odd from outside. They're opaque with steam, even the small panes in the door. The ocean wind normally keeps our kitchen chilly in the winter, but tonight a noticeable warmth washes over me as soon as I go inside. And the rich scent of burning wood is mixed with another aroma, something familiar.

Ragú. Maggie Baker is on tiptoes at the stove, giggling and struggling to control a large pot of furiously boiling pasta. Luke is laughing too, standing next to her, absentmindedly stirring a smaller pot while he watches Maggie struggle. He's in charge of the red sauce, it seems, and he's not doing a very good job. He is, after all, his mother's son.

The front of Luke's gray sweatshirt is peppered with small red dots. So are Maggie's sleeves. Actually, they're my sleeves. She's wearing my knit fisherman's sweater.

"Marty, you're just in time," she shouts, then bends in two, shrieking, and points her wooden spoon at a red circle newly arrived on Luke's cheek.

"Ow, that's hot. It's not funny." Luke launches into a laughing fit of his own, though, holding his arms in front of his face as if shielding himself from enemy gunfire.

Just in time or not, I decide to get out of my suit before going anywhere near either one of them. Maggie and Luke continue shouting in the kitchen, each of them giving the other instructions on what to do next, while I change into old jeans and a warm sweater. The clanging of pots is followed by a sound that might be Niagara Falls. I hope some of it went into the sink.

By the time I get back to the kitchen, things have calmed down and the food is actually on the table. The kerosene lamp is lit and two Christmas candles left over from last year are glowing amid the bowls. Maggie is already seated, beaming at her handiwork. Luke holds a chair for me, kitchen towel draped over his arm, as if he's the maître d'. Never mind the red polka dots.

It's quite a spread. A steaming bowl of linguine, a fresh garden salad, even garlic bread. I realize I must be ravenous. The Ragú smells divine.

The self-appointed maître d' pours a glass of Chianti for me, then awaits my approval, as if I might send it back for another vintage. "Sit," I tell him.

"I'd have made meatballs," Maggie says, "but there wasn't any meat."

A good mother would have meat in the house.

"And I'd have made cookies," she adds, "but there weren't any eggs."

Even a mediocre mother would have eggs on hand.

123

"This is wonderful," I tell her. "We don't need another thing."

Luke clears his throat and arches his eyebrows at me. Meatballs and cookies sound good to him. I pass him the pasta.

"Maggie, you're quite a cook. How did you learn?"

She shrugs, a pleased smile on her face. "I cook on Sundays," she says. "Howard always eats with his poker buddies on Sundays, so it's just Mom and me home for dinner. Mom says I shouldn't cook when Howard's home. He gets mad if anything goes wrong."

Howard Davis was quite an addition to that household.

Luke reaches for the bread basket, shaking his head. His expression tells me he knows all about Howard Davis. He and Maggie have been talking. Good. Maggie's going to need a friend in the months ahead. And when it comes to being a friend, Luke is the best.

We eat as if it's Thanksgiving in Italy, then move into the living room, closer to the woodstove. No need to fuss with the dishes, we all agree. They'll still be here tomorrow. I realize my claim even to mediocrity is slipping.

By eleven, Luke and I are all but asleep in our overstuffed chairs, and Danny Boy is snoring by the woodstove. Maggie is wide awake, though. She has the sofa bed all set up, and she's propped on two pillows, reading a *Glamour* magazine and painting her fingernails.

Luke rallies enough to bid us good night and head

for the stairs. Danny Boy stretches and yawns, then follows him. I steer toward my own room, relishing the thought of my old, heavy quilt.

"Don't read too much longer," I tell Maggie. "There's school tomorrow."

"I'm not going to school tomorrow," she says.

Luke stands still on the staircase. Danny Boy does too. He looks down at me, then stares up at Luke, as if one of us should give him an explanation.

I lean against my doorway. "You're not?"

"No."

This doesn't sound negotiable. I move back into the living room. "Maggie, it's the last day before the break. It would be crazy to skip."

"I want to go see my mom."

Of course she does.

"I called there today," she says. "They'll let me see her at one o'clock tomorrow. For half an hour."

She's a self-sufficient little thing.

"I was hoping I could ride over there with you— when you go to work. I don't mind waiting around. I'll watch your trial." She finishes a fingernail and smiles up at me. "It'll be educational."

I sit back down in the overstuffed chair. "Maggie, I know you want to see your mom. And she wants to see you. But tomorrow's the last day of school before Christmas. Don't miss it. You can go with me on Thursday. Thursday and Friday, if you want."

Luke steps back into the room. "I have to go in tomorrow," he says to Maggie. "I have practice."

He has to go in tomorrow for more reasons than that. Classes, for instance. I bite my tongue.

125

"But if you wait until Thursday, I'll go with you," he says. "If Mom will lend us the car, we can go to the mall while she's working. I still have Christmas shopping to do."

Yikes. Christmas shopping. All hopes of maternal mediocrity are dashed.

Maggie caps the nail polish, considering. The educational opportunities afforded by watching my trial apparently pale compared to Luke's idea. "Will you?" she asks me.

"Will I what?"

"Lend us the car."

I can't help but remember my first meeting with Maggie, the newly initiated driver. Hard to believe it was yesterday. "Yes," I tell her. "But Luke does the driving. All of it."

She laughs and turns out the lamp. "Okay, okay. I'll go to school tomorrow. And I'll go see Mom on Thursday. Thursday and Friday, just like you said."

Luke heads upstairs again, but I catch his eye before he disappears onto the second floor. I give him a thumb's-up, and he smiles. He really is the best.

During the weeks leading up to Buck Hammond's trial, I worried that I'd be unable to sell the temporary insanity defense to our jury. I worried that my unspoken doubts about the validity of that defense would render my words in support of it hollow, unconvincing. And so I returned, night after night, to the words of Mr. Justice Paxson, hoping his words would help me choose mine. Not all of them did.

> *Chief Justice Lewis has said that moral insanity bears a striking resemblance to vice, and further, it ought never to be admitted as a defense, until it is shown that these propensities exist in such violence as to subjugate the intellect, control the will, and render it impossible for the party to do otherwise than yield.*
>
> *And again, this state of mind is not to be presumed without evidence, nor does it usually occur without some premonitory symptoms indicating its approach.*

A striking resemblance to vice. Sounds like something Stanley would say.

CHAPTER 20

Wednesday, December 22

The front-page headline of this morning's *Cape Cod Times* proclaimed: "Defense Attorney Puts On Magic Show." The article accuses me of trying to pull an acquittal from thin air. Seeing myself identified in print as a defense attorney caused a momentary jolt. For the past six weeks I've thought of myself as Buck Hammond's lawyer, but never as a garden-variety defense attorney. I'd better get used to it, I guess.

The *Boston Herald* wasn't so jocular. "Justice Undermined" screamed its page-one banner. The article that followed condemned my "thinly veiled" call for jury nullification and criticized any juror who might "buy into" it. The reporter lambasted Judge Leon Long for his tolerance of my "subversive tactics." Generous quotes from District Attorney–Elect Geraldine Schilling, along with a few sarcastic remarks from Stanley, were sprinkled throughout.

It occurred to me as I finished the piece that I must be a defense attorney after all. No one called me for a comment.

The good news is that the news doesn't matter. Thanks to the street smarts of Judge Leon Long, our jury is sequestered for both the trial and the deliberations. From now until the verdict is returned, the members of the panel will hear none of the media hype. The press will try its case in the court of public opinion for the foreseeable future, of course. And, to some extent, the prosecution will too. But I will try mine only in this courtroom, before the men and women who will decide Buck's fate.

We're delayed this morning. Yarmouth police officers picked up Dominic "Nicky" Patterson late last night, and he's scheduled to face the music here before our trial resumes. Nicky is one of the Cape's better-known deadbeat dads. He gets hauled in every year or two, signs off on a payment schedule, makes a few installments, then disappears again. This time the Kydd has been appointed to defend him.

According to the courtroom clerk, Wanda Morgan, it was close to midnight when the Kydd got the assignment. He was still in the office when the night clerk called, intending to leave a message on the answering machine. Wanda shakes her head sympathetically when she delivers this news. She's at least as old as I am, but I think she's taken a shine to our young associate. I wonder how the Kydd feels about forty-something women.

The Kydd hustles into the courtroom and hurries down its crowded center aisle, scanning the front of the room for his new client. He doesn't seem to notice Wanda, though she clearly notices him. His eyes find only Harry and me. His grin is halfhearted.

"Where's dear old dad?" he asks, joining us at the counsel table. His eyes are bloodshot.

"Not here yet," I tell him.

"You're going down, Kydd," Harry threatens, leaning toward him and laughing.

The Kydd frowns at him. "Why the hell are we here?"

It's a valid question, but we all know the answer. Deadbeat dads are usually handled across the parking lot, in Family Court. There's only one way this particular deadbeat ended up in Superior Court. Judge Leon Long requested him.

"You're going down, Kydd," Harry says again, laughing harder.

"Stop it," I tell him, fighting back my own laughter. The Kydd's been dealt a lousy hand. And he hasn't been practicing law long enough yet to separate himself from it. There's nothing he can do. One of the county's chronic deadbeat dads is about to face a judge who views supporting one's children not only as a legal obligation but as a sacred moral mandate as well.

The errant father comes through the side door, cuffed, shackled, and flanked by armed guards. His clothes are disheveled and his hair sticks up at odd angles. He looks like he had a rough night. He doesn't know it yet, but his morning will be worse.

The reporters ask questions of anyone who'll give

them the time of day, and the TV cameras are rolling. This won't be tonight's top story—Buck has that slot sewn up for the week—but it's a strong candidate for second place. With Judge Leon Long presiding, even a routine child support hearing is newsworthy.

Harry and I move back to the row of seats at the bar. The guards deposit Nicky at the defense table and the Kydd starts talking to him at once. Nicky isn't listening. He'll regret that in a few minutes.

"Oyez, Oyez," the bailiff intones. Joey Kelsey is new at his job and he reads his morning litany from a cheat sheet cupped in the palm of his hand. "The Superior Court for Barnstable County in the Commonwealth of Massachusetts is now in session. All citizens having business before this honorable court should now draw near. May God save the Commonwealth and this great nation."

This announcement always makes me wonder who wrote the rules. Across the parking lot, in District Court, the bailiff just shouts "Court!" It's as if someone decided that the type of offenses heard in each courtroom should determine the length of its morning announcement. Commit a minor crime and you get one word. Do it up big and we'll write you a patriotic essay.

Judge Long strides to the bench, his radiant smile noticeably absent. His expression is stern and he bangs his gavel three times, each thud louder than the last. The room falls instantly silent. The judge glares at Nicky Patterson over the tops of his half glasses. Without a word, he turns toward the prosecutors' table.

Geraldine and Stanley are both here. Stanley is leafing through his notes, preparing for today's trial witnesses, paying no attention at all to the deadbeat dad. If Geraldine doesn't replace the Kydd soon, she may never get out of the courtroom. This morning, though, she doesn't seem to mind. She's on her feet, smiling at Judge Long. This is one case she's happy to have before him.

"Mr. Dominic Patterson." Geraldine holds both hands out toward the defendant, as if she's a game show hostess and he is the grand prize. "Need I say more?"

The Kydd gets to his feet. "Your Honor . . ."

Judge Long silences him with one hand, his eyes once again boring into Nicky. "The charges, Attorney Schilling. Read the charges."

She does. Nicky has two daughters, now ten and eight. He's been estranged from his wife and the girls for five years. He met his support obligations during the first two, but his contributions since then have been spotty, at best. His last partial payment was made more than eight months ago. All totaled, he's in arrears more than twenty-two thousand dollars, exclusive of interest.

The Kydd does what he can. There are only so many responses one can make to this sort of charge. Out of work . . . hard times . . . looking for a job . . . The Kydd asks the judge to approve a new payment plan, and he has one prepared. No wonder his eyes are bloodshot.

The Kydd hands his proposal to Wanda. Her eyes linger on him for an extra beat before she passes the paperwork up to the judge. I can't be sure, but I think the Kydd notices. The tips of his ears turn pink.

Judge Long doesn't respond to the Kydd's request, doesn't even look at his proposed plan. "Thank you, Mr. Kydd," he says softly, his eyes still focused on Nicky. "You may be seated now."

The Kydd crosses the room, drops into his chair, and rests his head in his hands. He knows this isn't good.

"Stand up, Mr. Patterson." The judge's voice is uncharacteristically quiet.

Nicky gets to his feet, looking like he's about to make excuses. That would be a mistake. Lucky for him the judge speaks first. It's almost a whisper. "What did you have for dinner last night, Mr. Patterson?"

"Huh?" Nicky is thrown by the question. He stares at the judge, then looks down at the Kydd for help. The Kydd shrugs at him.

Judge Long leans forward on the bench, his half glasses perched on the end of his nose. "What did you have for dinner last night, sir? What did you eat?"

"What did I eat?"

"That's right. What did you eat?"

Nicky stares at the Kydd, desperate for advice now.

"Mr. Patterson, did you have dinner with Mr. Kydd last night?"

Harry laughs out loud beside me, then covers his mouth and fires an apologetic glance toward the judge. I don't dare look at either one of them.

Nicky bites his lower lip and shakes his head. "Naw, I didn't have dinner with him. I don't even know him."

"Well, then, he can't help you with my question, can he?"

Nicky stares at the judge, blank.

"Dinner, Mr. Patterson. What was it?"

Nicky gives up on the Kydd. His eyes dart around the room for a few moments, as if he might find someone else to come to his aid. Finally, he faces front and looks up at Judge Long. "You want me to, like, name the foods?"

The judge sits back in his chair, smiling at Nicky. But anyone who knows Judge Leon Long can see it's an ominous smile. His voice is still barely more than a whisper. "That's right, sir. Name the foods."

"Well . . . I . . . uh . . . I ate at Zeke's."

Laughter erupts in the gallery. Harry leans forward and lowers his head to his knees, his shoulders shaking. I turn away from him and cover my mouth with both hands; I might have to leave the room.

The Kydd buries his face in his arms on the defense table. He's digesting one of the many cruel realities of practicing law: No matter how bleak a case may look, it can always get worse.

Zeke's is a strip joint in Hyannis.

Judge Long sits perfectly straight in his leather chair and bangs his gavel again. The laughter stops. But Harry's shoulders keep shaking.

"The food, Mr. Patterson. I don't want to hear about anything but the food."

The hissing steam radiators have barely begun to heat this room, but Nicky is sweating. "I . . . uh . . . I got the special."

Judge Long leans forward again. "And what was

the special, Mr. Patterson? Remember, just the food."

"Meat loaf," Nicky says, "with mashed potatoes."

The judge nods. "Vegetable?"

Nicky swallows. "Green beans."

"Beverage?"

Nicky swallows again. "I had a beer."

The judge glares at him.

"Two."

Judge Long stands and paces behind the bench, his arms folded across his pleated robe, his eyes on the floor. Minutes pass. The room is silent. Nicky, it seems, isn't breathing. Finally, the judge stops pacing, removes his glasses, and glares at Nicky again. "What did your children have for dinner last night, Mr. Patterson?"

Nicky freezes. "I dunno."

"You dunno?" The judge isn't whispering anymore. "You dunno?"

"No."

"You ate your meat loaf and your mashed potatoes and your green beans—all the while not knowing what your little girls had to eat, Mr. Patterson?"

Nicky opens his mouth, but nothing comes out.

"You drank your beer and then ordered another—not knowing what they had to drink?"

Nicky stares at his shoes.

"Do they have milk in the house, Mr. Patterson? Do they have orange juice?"

"Prob'ly."

"Prob'ly? Prob'ly's not good enough, Mr. Patterson. Not good enough for those two little girls."

The judge sits down again and picks up the Kydd's

proposed payment plan. He puts his glasses back on, skims the proposal for less than a minute, then sets it on the bench and leans toward Nicky.

"I'll tell you what we're going to do, Mr. Patterson." Judge Long's voice is low again—and threatening. "We're going to send you home."

Nicky is stunned.

"We're going to send you home with a new payment plan."

Nicky wears the smile of a man who can't quite believe his good fortune.

"Here's the plan."

Nicky leans forward, eager to please.

"You're going to be back here tomorrow morning at nine o'clock, Mr. Patterson, with a bank check for twenty-two thousand dollars."

Nicky swallows his smile. "I ain't got it, Judge. I ain't got that kind of money. Honest."

"Then get it, Mr. Patterson. After you deliver the bank check, I'll enter an order that allows you to pay off the interest over time." The judge takes his glasses off again and points them at Nicky. "Provided, of course, that you make your future payments on schedule."

The Kydd is on his feet, trying to bring an end to this session. They've got twenty-four hours. They may as well take it. But Nicky won't budge. He's shaking his head at Judge Long. "Get it where?"

"You drive, Mr. Patterson?"

"Yeah, I drive. Course I drive."

"What do you drive?"

"Chevy pickup. Two-fifty diesel."

"Old?"

Nicky hesitates. "Not really. A year."

"Sell it."

The Kydd elbows Nicky Patterson out from behind the table and shepherds him toward the center aisle.

"Nine o'clock sharp," the judge says to Nicky's back. "Oh, and one more thing, Mr. Patterson."

The Kydd and Nicky are almost at the back doors, but they turn and face Judge Long.

"You show up without that check," the judge says, "you'd better bring your toothbrush."

CHAPTER 21

Sequestered jurors seem to meld. Fourteen strangers, with nothing in common but the case before them, somehow take on a single personality as soon as they are quarantined. It happens almost every time. Some panels are reserved and distant. Some are angry. Others are warm, sympathetic.

Ours is worried. Worried about convicting a man who has already suffered so much. Equally worried about not convicting a man who shot another in cold blood. It's all written on their faces.

They file through the side door, wrapping up whispered conversations, their expressions tense, sober. Judge Long greets each of them, his radiant smile back where it belongs. He invites them to take their seats, and the crowd in the gallery sits as well. Every bench in the courtroom is full. Even the aisles are jammed.

Chief Tommy Fitzpatrick reclaims the witness box, hat in his lap. The judge reminds him that he is still under oath and the Chief nods his understanding. He's been in the witness box a few times before. He knows the rules.

The jurors have had all night to reflect on the damning testimony Stanley elicited yesterday. No doubt Buck's words—*I wish he'd get up, so I could kill him again*—echoed in their minds throughout the night. Now it's my job to make the jurors understand those words. It's my job to make them feel what Buck felt that morning. None of us can, of course. Not completely. But we're sure as hell going to give it a shot. And the Chief of Police is going to help.

"Chief Fitzpatrick, tell us about Billy Hammond. What happened to him?"

I just broke the cardinal rule of cross-examination. Questions posed during cross should never be open-ended, should always call for yes or no answers. But that rule doesn't apply here. Not in this case. Adverse witness or not, Chief Tommy Fitzpatrick can talk all day as far as I'm concerned. As long as he's talking about Billy Hammond.

Stanley clears his throat and stands, then heads for the bench. "Your Honor, this isn't about the Hammond boy."

"It most certainly is." I respond to the jurors, not to Stanley. A few of them look startled. It's the first time they've heard me raise my voice.

I turn to the judge. "It is about the Hammond boy, Your Honor. That's *all* it's about."

Judge Long puts his hands in the air to silence both of us. "I'll allow the testimony," he says, "but I'm going to give them a limiting instruction."

I return to my seat. A limiting instruction is fine with me as long as the facts come in. By the time the Chief of Police tells the story of Billy Hammond's death, the limiting instruction should be a distant memory. And the jurors, I hope, will use the evidence the way it should be used: to conclude that justice, albeit a rough justice, has already been served.

Stanley pauses at our table on the way back to his seat. "This judge," he whispers, glaring at me as if I had personally appointed Judge Long to the bench, "is despicable."

I wonder what Stanley whispers about me.

"Ladies and gentlemen," the judge says, "the defendant has raised a temporary insanity defense. The testimony you are about to hear is relevant to the defendant's state of mind and should be considered by you when you evaluate that defense. It should not be considered for any other purpose."

Buck lowers his head to his arms on the table and Harry rests a hand on his shoulder. I'd all but lost sight of the fact that Buck and Patty will have to listen to this testimony too. The Chief's words—essential for Buck's defense—will bring him and Patty to their knees. Again.

I turn to check on Patty in the first row. She's already weeping.

The judge concludes his instruction and the jurors nod their acquiescence at him. Their intentions are good; they plan to comply with the judge's admonition, to limit their use of this evidence. They'll compartmentalize the information they are about to hear, use it only for its proper purpose.

I sure as hell hope not.

"Let's begin on June nineteenth, Chief. What happened to Billy Hammond?"

Stanley clears his throat again. "Your Honor, I'm sorry, but I have to object once more. This witness isn't competent to testify about what happened to another person—especially a dead person."

Judge Long leans back in his chair and takes a deep breath. He taps his fingertips on the bench and shakes his head, peering over the rims of his half glasses at Stanley. He's annoyed by the repeated interruptions. But I'm not.

This is the kind of objection I hoped Stanley would raise. I'll have to rephrase my question, and the Chief's cross-examination will take longer than it should, but eventually the jury will hear the facts. They'll hear them from the Commonwealth's witness, not ours. And my gut tells me these jurors won't appreciate Stanley's attempts to muzzle his own witness.

Judge Long removes his half glasses and shifts his gaze to me, rubbing the bridge of his nose. I look back at him and raise both hands toward the bench. No need for a ruling. I know what to do.

"Chief Fitzpatrick, you led the investigation into the disappearance of Billy Hammond, did you not?"

Stanley drops into his chair before the Chief answers.

"I did."

"Tell us, sir, what prompted that investigation."

Stanley shifts in his seat but doesn't get up. Judge Long sighs and shakes his head.

"The 911 dispatcher got a call from a woman at about eleven o'clock that morning. It was a Saturday—June nineteenth. The caller could barely speak; she was hysterical. Turned out to be a summer neighbor of the Hammonds. She'd been weeding her garden, she said, and had spoken with Billy as he passed her house on his way to the beach."

Stanley stands and clears his throat again, apparently anticipating my next question. "Your Honor, we're headed for unadulterated hearsay."

There are twenty-three exceptions to the hearsay rule and this testimony arguably falls within three of them. One, though, is a perfect fit.

"Excited utterance, Your Honor. The statement is admissible if it relates to a startling event made while the speaker was still under the stress of the moment. If that exception doesn't apply here"—I turn to face the judge—"then it doesn't apply anywhere."

Judge Long looks down at me but I turn away from him, face the panel again. If he's going to allow the testimony, I don't want him to say so yet. I want to get one more argument in front of the jurors—and in front of Stanley—before the judge rules.

"But if the Court prefers, Your Honor, we'll call the neighbor during our case in chief. She's spending the Christmas holidays in her South Chatham cottage. I spoke with her this morning."

Hearsay is only hearsay if the person being quoted is unavailable to testify. If the neighbor is available for trial, then the Chief's testimony isn't hearsay in the first place; it doesn't have to qualify as an exception.

I face Judge Long again. He arches his eyebrows, then looks at Stanley for a response.

Stanley sinks to his chair without a word.

I steal a glance at the defense table. Harry winks. It worked.

The last person Stanley wants in front of this panel is the Hammonds' hysterical neighbor. If Stanley persists with his objections—even the valid ones—I'll call the neighbor to the stand to fill in the blanks. If Stanley keeps quiet and lets the Chief tell the whole story, then the neighbor's testimony won't come in. It will be excluded as cumulative.

Judge Long looks at the jurors, then at Stanley, and finally at me. "I'll allow it."

I face the witness box again. "Chief, you were telling us about a conversation between Billy Hammond and his neighbor."

The Chief looks comfortable in the witness chair. He always does. He enjoys the ease of a man who plans to tell the truth—nothing more, nothing less.

"Yes," he says. "The neighbor told Billy he looked like he'd grown three inches since she'd seen him last. Billy laughed and said he probably had. She turned back to her weeding but stood up a few moments later to stretch."

The Chief pauses for a sip of water.

"She was facing the beach at the time. She saw Billy approach a van idling at the far end of the parking lot. He was reaching out to pat a dog in the front seat. Then Billy vanished. She ran to the road and started for the beach, but the van peeled off before she got there. She found a fishing pole where the van had been."

"Billy Hammond's fishing pole?"

"Yes." The Chief turns from the panel and looks—apologetically, it seems—at Patty. "His mother identified it."

The members of the panel turn toward Patty too. Her eyes are wide, tear-filled, and she's biting her lower lip, all the horror of that moment written on her face.

It takes a while for the jurors to return their attention to the Chief. I remain silent until they do.

"What happened next?"

"Well, as I said, it was a Saturday. One of my men called me at home and I joined the officers at the scene right away. The neighbor had gotten a good look at the van. She'd also had the presence of mind to memorize its license plate. We traced the plate immediately. Then I alerted the state barracks and they set up checkpoints at both bridges. We didn't want that van leaving Cape Cod."

"Did it?"

The Chief looks at the hat in his lap and shakes his head. "No."

"Where did it go?"

He looks up at the panel again and takes a deep breath. "A state trooper found it the next day—Sunday—at about five in the afternoon. It was backed into a thicket of bushes at the Cape Cod Canal."

The Chief looks down at his hat again, then up at the panel. "Empty."

"Let's back up a moment, Chief. You say you traced the plate. What did you learn?"

"The van was registered to a Hector Monteros. We did a background check on him as soon as we got the ID, then put out an APB."

Stanley clears his throat yet again.

"What did the background check tell you about Monteros?"

Stanley jumps up and his chair topples backward once more. "Objection, Your Honor!"

"Counsel"—Judge Long waves his arms like a traffic cop—"approach."

Stanley and I hurry to the judge's bench, to the side farthest from the jury.

"Where are you going with this, Counsel?" Judge Long directs his question to me, in a whisper.

"Monteros was on the county's registry of known sex offenders, a repeat pedophile."

The judge shakes his head emphatically before I complete the sentence. "Not coming in."

"State of mind, Judge. That information was conveyed to the parents—to the defendant—before Monteros was arrested. Surely it goes to state of mind."

Judge Long shakes his head even harder. "No way. I'll allow testimony about what happened to this child. That's all. No prior acts."

He's right, of course. Even if Monteros were alive and sitting in the courtroom, evidence of his prior bad acts wouldn't be admissible. Not unless he opened the door by offering evidence of good character. And no lawyer with a license would let him do that.

Stanley rights his chair again and sits, and I return to my post in front of the jury box. Twenty-eight eyes search mine. They want to know what information I'm being forced to swallow. They want to know what I know—more important, what Buck Hammond knew—about Hector Monteros.

I'd like to tell them to remember this moment. I'd like to tell them to keep it in mind as they listen to the Chief's testimony. I'd like to tell them to read between the lines, to fill in the blanks, to figure it out for themselves.

I can't, of course. I can't say any of those things. Not now. Not ever.

CHAPTER 22

Silence settles on the courtroom like cloud cover. The jurors' gazes rest on Tommy Fitzpatrick. Mine does too. But I'm in no hurry to resume questioning. The longer the pause, the more memorable the hole in the testimony. At least that's my theory.

Finally, Judge Long leans forward and catches my eye. "Counsel," he says, "you may proceed."

I smile up at him, as if I'd been awaiting his permission.

"You told us yesterday, Chief, that Hector Monteros was the main suspect in the disappearance of Billy Hammond, is that correct?" I turn to scan the faces in the jury box as I ask the question.

"That's right," he answers.

I face him again. "Who were the other suspects?"

His smile is barely perceptible. He knows where this is going. "There weren't any other suspects," he says.

"Never?"

"Never."

"To this day?"

He nods. "To this day."

"You also told us you were hoping—initially, at least—that Monteros would lead you to Billy Hammond, correct?"

"Yes."

"That wasn't necessary, though, was it?"

"No."

"Why not, Chief?"

He takes a deep breath. Stanley shifts in his chair and Judge Long looks over at him, no doubt anticipating an objection. Stanley doesn't get up, though. I walk to the jury box and lean forward on its banister, my back to the witness.

"We found the boy," the Chief says. "We found his body. Early Monday morning, the twenty-first, at about half past one."

I continue to stare at the panel. "Where did you find Billy Hammond's body?"

Water pouring from pitcher to glass is the only sound in the room. Silence surrounds us, weighs on us, while the Chief sets the pitcher down and pauses for a drink. "We had canine units working the canal. Two of them; one on each side. They started combing the area late in the day Sunday, as soon as the van was located."

Another pause. Another swallow.

"One of them found the boy's body. It was buried in a shallow grave, under thick brush, about a hundred yards behind the power plant."

The jurors are silent, their eyes riveted to the witness box. Their expressions are fixed; no emotion in sight.

"Tell us about Billy's body, Chief. What condition was it in?"

Stanley's creaking chair tells me he's getting up again. "Your Honor, please. Counsel is crossing the line here. This is nothing but inflammatory."

Judge Long shakes his head. "I've already ruled on this, Mr. Ed-gar-ton the Third. I'll allow testimony about what happened to this child. The information is relevant to the defendant's state of mind and I'll allow it for that limited purpose."

The judge turns toward the witness box. "Chief Fitzpatrick, keep it brief. Just the facts."

The Chief nods up at the judge. His eyes rest briefly on Buck before he faces the panel again. The jurors stare back at him, not blinking. "The boy was bound and gagged," he tells them. "Naked." Tommy Fitzpatrick almost swallowed the last word. If the jurors got it, their faces don't say so.

"An oil-stained towel was stuffed in his mouth. Thin metal cables were twisted around his ankles and wrists. They'd worn through the skin in some spots, exposing the bone."

The Chief takes a deep breath, shakes his head, and looks at Buck again. "There were no other marks on his body."

Two jurors in the front row close their eyes. The

other twelve don't move a muscle. I wait until all eyes are open and on me, then turn to face Buck and Patty. Buck's head rests in his arms on the table, his body rigid. Patty lifts her face skyward, eyes closed, cheeks drenched. Neither one of them makes a sound.

The Chief wipes his eyes. "Twenty-seven years I've been on the force. I've never seen anything worse."

"Objection!" Stanley's face is beet red, his forehead vein bulging.

"Sustained!" Judge Long isn't happy either. "Chief Fitzpatrick, please, sir. Answer only the question asked. And give us the facts, nothing more."

More than a decade I worked in this courtroom as a prosecutor. Not once did I hear Tommy Fitzpatrick express an emotion. Until now.

The Chief looks up at the judge, wiping his eyes again. "I'm sorry, Your Honor. I apologize."

Judge Long turns to the panel. "The jury will disregard the witness's last statement."

They nod at him, compliant.

"How did you know the dead child behind the power plant was Billy Hammond, Chief?"

The Chief shifts in his seat. "Well, we felt pretty confident about it from the start. Everything fit. We couldn't say for sure, of course"—the Chief gestures toward Buck—"until his father identified the body."

I cross the room again to stand behind Buck, who manages to lift his head from the table to face the Chief. "When did he do that?"

"Right away," the Chief says, looking back at Buck. "Mr. Hammond was waiting at the morgue when the body arrived—at about two forty-five that morning. We'd called from the road and asked him to meet us there, so we could get a positive ID as quickly as possible. We'd also called the coroner in to do an immediate autopsy. Mr. Hammond identified his boy before it started."

"Were you present, Chief Fitzpatrick, when Mr. Hammond identified his son?"

"I was." The Chief stares at the hat in his hands.

"Describe for us, if you can, Mr. Hammond's demeanor at that time."

Stanley stirs but says nothing.

For a few moments the Chief seems unable to tear his eyes from his hat. Finally he looks up, his eyes glistening, and speaks directly to the panel. "He collapsed. Fell to his knees at first, then put his face down on the floor, his cheek pressed against the linoleum. I knelt beside him, said I was sorry."

The Chief shakes his head slowly. "Hell of a thing to say to a man at a time like that. Words are no good sometimes."

"What did Mr. Hammond say?"

The Chief shrugs and looks down at his hat again, blinking. "Mr. Hammond didn't say anything. Banged his head against the floor. Kept banging it, harder each time. It took three of us to stop him."

"What happened next?"

The Chief's expression grows puzzled. "He quieted. He just stopped. He got up and sat on a bench in the hallway, outside the autopsy suite. Said he wanted to wait. To wait for Billy, he said. I assumed he meant wait for the coroner's report on Billy."

"Do you know what Mr. Hammond did next?"

The Chief takes another swallow of water. "He was still sitting on that bench when I left the building. I remember because I asked if I could get him a coffee—or anything."

"What did he say?"

The Chief shakes his head. "He didn't say a word. Didn't even seem to hear me."

"Chief Fitzpatrick, why did you leave the morgue?"

"I'd just gotten a call from my dispatcher. The army chopper transporting Monteros back to Chatham was in transit, due in Chatham a little before five. My night shift is thin to begin with. I needed to call in extra officers, make preparations."

"And when was the next time you saw Mr. Hammond?"

"When I went back. He was sitting in that same spot on the bench outside the autopsy suite. I don't think he'd moved."

"Why did you go back to the morgue, Chief?"

"To talk to the coroner. I wanted to issue the charges before Monteros landed. Didn't want to wait for the written autopsy report."

Buck loses his battle with gravity and lowers his head to the defense table again. I leave his side and walk slowly across the courtroom toward the jury box. "Charges against Hector Monteros?"

"Yes."

I lean against the wooden railing, facing the jurors again. "After speaking with the coroner, Chief, how many separate charges did you file?"

"Three."

I study the jurors as they stare at the Chief. "What were they?"

"First-degree murder. Kidnapping. Forcible rape of a child."

No visible reaction in the box.

I travel the length of the courtroom again, back to Buck's side, and face the jurors in silence. I want them to look at me. When they do, I turn my own eyes to Buck.

They do too.

Silence. I want them to look hard at this man. I want them to digest the fact that on the morning of June 21, he received the same information they just did. I want them to imagine what it was like for him, receiving that information about his little boy. And I want them to react.

But they don't.

"Chief Fitzpatrick, what was the cause of Billy Hammond's death?"

The Chief turns from the panel to Buck, then looks up at me. "Asphyxia. The medical examiner found minute hemorrhages in the lungs and heart, meaning death was caused by a lack of oxygen. The boy suffocated."

"Did you give Mr. Hammond that information while you were both at the morgue?"

"Yes."

"Did you tell him what specific charges you planned to file?"

The Chief nods and turns back toward the jurors. "Yes, I did. I felt I owed him that much. Otherwise he and his wife"—the Chief gestures toward Patty with

153

his hat and shakes his head—"they'd hear it on the radio. Or on TV. I couldn't let that happen."

"How did Mr. Hammond respond?"

The Chief shakes his head again, slowly. "He didn't. He never said a word."

"Your office later received the results of DNA tests conducted on both Monteros and Billy Hammond, is that right, Chief?"

"Yes."

"Were they conclusive?"

He nods. "They were."

"Tell the panel, if you will, what was found beneath Billy's fingernails."

The Chief nods again and swallows hard. He knew this was coming. "Skin fragments," he says. "The coroner scraped skin fragments from under the boy's fingernails. DNA testing established that Hector Monteros was the source. The boy fought. He fought for his life."

At least half of the jurors shift in their seats, look away from the Chief, away from me too. Their faces are closed; they don't want to hear any more.

I look over at Harry. He runs four fingers across his neck as if decapitating himself. He's telling me: You're done. Sit down. Shut up.

But I can't. Not yet. I have one final, burning point to hammer home.

"When Billy Hammond disappeared, Chief, did your office open a file?"

He takes another drink of water and his eyes open wide. He seems surprised by the question. "Of course."

"An accordion pocket with manila folders inside, a place to file reports, record telephone numbers, organize correspondence?"

"That's right."

"A file you planned to use throughout the investigation?"

"Yes."

"A file you'd need to consult until the investigation ended, is that right?"

"Well, of course."

"What's the current status of that file?"

The Chief stares at me for a moment, a glimmer of understanding in his eyes. Then he turns to the panel and looks slowly at each person. "It's closed."

CHAPTER 23

The conference room looks like a paper recycling center gone amok. Documents, manila folders, and legal pads litter the table, chairs, and floor. A half dozen courthouse-generated printouts hang from the ceiling-high bookcases, thumbtacked at eye level. They're rap sheets, a couple of them long enough to touch the floor.

The Kydd sits in the midst of it all, jacket and tie gone, sleeves of his wrinkled shirt rolled up to his elbows. He's traded his contacts for an old pair of horn-rimmed glasses. He's immersed in a file, leaning into the single arc of soft light thrown across the table by an old brass lamp. He doesn't look up—doesn't seem to notice—when I join him.

"A little light reading, Kydd?"

He lifts his eyes from the page and blinks, then points with his file toward the printouts. "Any of these guys . . . ," he says, shaking his head and tossing his glasses on the table. "Any one of them could've done Howard Davis. They all had trouble with him. And they're all up to the job."

I sink into one of the old upholstered chairs and the Kydd leans back in his. "I took a look at the crime scene photos," he says, "then decided to start with the most recent releases."

That makes sense. Whoever murdered Howard Davis was enraged. If it was one of his parolees, it was almost certainly a recent release. Not someone who wasted much time planning; not someone who weighed the pros and cons in any detail.

"Howard Davis got six new assignments during the past four weeks."

I rest my head against the chair's soft spine and look toward the rap sheets. "Anybody interesting?"

The Kydd leans forward and points to one of the shorter printouts. I recognize the intensity in his eyes. He's on to something.

"Yep," he says. "Frank Sebastian. He's pretty interesting. Out three weeks and already hauled in once for violating parole. Nothing big—just failed to check in with Howard Davis when he was supposed to. He got off with a warning."

The Kydd stares at the floor, elbows on his knees, then looks up at me. "He screwed up again, though— big this time. Knocked over a gas station with two other thugs late Sunday night. One of the conditions of parole was that Sebastian refrain from enjoying the company of these particular gentlemen. The surveillance camera got good shots of all three of them. The station owner fingered them, too, in a photo lineup on Monday."

I sit up straight and the Kydd nods at me. "Revocation hearing scheduled next week, first thing Tuesday. Old Frank's going back to the Big House right now, for parole violation. No need to wait for the armed robbery trial."

The Kydd straightens up and runs his hands through his hair. "Trouble is, he hasn't been picked up yet. He's running."

A low whistle sails into the room. Harry fills the doorway. "You're good, Kydd," he says, throwing his jacket and briefcase on top of the cluttered table. "You're damn good."

The Kydd grins. "Damn good" is the highest praise Harry doles out.

"Anything from the lab?" Harry crosses the room and drops into the chair next to mine, loosening his tie.

"Not yet," I tell him. "Geraldine says we'll have everything by the end of the day tomorrow."

Harry leans back in his chair, adds his scuffed shoes to the chaos on the table, and winks. "Cross your fingers."

We all laugh. The chance of finding a match of any kind with Frank Sebastian is slim to none. Pointing a finger at a third party to create reasonable doubt is one thing. Proving that the third party is, in fact, guilty is quite another. It happens only in Hollywood scripts and *Perry Mason* reruns.

"We do have a small problem," the Kydd says, his tone apologetic. "When Sebastian got hauled in the first time, for failing to report, our friend Stanley wanted to lock him up on the spot. A violation is a violation, Stanley said. It was Howard Davis who convinced Judge Long to give Sebastian another shot. Davis told the judge to ignore Stanley, said Stanley would lock up every last Boy Scout in the county if he could."

Harry and the Kydd laugh out loud, and I reluctantly join them. It's really not funny, though. The prosecution will have a party with that information. We'll end up arguing that Frank Sebastian murdered the one guy who spoke up for him. Sometimes I hate this business.

Harry leans over and gives me a pretend punch on the arm; he knows what I'm thinking. "Not a big deal," he says. "Davis wasn't going to give Sebastian a break on this one. And Sebastian knew that. That's why he's on the run."

"Listen to this." The Kydd's grinning again, holding up the transcript. "Stanley told Judge Long that he had no discretion. Stanley said the judge was duty-bound to send Sebastian back to prison; the rules don't allow for anything else."

Harry laughs again. "The rules according to Stanley?"

"He told the judge he shouldn't listen to Davis, that Davis is a disgrace to the criminal justice system." The Kydd looks up from the transcript, eyes wide as if he can't believe what he just read. "Stanley actually said that."

Harry leans back in his chair, hands behind his head. "Can't argue with that. I hate to agree with Stanley about anything, but he's got a point there."

"What was the ruling on that one?" I ask.

The Kydd shakes his head, his grin growing wider. "Judge Long didn't respond. But Howard Davis did. Davis asked the judge, 'Where the hell'd you find this little guy?'"

We're all laughing again.

"That's how the transcript ends," the Kydd adds, pointing at the document in case we don't believe him, "with 'Where the hell'd you find this little guy?'"

Harry stops laughing and looks sympathetically, almost mournfully, at the Kydd. "You know you've had a bad day," he says, "when you feel a kinship with Howard Davis at the end of it."

"End of it?" The Kydd shakes his head. "I've got two more files to review."

"Not tonight you don't," Harry says.

The Kydd arches his eyebrows at me. I shrug.

Harry stands and takes his wallet from his back pocket. "You look like hell," he says, pushing a fifty into the Kydd's shirt pocket. "Go get a steak."

"What? I don't want a steak."

"Then get a lobster," Harry says. "Get whatever the hell you want. But whatever you get, order a decent wine with it. Then go home and get some sleep."

The Kydd leans back and looks up at the ceiling, considering.

"You look like hell," Harry repeats. "Get out of here."

The Kydd puts his hands in the air, surrendering. "Okay, okay," he says. "Lobster sounds pretty good now that you mention it."

Harry slaps him on the back and heads for the steep staircase that leads to his second-floor apartment. The Kydd starts packing his briefcase. I head up to my office to do the same.

The Kydd's car is barely out of the driveway when the door between my office and Harry's living space opens a crack. "Hey, Marty," Harry whispers. "Come here a minute."

I leave my desk and walk toward the door, but I can't see him. He's behind it. "Why are you whispering?"

He doesn't answer.

I open the door and Harry whisks me inside, closing it behind us. I'm stunned.

Harry's living room, normally something of a mess, is transformed. It's uncluttered—tidy, even—lit only by the glowing logs in the fireplace. On the coffee table is an ice bucket, a fine Fumé Blanc perspiring in its cubes, and two long-stemmed wineglasses. An even longer-stemmed yellow rose (my favorite color) stands tall in a vase between them. The mellow sounds of a saxophone drift softly through the room.

"One hour," Harry says, slipping both arms around my waist and pulling me close, beginning his signature version of a slow dance. "Let's take one . . . goddamned . . . hour . . . for us."

My mind jumps back to the image of Harry stuffing a fifty in the Kydd's shirt pocket. I feel like a high school senior whose prom date just bought off the little brother. I look up into Harry's hazel eyes and drape my arms over his shoulders. He pulls me even closer then, pressing his cheek against mine.

"You're good," I tell him. "You're damn good."

CHAPTER 24

The chefs aren't cooking tonight. They don't have time, Luke said when I called. I'd hung up before I wondered what was keeping them so busy. Then I decided I'd better go home.

Cape Wok is decorated with tiny green lights and red tinsel garlands. The owners are happy to see me, as always, and they should be. I've put one of their daughters through college already. And there's little doubt that I'll educate the other one before my son reaches adulthood.

Our dinner is ready, small white boxes with tin handles packed in two brown paper bags, each one carefully stapled closed. The owners wave as I leave, wishing me a Merry Christmas and saying they hope to see me again soon. None of us has any real doubt that they will.

The spicy aromas of Szechuan shrimp, orange chicken, and fried rice fill the Thunderbird, then merge with the smell of burning wood when I pull into our driveway. Luke is at the kitchen counter when I come through the door, piling mounds of whipped cream on two mugs of steaming hot chocolate. He puts his nose in the air and sniffs, then closes his eyes as a satisfied smile spreads across his face.

"All right! Cape Wok!"

My stomach knots a little—a guilt spasm. In our house, Chinese takeout is comfort food.

There's another smell, I realize, competing with the spices, the wood, and the chocolate. Again, it's familiar, but it's not Ragú. It's something sweet. I can't name it.

I park the bags on the table and then notice that it's clean. In fact, the whole room is clean. Last night's dishes have been washed and put away. The pots and pans are spotless, shiny even, hanging from their hooks over the gas range, and the counters have been wiped down. It's nice to have a girl around the house.

The living room, though, is another story. The furniture's been moved and the relocated couch holds two cardboard boxes, tissue paper and tree ornaments spilling over their sides. A wide red ribbon decorates the staircase banister, tiny white lights dancing around it. Bing Crosby croons in the corner.

The crèche sits on the coffee table, the nativity scene characters scattered around in no particular order. A cow stands alone in the center of the barn. The baby in his manger is somewhere out in the field, his mother unaccounted for. A handsaw is on the table too, three unshepherded lambs meandering across its blade.

And there's a tree. That's the other smell. In the middle of our living room, in front of the picture window, stands a tall, scrawny pitch pine, a Cape Cod native not normally selected for Christmas duty. Not even by Cape Cod natives.

I turn to face Luke, who followed me in from the kitchen. He's beaming. He points one of the dripping mugs at the saw, the other at the scarecrow tree. "We chopped it down today," he says, "just before dark. It's a beauty, huh?"

Beauty's a stretch.

Luke hands one mug up to Maggie, who's seated on the top rung of a ladder, crooning with Bing about a white Christmas and stringing unlit bulbs around the highest branches. He holds the other one out toward me, but I shake my head. Hot chocolate is not my drink of choice with Szechuan shrimp. Luke shrugs and inhales half of it in one swallow.

Maggie stops crooning long enough to take a gulp from her mug. She comes up with a whipped-cream mustache. "Check out your bedroom," she says. "We've got a surprise for you."

These days, surprises make me nervous. I head for the bedroom door with Luke on my heels, Maggie scrambling down the ladder to follow. There's a faint glow in the darkened room, the kind thrown by the last embers burning in a fireplace.

My stomach knots again. I don't have a fireplace.

Danny Boy's bed, normally in Luke's room, is here instead. A wicker oval lined with an old pad and worn blankets, it's pressed against the wall beside my bed. And a night-light—one I haven't seen since Luke was a toddler—is plugged in above it. A yellow, giddy dish dashes over the outlet with an equally enthusiastic spoon.

Danny Boy isn't in his bed, though. He's curled on the braided rug beside it, his eyes alert and focused on a small, dark-brown bundle inside. His tail thumps to greet us, but his steady gaze doesn't move. The bundle lifts its head and opens moist, chocolate-colored eyes. A puppy.

Maggie bends and scoops up the small dog. "We found him in the woods," she says. "Someone must have dropped him off at the edge of the highway, and he wandered into the woods, away from the traffic. He was scampering around from tree to tree, all alone, whimpering."

"We couldn't just leave him there," Luke adds. "He'd have frozen."

More likely he'd have been a coyote's dinner. Better keep that thought to myself.

"We named him Charles," Maggie says, scratching the puppy's floppy ears.

Charles? A mental picture of the Prince of Wales pops into my head, uninvited.

"He looks like a Charles, don't you think?" Maggie hands the prince's namesake to me.

Charles looks up, as if awaiting my opinion of his christening. He drops his lower jaw, and his long tongue falls over one side of it. He looks like he's smiling. And he's far more charming than the prince.

"He does," I agree. "He looks like a Charles."

"Danny Boy has been taking care of him since we got home," Maggie says, bending again to pat the old dog. "Like a mother hen."

This news is somewhat surprising. "Maggie, Danny Boy is—well—he's a boy."

"I don't care," she says. "He's been acting like a mother hen."

Charles raises his face toward mine, his smile widening, confirming Maggie's account of Danny Boy's maternal attentions.

"Watch out," Luke warns. "He's got a wicked case of dog breath."

"He's a dog," I tell him. "He's supposed to have dog breath."

"Anyway," Maggie says, "we thought Charles should sleep with Danny Boy, but not upstairs. Charles can't handle the steps yet."

I examine the warm bundle in my arms. He has sizable paws. He'll handle the steps in no time.

"So we moved them in here," Maggie continues. "But it's temporary. When I go home, Charles can live with Mom and me."

Charles smiles again. He approves.

Maggie's face brightens and her eyebrows arch, an idea dawning. "And Luke and Danny Boy can visit."

Danny Boy's ears perk up and his tail thumps the floor again at the mention of his name. He doesn't realize he's a mere pawn in this plan.

"I was never allowed to have a pet before," Maggie says. "Howard hates animals. But now"—she shrugs, reaching over to scratch Charles's ears—"I can."

Howard Davis for Charles. A good trade if ever there was one. I bite my tongue.

Maggie and Luke head back to their tree trimming and Danny Boy follows, leaving Charles and me to get acquainted. I sink into the old rocker at my bedside and nestle Charles, still smiling, in my lap. In the space of three days, we've added a teenager and a dog to the household. Maybe it's time to build an addition.

By the time Buck's trial was a week away, I had almost convinced myself that my own misgivings about the temporary insanity plea were irrelevant. The only meaningful thoughts on the matter, I told myself, are those of the experts: members of the medical and psychiatric community. Surely, I thought, Mr. Justice Paxson would agree.

He didn't.

Physicians, especially those having charge of the insane, generally, it would seem, have come to the conclusion that all wicked men are mad, and many of the judges have so far fallen into the same error as to render it possible for any man to escape the penalty which the law affixes to crime.

We do not intend to be understood as expressing the opinion that in some instances human beings are not afflicted with a homicidal mania, but we do intend to say that a defense consisting exclusively of this species of insanity has frequently been made the means by which a notorious offender has escaped punishment.

One thing seemed certain the night I read those words. Harry should handle the experts.

CHAPTER 25

Thursday, December 23

The judge is missing. Buck Hammond is seated and the attorneys are ready. Today's witnesses are present and the press is hyperactive. The jurors aren't here yet, though. There's no judge to call for them.

Joey Kelsey, the newly hired bailiff, is antsy. He was just getting comfortable with the morning routine; he doesn't like this wrinkle. He's consulted his cheat sheet more than once, rehearsing, I guess. But it's almost nine-thirty, and the bench is empty.

Stanley is agitated. He must have arrived later than usual this morning; his hair is still wet from his morning shower. Even so, he beat Harry and me to the courtroom. And he checked his watch when we arrived.

The crowd in the gallery has grown impatient and

noisy. Harry and I are seated at the defense table, leaning back in our chairs and laughing. Stanley fires an admonishing stare in our direction, mouthing "you people" before averting his eyes. It seems J. Stanley Edgarton the Third disapproves of our lack of decorum.

But Harry and I have good reason to laugh. We know where Judge Leon Long is. It's Thursday morning before Christmas. He's in traffic court, ripping up parking tickets, bestowing his annual gift upon the citizens of Barnstable County. And Geraldine, no doubt, is enduring the festivities. Too bad Stanley couldn't join them.

Stanley did, though, receive a small surprise of his own this morning. When Harry and I set up at the defense table, Stanley was visibly flustered. He informed us that he had arrived early, though not as early as usual, and had found the courtroom dark, as it always is when he arrives. But when he flipped the switch that lights the old courtroom's four ornate chandeliers, he found Nicky Patterson already seated on the front bench. He'd been waiting in the darkness.

Stanley apparently didn't like the idea that someone beat him to the courtroom—even someone not involved in his case. "He made himself right at home," Stanley complained. "You'd think he owned the place."

I wondered who Stanley thinks does own the place.

"It's okay," Harry consoled him. "He doesn't look like he's having a good time."

And he doesn't. Nicky is still seated on the front

bench, alternately biting his nails and pulling an envelope from the inside pocket of his jacket, checking its contents. The Kydd isn't here yet, and it's clear from the darting of Nicky's eyes—from the clock to the back doors to the clock again—that he doesn't want to face Judge Leon Long alone. Whatever he's got in that envelope, it isn't enough.

The Kydd rushes into the courtroom and almost runs down the center aisle. He's a half hour late. He nods at Nicky and Nicky waves to him as if greeting the Messiah. The Kydd stares at the empty judge's bench as he heads for our table. He loosens his tie, a man freeing himself from a noose.

"He's not here?" The Kydd can hardly believe it.

"Not yet," I tell him.

"Merry Christmas," Harry adds.

"The electricity went out," the Kydd says. "My alarm didn't go off."

This happened more than once last winter, during our joint tenure with the DA's office. It was the Kydd's first winter on the Cape, his first winter north of the Mason-Dixon line, for that matter. I explained to him several times that ocean winds wreak havoc with overhead wires. On Cape Cod, I told him, wintertime electricity is a gamble. A battery-operated alarm clock is a must. Obviously, he wasn't listening.

I roll my eyes at him. "You're not in Georgia anymore, Toto."

He ignores me.

Harry tosses his head toward Nicky. "Does he have the twenty-two thousand?"

The Kydd closes his eyes and releases a long sigh,

shaking his head. He pulls a chair up to our table and drops into it, leaning forward and lowering his voice. "Turns out child support isn't the only unpaid bill. He owes more on the damned truck than it's worth."

Harry laughs. "That's a shock," he says. "So what's he got?"

"Half. He borrowed it from his parents. That's all they had."

"His parents?" I steal another glance at Nicky. "He has parents? How old are they?"

The Kydd rests his chin on his hands. "Old."

Harry lets out a soft whistle. "Stealing from the elderly to give to the children—all the while patronizing Zeke's." He leans forward on his elbows and shakes his head. "I don't see a happy ending here, Kydd. Judge Leon Long isn't going to like this version of Robin Hood."

The Kydd waves him off with both hands, then points his pen at the empty bench. "Speaking of Judge Leon Long, where the hell is he?"

Harry grins. "Think, Kydd. And take a look at your calendar."

The Kydd pulls a monthly planner from his brief-case, opens to December, then laughs out loud. "Damn," he says, "I wanted to watch."

"Don't worry," I tell him. "Geraldine will memorize the details, and she'll share them—a hundred times—with anyone who will listen. It'll be May before she stops raving about Judge Leon Long's annual obstruction of justice, his blatant disregard for the county's coffers."

As if on cue, Geraldine blasts through the back doors and strides down the center aisle, sending men and women alike fleeing from her path. She opens the gate to the inner sanctum and slams it shut behind her. The room falls silent.

Stanley jumps to his feet, but Geraldine doesn't acknowledge him. Instead, she stops at the defense table and points out the window, toward the District Courthouse. "I need a judge."

Harry leans back in his chair, smiling at her. "Get in line."

"I'm not kidding," she says. "If he's going to play this little game every year, he needs to show the hell up."

"He's already over there," I tell her. "He's not here. He's probably waiting for you."

"He's not over there," she snaps. "I just left. It's standing room only in that courtroom and there's no goddamn judge. He told the magistrate to stay home, and now he hasn't shown up."

Harry straightens in his chair, his smile erased. My stomach tightens and I get to my feet, though I'm not sure why.

Geraldine heads toward chambers, Stanley on her heels like a nervous poodle. She pounds on the door. No answer. She looks toward Joey Kelsey and arches her eyebrows. Joey checks his cheat sheet—even he doesn't know what he expects to find there, I'm sure—then shrugs.

Geraldine opens the door and disappears, but Stanley doesn't follow. He freezes in the doorway and screams.

I'm in chambers before I realize I've moved. The judge's desk chair is swiveled toward the door. Judge Leon Long is sprawled on the floor in front of it. Facedown on the plush carpeting. A knife in his back.

CHAPTER 26

Geraldine slams the phone into its cradle. Simultaneously, it seems, screaming sirens fill the air. The fire station is adjacent to the Barnstable County Complex, just on the other side of the parking lot. Help should be here in minutes.

Harry and the Kydd stand side by side in the doorway to Judge Leon Long's chambers, forming a human blockade against the press corps. Even so, bright lights from television cameras and erupting flashbulbs flood the room. Photographers strain against each other for a shot of Judge Long's prostrate form, more than a few of them standing on chairs. From behind them, faceless reporters shout questions to Geraldine and me.

"Is the judge dead?"

He's not, but we don't say so. I am unable to speak. Geraldine, I think, simply chooses not to.

"Is he breathing?"

He is. I'm on my knees beside him, holding his hand in both of mine, forcing myself to find words, to urge him to hang on. His pulse is weak but detectable, even to an amateur like me. "You're going to be okay," I whisper. I don't recognize my own voice. "Help is coming. You're going to be fine."

I hope I sound more certain than I am.

Court officers shout directions above the chaos in the courtroom, and Harry and the Kydd abandon their post. Seconds later, four emergency medical technicians appear, three men and a woman. They crowd into the small chambers, two of them steering a stainless steel gurney, the others carting sacks of equipment into the room, unpacking as they move.

Geraldine and I back up against the wall and inch along it toward the doorway, careful to avoid the working technicians and their gear. We emerge into the courtroom to find Harry, the Kydd, and Stanley lined up in front of the judge's bench in stunned silence. Joey Kelsey is backed against the jury box, eyes glazed. All four of them look paralyzed.

A barrage of Barnstable police officers has already arrived and they've pushed the throng of noisy onlookers—press corps included—behind the bar and into the gallery. The crowd is worked up, almost panicked, and the photographers continue shooting, random pictures of utter chaos, it seems. The reporters are still pelting Geraldine and me with questions. We're still mute.

Two court officers lead Buck Hammond toward the side door, his cuffs and shackles back in place. Buck's expression tells me that someone, probably one of his escorts, has filled him in. His gaze meets mine as he approaches the doorway. His eyes ask his questions before the door closes behind him. Why Judge Long? And why now?

The police clear a path down the center aisle just in time. The EMTs hustle through, one at each end of the gurney, the others on either side of it, holding IV bags above their shoulders. One of the bag holders, the woman, relays information into a two-way radio as she runs down the center aisle beside Judge Long's motionless body. They disappear into the hallway and the courtroom's back doors slam shut behind them.

Abruptly, the room is silent, its occupants still.

Stanley is the first to emerge from paralysis. He walks slowly from the judge's bench toward the gallery, stepping on the plush carpeting carefully, as if precariously balanced on a high wire. His lower jaw hangs slack and his breathing is quick, shallow. His mud brown eyes bulge from their tiny sockets. He raises one hand and points a stubby index finger at Nicky Patterson.

"You," Stanley whispers.

Nicky is still in his original front-row seat. His eyes grow wide as Stanley approaches, and he clutches his envelope, as if he thinks Stanley might take it from him.

"It was you." Stanley's voice is louder now. He continues to point at Nicky, but his eyes dart around the room.

A Barnstable police officer materializes at Stanley's side. Sergeant D. B. Briggs, his badge says. Geraldine joins the pair, her pale green eyes fixed first on Stanley, then on Nicky Patterson.

Nicky turns and looks at the faces in the second row, as if he's certain Stanley is speaking to someone else.

"Officer," Stanley calls out to the cops in general, "arrest this man."

Nicky stands but he can't go anywhere. A half dozen uniforms surround him, all looking at Sergeant Briggs for direction.

The Kydd snaps out of his trance next. He rushes toward the gallery, glaring at Stanley. "Arrest him? For what?"

"For murder."

Stanley's arm is still outstretched. And his index finger is closer to Nicky than it should be. If Nicky's a murderer, that is. Stanley doesn't seem to realize.

"For the murder of a Superior Court judge who was about to put him behind bars."

"Judge Long isn't dead," I say, still frozen to my spot outside the chambers doorway. No one pays attention.

Men and women in the first few rows—newly informed of a murderer in their midst—scramble from the benches into the aisle and head for the back of the room. No one leaves, though. Instead, they huddle in small groups against the back wall to watch. They're not sure what's going to happen next, but they are sure they don't want to miss it.

The Kydd grabs Stanley by one elbow and spins him around. "What the hell are you talking about?"

"He was the only one here." Stanley's answer isn't directed toward the Kydd. He's speaking to Geraldine and Sergeant Briggs, no one else.

The Kydd doesn't take kindly to being ignored. He inserts himself in the center of the law enforcement trio. "What do you mean?" He gestures to the crowd. "There are hundreds of people in this room."

Stanley shakes his big head, his forehead vein working overtime again. "Early this morning," he says, still addressing Geraldine and Sergeant Briggs. "I found him sitting on this bench in the darkness when I arrived. Alone. He was alone with the judge—the same judge who told him to bring his toothbrush, I might add—and now the judge has been murdered."

I'm surprised to hear Stanley mention the toothbrush. He was paying more attention yesterday than I thought. "Judge Long isn't dead," I repeat. Still, no one seems to hear.

Stanley wheels back toward Nicky, pointing again. "You don't have it, do you? You don't have the twenty-two thousand dollars. Judge Long was going to put you away and you knew it."

Nicky shakes his head and parts his lips, but no sound comes out.

The Kydd raises both hands to cut him off. "Shut up," the Kydd orders. "Don't say a word."

Nicky's face says there's no danger of that.

The Kydd towers over Stanley. "That's ridiculous,"

he says, looking down at Stanley's comb-over. "Even you can't believe that." The Kydd's drawl is more pronounced than usual. "If he'd murdered the judge, he'd have gotten the hell out of here. He wouldn't have sat on the front bench waiting for the rest of us to find the body."

I consider announcing again that Judge Long isn't dead, but it seems futile.

Stanley doesn't look at the Kydd. He faces the uniforms surrounding Nicky, his eyes darting from one cop to the next. "What are you waiting for? Didn't you hear me?"

Stanley points at Nicky yet again, as if he thinks the officers don't know who he's talking about. "I just told you people that this man attacked a Superior Court judge. Arrest him. Now."

Nicky gapes at the cops. The cops stare at Sergeant Briggs. The sergeant turns a questioning eye toward Geraldine. No one's taking orders from Stanley.

"You people," Stanley says to no one in particular, folding his thick arms across his chest.

Geraldine remains silent for a moment, staring at Nicky. She presses two fingers against her lips, no doubt wishing there were a cigarette between them. Finally, she takes a deep breath and returns Sergeant Briggs's stare. "Take him in," she says.

"You can't be serious." The Kydd faces Geraldine, his eyes wide. This is his first battle with our former boss, but he and I have both seen Geraldine at war. It'd be easier to take on the armed forces of a medium-sized country.

Geraldine stares up at him and almost smiles before

she narrows her green eyes. "Your client had motive, Mr. Kydd."

The Kydd's eyes open even wider. Geraldine never called him "mister" when he worked for her.

"He had opportunity. And his opportunity was exclusive." Geraldine turns to Nicky, who's now cuffed, then looks back at the Kydd. "I'm quite serious, Mr. Kydd. Quite."

CHAPTER 27

Judge Beatrice Nolan was appointed to the Superior Court bench fifteen years ago. She brought along a fiery temper. And it's not just lawyers and litigants who bear the brunt of her outbursts. She abuses her courtroom staff as well.

Beatrice Nolan is a narrow woman—truly. Her shoulder-length, dark gray hair is the texture of steel wool. Severe features—pinched eyes and anemic lips—punctuate her long face. Her complexion, though, is uncommonly smooth for a woman her age. Not a laugh line in sight.

The chief judge called upon Beatrice this morning to preside over the remainder of *Commonwealth versus Hammond*. He postponed a civil suit that was scheduled to begin in her courtroom today. I'm certain she didn't appreciate his meddling with her schedule. There's one thing every lawyer in the county knows about Beatrice Nolan. She doesn't like criminal cases. They're messy.

The chief judge gave Beatrice our trial briefs and the list of exhibits already admitted into evidence. He asked her to spend the balance of the morning reviewing them. Then he directed the court reporter to begin printing the transcript of the testimony received so far. And he told the rest of us to stay put. I didn't, though.

Harry stayed behind to oversee the transition while I ran through the parking lot in the snow to the House of Correction. I wanted to check on Sonia Baker, find out how her meeting went with Prudence Nelson. One look at Sonia answered the question. It didn't go well.

"What a bitch!" Sonia shouted into the telephone.

"She can help you," I countered.

"I don't care." Sonia was as worked up as I'd ever seen her. "I don't want her help. I don't want to answer any more of her nosy questions. I don't want to listen to any more of her arrogant lectures. I don't want to see her again—not ever. She's a condescending bitch."

I stayed with Sonia for almost an hour, trying to calm her, trying to convince her to meet with the doctor again, to give it another shot. She refused. I wasn't entirely surprised. Prudence Nelson isn't known for her bedside manner.

I returned to the Superior Courthouse, searching my brain for an alternate expert on battered woman's syndrome, but I came up empty. Then I began searching my brain for a way to convince Sonia to change her mind. Prudence isn't the only Massachusetts psychiatrist well versed in battered woman's syndrome, and I don't particularly like her myself. But as expert witnesses go, she's the best.

When I got back to the courthouse, Harry assured me I hadn't missed a thing. He'd spent the time pacing the hallway, he said, phoning Cape Cod Hospital more often than he should have. The exasperated unit secretary gave him the same message each time: The judge is in surgery and won't be out anytime soon; no word yet on his condition.

When he wasn't busy bothering hospital personnel, Harry was lamenting the appointment of Judge Leon Long's replacement. Judge Beatrice Nolan is bad news. She's especially bad news for Harry.

After lunch the chief judge moved our entourage, TV cameras and all, into Judge Nolan's cramped courtroom. It's a former storage area, windowless and dank, at the back of the first floor. The only real courtroom in the building—the main one upstairs—is off-limits because it's a crime scene.

Stanley, of course, rolled his TV table into our new venue at once. He positioned his star witness against the judge's bench, facing the jury box, front and center in the dingy room. Stanley can barely wait to show his videotape again. He actually patted the box when he was done—stroked it—as if it were a pet.

Judge Nolan emerges from chambers in a huff and her bird eyes dart around the room before settling on our table. They confirm what Harry and I already know. She's not happy about her new assignment. And she knows we're not, either.

Harry and Beatrice have a history.

When young Harry Madigan arrived in Barnstable County fresh out of law school, Beatrice Nolan took notice. That was twenty years ago. Beatrice was already ten years into her private practice. She offered to take the young Harry under her wing. Give him guidance. Show him the ropes.

The problem—one of them, anyway—was that Harry had been hired by the Barnstable County Public Defender's office. From day one, he was a criminal defense lawyer. Beatrice Nolan's practice was limited to trusts and estates. The only ropes she could show him, the civil side of the law, had nothing to do with Harry's job.

Besides, Harry says, she scared the daylights out of him. Even then, when her hair was brown.

Turns out the ropes Beatrice wanted to show Harry had nothing to do with the practice of law, civil or criminal. She began cornering him at County Bar Association meetings. She started monopolizing him at the local watering hole, the Jailhouse. She stood too close, Harry says, touched him too often. She draped her arm across the back of his chair, set her hand on his knee on one occasion.

Twenty-six-year-old Harry Madigan was mature about it, of course. He hid.

Harry quit going to County Bar Association meetings, even though he'd barely begun. At the Jailhouse, he switched chairs as soon as Beatrice sat down. He stood if he couldn't see both of her hands. One night, he says, he jumped up so fast he knocked the table over, and a half dozen people lost appetizers and drinks.

But Beatrice Nolan was not deterred. She left messages with his secretary, proposing coffee, lunch. She began parking her car next to his in the courthouse lot. She plastered notes on his windshield, suggesting after-work cocktails, a movie, perhaps. Her phone number, Harry says, turned up in the damnedest places.

He admits he panicked. And not only because Beatrice scared him. He was having difficulty meeting anyone else. Younger women fled, he says, when Beatrice made a beeline for him. She scared the daylights out of them, too.

Harry also admits—most of the time—that he didn't handle it very well in the end.

He went to the Jailhouse one night after a long day in trial, looking for nothing more than a cold beer and a burger. He scanned the place for Beatrice, as he always did then, before he went in. He didn't see her. So he settled on a stool at the bar.

Another newly graduated attorney, a young woman Harry had noticed around the courthouse more than once, sat a few stools away. She smiled at him when he arrived, then looked down at her glass of wine. He was planning his opening line—and it would have been brilliant, he swears—when Beatrice approached from behind. He didn't hear her coming.

Beatrice latched on to his shoulders and massaged, Harry says, until he squirmed off the stool and out from under her grasp. The young attorney who had smiled at him left her stool too, then, and disappeared into the crowd.

That's when he lost it.

Harry claims not to remember his exact words, but he's pretty sure they were graphic. In essence, he says, he told Beatrice Nolan to keep her hands to herself. Then he told her to get lost—for good. And he wasn't quiet about it. The bar crowd hushed. Beatrice froze. He blasted her.

And she hasn't spoken a civil word to him since.

There aren't many people who've worked at the County Complex for twenty years. Most county employees don't know anything about the scene at the Jailhouse or the events leading up to it. Even the old-timers—the few who were around back then—have long since forgotten about it.

But Beatrice hasn't.

Members of the courthouse staff comment frequently on the open animosity Judge Nolan shows toward Harry Madigan. No one can figure it out. When I first started working at the DA's office, my coworkers routinely—and nonchalantly—referred to Harry as "that big guy Judge Nolan throws in jail all the time." I didn't believe it. Not until I saw it for myself.

Beatrice has always done her best to steer clear of criminal cases, but no judge in Barnstable County can avoid them entirely. During my decade of prosecuting, I tried a half dozen cases before her. In half of them, Harry Madigan was my opponent. All three times, he landed in jail.

Any criminal defense attorney worth his salt spends some time in lockup. But Harry has served far more hours than most, the vast majority at the behest of Judge Beatrice Nolan. "Insubordinate," she calls him.

I wonder if she knows what he calls her.

Judge Nolan signals the bailiff and he leaves to summon the jury. We're stuck. Beatrice Nolan is our judge. Worse, she's Buck Hammond's judge. And there's not a damn thing we can do about it.

Harry stares up at her for just a moment before setting his jaw and turning back to Buck and me. "Damn," he mutters, "I wish I'd packed."

CHAPTER 28

Judge Nolan issued a stern greeting to our jurors as they took their seats and looked around the room, surveying their new surroundings. She told them Judge Leon Long had fallen ill and would be unable to continue the trial. Their faces registered concern for Judge Long, disappointment for themselves. The atmosphere in this courtroom is decidedly darker than that in Judge Long's. And it's not only because the room has no windows.

Stanley could barely wait to begin. He's downright ebullient about today's personnel change. Beatrice Nolan is his kind of judge, a courtroom drill sergeant. She consistently handles criminal defendants by the book. And then she throws it at them.

The meat of Stanley's case came into evidence yesterday. He got all he needed to establish the elements of first-degree murder: A man is dead. The defendant killed him. The killing was premeditated. Stanley also got a rare prosecutorial bonus: it all happened on TV.

Today Stanley needed to establish one final element: sanity. Because we've raised the issue, it's incumbent upon the Commonwealth to prove that Buck Hammond was sane at the moment he pulled the trigger. Stanley closed his case this afternoon with two expert witnesses who said exactly that.

The first was Malcolm Post, a Johns Hopkins–educated psychologist who's been in private practice for more than twenty years. Dr. Post testified that he examined Buck Hammond for competency and criminal responsibility on June 22, the day after the shooting. The doctor conducted a forty-five-minute interview, during which Buck denied suffering hallucinations or delusions. Buck told the doctor he had never been treated for a mental disorder and had never sought help from any mental health professional.

Dr. Post told the panel that Buck's answers to questions were "straightforward, not rambling, not confused." The doctor testified in a relaxed, nonconfrontational manner, using simple terms; no showy words, no scientific jargon. The jurors seemed to like him.

Next Stanley called Dr. Sheldon Turner, Professor of Psychiatry at Tufts Medical School. Dr. Turner testified that he examined Buck for almost three hours on October 25, about four months after the shooting. Before the examination, Dr. Turner reviewed police reports and other court documents, including our expert psychiatrist's written evaluation. He also watched the videotape, of course.

In response to carefully worded questions from Stanley, Dr. Turner gave his professional opinion that Buck Hammond was criminally responsible at the time he shot Hector Monteros. The doctor testified that Buck was fully able to tell right from wrong, knew he was violating the law, and was capable of controlling his actions. Simply put, the doctor concluded, Buck chose to kill.

Harry cross-examined both men, which didn't take long. No lawyer can do much with an adverse witness who's a competent expert, but Harry did what he could. Both doctors acknowledged they were being paid by the Commonwealth for their testimony. Both admitted they had testified in dozens of cases for the prosecution. Dr. Post said he's appeared only once on behalf of a criminal defendant; Dr. Turner not at all.

Most significantly, both experts conceded that Buck Hammond had suffered severe trauma just hours before the shooting. The ultimate human tragedy, they agreed.

Stanley declined redirect and thanked both physicians repeatedly for their testimony. Then, with his tiny eyes beaming and his stance triumphant, he rested his case. For a moment, I thought he might take a bow. It's time—at last—for my deferred opening.

The podium is against the wall opposite the jury box. Harry offers to move it for me, but I shake my head. I'd rather be free to walk around while I open, move closer to the jurors than the podium would allow. Besides, I intend to be brief.

I leave my seat and walk toward the jury box. "Ladies and gentlemen . . ."

Beatrice's gavel pounds a half dozen times. It sounds like an angry woodpecker.

"Counsel," she barks, "what are you doing?"

A moment passes before I realize she's speaking to me. "Getting started," I tell her.

"Getting what started?" Beatrice's bird eyes are as wide as I've ever seen them.

"Our case. Our defense. The Commonwealth just rested." Stanley's wrap-up was pretty dramatic. I can't imagine how the judge missed it.

"I'm well aware of that, Counsel. You'll recall I was here when it happened."

I turn to Harry. I'm at a loss. He's not, though. His expression says he knows exactly what's going on.

The judge leans back in her chair, arms folded across her robe, gavel still in hand. "Call your first witness, Ms. Nickerson."

"But Your Honor, we haven't opened."

"You most certainly have."

"No, we haven't, Judge. We deferred."

Beatrice holds up her copy of the trial transcript. "You did no such thing."

"Your Honor, if you'll give me a moment"—I move to the bench and reach up for the printout—"I'll show you the spot. The defense opted to defer opening. Judge Long allowed it."

Beatrice yanks the transcript backward with both hands, as if it's her purse and I'm about to snatch it.

"Judge Long is not presiding over this trial, Counsel." She enunciates each word carefully, as if she's speaking to a dull-witted child. "I am."

I stare at her, silent, and I realize this isn't about me. And it's certainly not about Buck Hammond. It's about Judge Beatrice Nolan. She holds the reins in this courtroom. She wants us to know that her power is absolute.

For the moment, at least, she's correct.

"You addressed the jury, Counsel. If you didn't say everything you should have said, that's too bad. But it's your problem, not mine. You don't get a second shot." She leans toward me and bangs her gavel, just once, for emphasis. "Not in *my* courtroom."

Harry gets to his feet. He shakes his head at me, his eyes telling me to forget it. There's no point in trying to reason with Beatrice. Let's get on with the case.

It doesn't feel right, though. I didn't intend to be that brief.

Harry buttons his suit coat and straightens his tie—almost—as he leaves the table. "Your Honor, the defense calls Dr. Martin Simmons to the stand."

The doctor rises in the gallery and heads for the witness box. Harry moves toward the front of the room, his eyes still telling me to let it go. The judge stares down at me, almost smiling, victorious.

Harry stops on his way to the witness box and leans toward me. "I could be wrong," he whispers, "but I don't think she likes you."

CHAPTER 29

Dr. Martin Simmons is Chief of Psychiatry at Massachusetts General Hospital. He's a handsome man in his mid-sixties, with salt-and-pepper hair, a friendly manner, and a build that suggests he takes good care of himself. More important, he's an intelligent, compassionate person. His sympathy for Buck and Patty is genuine.

The doctor has spent a lot of time with Buck, more hours than necessary for trial purposes. Buck said he didn't mind those hours; he sort of liked thinking about the doctor's questions. He told me he felt a little better after each session with Dr. Simmons. Buck surprised himself, I think, when he said that.

Harry marched through the preliminaries—the doctor's education and professional experience—

quickly. He wants to get to the point before Stanley—and Beatrice—start interrupting.

Dr. Simmons just told the panel that Buck was in the midst of a psychotic episode when he shot Hector Monteros.

Harry pauses to let the jurors absorb the doctor's testimony. A few jot quick notes.

"Tell us, Dr. Simmons, what is a psychotic episode?"

The doctor nods and turns toward the jury, his expression animated. He's eager to share the specifics of his field with people who are interested. But I'm not sure these people are. The jurors are all listening, that much is clear. But most of their faces are blank. A few look downright skeptical.

"An individual suffering a psychotic episode experiences impaired contact with reality during a specific period of time. The duration of a psychotic episode varies from patient to patient, as does the degree of impairment. If impairment is limited, the individual loses contact with a fragment of reality but retains clarity with regard to other facets of life. In serious cases, impairment can be complete. The individual's mind is severed from the real world."

"Before we get into the specifics of Mr. Hammond's diagnosis, Doctor, can you tell the jury what precipitated his psychotic episode?"

Stanley stands, clears his throat. "Your Honor, please, we've heard all this before."

"Approach." Judge Nolan sighs and shakes her head at Harry as he and Stanley near the bench. She leans toward them, lips pursed, eyes narrowed. Her pinched expression says it all. She doesn't know what Harry's up to, but she's sure it's nothing good.

"Mr. Madigan, where are you going with this?"

I wonder why the judge bothered to call a sidebar. She hasn't lowered her voice at all. If I can hear her, then the jurors can too. And the press, no doubt, isn't missing a word. We'll hear this exchange again—more than once—on the evening news.

"Where am I going?" Harry doesn't lower his voice either. In fact, he's louder. "My client has raised a temporary insanity defense, Your Honor. This is our expert psychiatrist. I'm *going* into the relevant facts." Harry's volume has amped up another notch. If old Beatrice plans to shut him down, everyone in the room is going to hear his protests.

Stanley clears his throat again; he wants a turn. "Your Honor, the Chief of Police testified at considerable length about the boy. We don't need to hear it again." Stanley shakes his head. "Besides, it's inflammatory."

"Inflammatory?" Harry's shouting now, his hands in the air. "Of course it's inflammatory."

Harry wheels around and points at Buck, then looks straight at the jury. He's not even pretending to address the judge. "This man's son—an innocent seven-year-old child—was raped and murdered. You bet it's inflammatory. Inflammatory enough to push a reasonable man over the edge, make him snap. That, Judge"—Harry turns and glares at Beatrice again—"is the point."

Judge Nolan sits up straight, her nostrils flaring. She's not happy about Harry's speech. And she agrees with Stanley. She'd agree with Satan if he were arguing with Harry.

"You will lower your voice, Counsel." Judge Nolan actually puckers her lips when she says this, but it's pretty clear she doesn't plan to kiss anyone.

"I'll do no such thing, Judge." Harry turns and points at Buck again. "You have no right to shut down this man's defense."

Now he's done it.

The judge holds up both hands, palms out, to call for silence. She removes her bifocals and sets them carefully on the bench. She leans on her elbows, eyes closed, and massages first the bridge of her nose, then her right temple. Her message wouldn't be any clearer if it were flashing in neon: Harry Madigan, not ten minutes into his direct, has given her a migraine.

Finally the judge opens her eyes. She takes a deep breath, folds her thin arms across her black robe, and tucks her hands inside its wide sleeves. "Mr. Madigan," she says, her voice lower but still perfectly audible, "no one is shutting down this man's defense. But I will shut you down, sir, if you get on your soapbox again."

She keeps her eyes on Harry and points at Dr. Simmons. "If your witness has a medical opinion, Mr. Madigan, you'd better get to it. This case is about the shooting death of Hector Monteros. We're not here to belabor the details of an unrelated murder."

"Belabor the details? Unrelated murder?" Harry's bellowing now, again directing his words to the panel, not Beatrice.

The jurors' gazes move between Harry and the

judge, question marks on their faces. They seem unsure what to make of this shouting match. The elderly schoolteacher watches Beatrice carefully. I'm worried about her.

Harry turns to look at me and it's my turn to give him a sign—an index finger pressed vertically against my lips. It means shut up and go where she's pushing you; we need the medical opinion. Continue this argument later.

Telling Harry to let go of a fight with Beatrice is like asking a hungry dog to abandon a ham bone. He frowns at my signal and clenches his teeth. After a moment, though, he nods and sighs. We do need the medical opinion. He may as well get it into evidence. He could land in a jail cell anytime now.

Harry turns his back on Beatrice and Stanley, dismissing them both, and walks toward the witness box. Stanley stands alone by the bench, looking stranded for a moment, before returning to his seat. Beatrice, of course, looks perturbed.

"Dr. Simmons, did you examine Mr. Hammond at my request?" Harry's voice is almost normal now; he's working at it. His fists are clenched but he's trying hard to appear relaxed, as if the verbal sparring of the past few minutes never happened, as if his prior question isn't begging for an answer.

"I did." The doctor looks puzzled, then relieved. He doesn't know why the battle ended, but he's glad it did.

"When did you examine him, sir?"

"On four separate occasions." The doctor opens his chart on the ledge of the witness box and pulls a pair of glasses from his jacket pocket. He settles them on the edge of his nose and looks down to read. "September tenth, sixteenth, and twenty-fourth of this year, for about two hours each time. Again on October eighth, a little longer that day."

"More than eight hours of clinical evaluation?"

"That's right." The doctor leans back in the chair, glasses once again in his hands.

"And did you reach a conclusion, Doctor, about Mr. Hammond's mental state on the morning of June twenty-first, the morning of the shooting?"

Dr. Simmons is a seasoned witness. He knows the drill. Answer only the question asked.

"I did."

"Can you state that conclusion to a reasonable degree of medical certainty?"

"I can."

Harry pauses and turns, beaming at Beatrice. "Judge Nolan is awfully eager for you to share your opinion with us."

Dr. Simmons looks up at the judge, unsure. She glares back at him, arms still folded across her chest, hands still tucked in her sleeves. After a moment, the doctor gives up on her and turns back to the jurors. They assess him critically.

It's plain to everyone in the room that Beatrice doesn't like this doctor and, for the jurors, that makes him suspect. Beatrice is, after all, the judge. The robe imparts a great deal of authority, commands a great deal of respect. No matter who's wearing it.

"As I said, Mr. Hammond suffered a psychotic episode that morning. It was a limited episode in that he lost contact with a fragment of reality—and had a jumbled perspective on other fragments—but he didn't lose everything. He was still functioning."

"Which fragment did he lose?"

"His son's death. Mr. Hammond's mind rejected it outright."

"Denial?"

Dr. Simmons shakes his head. "No. It wasn't that. Denial is a normal reaction to death—particularly a death so unexpected. What Mr. Hammond experienced that morning was an actual break from reality. In his world—in his mental universe, if you will—the boy's death hadn't happened. It wasn't a fact he rejected; it was a fact that didn't exist in the first place."

"And which fragments were jumbled?"

"The events of the prior forty hours. With the exception of his son's death, every event was clear in Mr. Hammond's mind when he stood beside the airport hangar that morning. But the timeline was mixed up; the occurrences were out of order."

"For example?"

"The most obvious example was also the most significant: his son's abduction. Mr. Hammond knew Billy had been grabbed by a dangerous man. He knew his boy's life was in jeopardy. But he had no handle on how long the boy had been gone."

"And he didn't know his son was dead?"

"No." Dr. Simmons turns from Harry to the panel and takes a deep breath. "When Mr. Hammond raised his rifle that morning, he believed he was fighting for his son's life." The doctor shakes his head. "It's hard to understand. I know that." He gestures toward the defense table, as if the best evidence of what he's telling them is seated here. The jurors' eyes follow, settle on Buck.

He's sitting upright, dry-eyed, staring straight ahead. He looks like a man whose mental universe is nowhere near this courtroom.

Harry paces in front of the witness box, one fist against his mouth, the other in his pants pocket. I recognize the expression on his face and it worries me. If I'm reading him correctly, he's about to buy a one-way ticket to lockup. And I don't want to have to finish this trial alone.

He stops pacing and his face registers a decision. He hasn't looked in my direction. This isn't good.

"Doctor, you say Mr. Hammond knew the man who abducted his son was dangerous. Can you be more specific?"

Beatrice is unaware of what's coming. She wasn't the judge when we tried to get it in the first time. At the moment, even Stanley seems not to realize.

Dr. Simmons looks surprised. He wasn't in the courtroom when Judge Long excluded the evidence. He assumed the jury already knew. "The police told him," he says.

Stanley rouses, but not fast enough.

"They told him they'd traced the van's license plate to a Hector Monteros. They told him Monteros was a violent sex offender."

Stanley erupts. "Objection, Your Honor! Objection!"

The doctor keeps talking. "On the mandatory registry. A repeat pedophile."

"Your Honor! Objection!" Stanley stamps both feet repeatedly on the worn carpeting of the court-room floor. A bona fide temper tantrum.

Everyone else in the room is quiet. The jurors appear frozen, their eyes locked on the witness box.

Beatrice pounds her gavel. Its thuds and Stanley's sputtering are the only sounds in the room. Stanley is ballistic. His blue forehead vein is pounding. He's shrieking at Beatrice, his voice an octave higher than usual. But Beatrice isn't listening. She's on her feet now, pointing her gavel at Harry.

"Mr. Madigan, your examination of this witness is over. One more word and I'll hold you in contempt. You can spend Christmas behind bars as far as I'm concerned. And if I were you, sir, I wouldn't make plans for New Year's Eve."

The judge turns her icy stare—and her gavel—on Dr. Simmons. "The county can provide accommodations for you as well, Doctor, if need be."

The doctor's eyes grow wide. He's speechless for a moment, then recovers. "Me? What did I do?"

This is a first. Beatrice sends Harry to the pokey with a great deal of ease, but as far as I know she's never threatened to throw his witness in with him. I'm surprised she'd allow him the company.

The jurors still haven't moved, but their eyes have. A few stare at Judge Nolan. Most focus on Buck. He's motionless.

Harry finally looks at me—that look that always takes my breath away—as he takes his seat. He's satisfied, happy even. He'll gladly serve whatever time Beatrice metes out, holidays or not. I can take it from here.

CHAPTER 30

If it's true that cats have nine lives, they've got nothing on Harry Madigan.

Beatrice Nolan excused the jury for a twenty-minute recess. She summoned additional court officers to her crowded courtroom, bringing the total to four. She told the court reporter we were to stay on the record. In short, she set the stage for her well-rehearsed one-woman show. She was about to throw Harry in jail. Again.

Harry had a different idea.

He told old Beatrice we'd take an interlocutory appeal. Kevin Kydd would be in front of the appellate panel within the hour, he said. Harry conceded that the Court of Appeals doesn't often allow interlocutory challenges—issues appealed in the midst of trial, before the final verdict is in. But it might just be interested in this one.

Harry stood in front of the bench and held up both hands to count out the number of times Beatrice has locked him up. He ran out of fingers. Without a trace of unpleasantness in his voice, Harry told Beatrice that the appellate court might wonder why a member of the bar—a member in good standing, no less—has been jailed so many times by the same judge. We'd like to be heard on that issue, he said.

Harry actually smiled at her then. Beatrice didn't smile back.

And it's not just the repeated lockups we'd ask the higher court to consider, Harry told her. We'd seek a review of the ruling on its merits. This was the defense psychiatrist, after all. It was his job to determine what facts Buck knew—and what facts he didn't know—when he pulled the trigger. The doctor would have been guilty of malpractice had he not factored in Buck's knowledge of Monteros's history.

Harry's not very veiled threats gave Beatrice Nolan pause. If there's one thing that matters to Beatrice, it's her standing with the courts of appeal—her reversal rate. She may have ice water in her veins, but it seems to keep her brain fueled. She is careful with her evidentiary rulings, meticulous in her written opinions. Technically, at least, she's usually correct.

There's also the Jailhouse incident, of course. Probably best, from Beatrice's perspective, not to memorialize it in a published appellate opinion.

In the end, Beatrice dismissed the extra court officers and settled for giving Harry a lecture. This was his final warning, she said. He was skating on mighty thin ice. Harry did his best to feign concern. When Beatrice is on the bench, Harry is lucky to have any ice at all.

Stanley's cross-examination of Dr. Simmons was by the book. Stanley scored a few points, but he lost a few too. This doctor has been cross-examined before. He's pretty good at it.

Harry's redirect was brief. He just wrapped it up, a few minutes past four.

Judge Nolan excuses Dr. Simmons and he heads for the side door, keeping his eyes at all times on the judge. Good instincts.

All in all, it was a decent day for the defense. The expert witnesses basically canceled each other out. One side's experts said Buck knew what he was doing; the other side's said he didn't. This is usually the way it plays out in insanity cases. The jurors will probably disregard all of the psychiatric testimony. They will decide Buck's fate based on other factors, and hang their hats on the insanity plea only if necessary.

Harry is packing up his day's trial notes. He uses an old schoolbag to cart his files back and forth to the courthouse and he has it open on our table, filling it with folders and notebooks. I give him an elbow. When he looks up at me, I move my eyes to the judge. She's glaring at him.

Harry looks at Beatrice, then back at me. I shrug. I don't have any idea what she's mad about now.

"What are you doing, Mr. Madigan?" Beatrice leans forward on the bench and folds her hands together, as if praying for patience.

"Packing up?" Harry looks down at his schoolbag, checking to make sure he's not doing something criminal instead.

"And why would you be packing up, Mr. Madigan?" Beatrice enunciates each word carefully again. Apparently, I'm not the only dull-witted child in the room.

Harry looks at me and I shrug again. He leans back in his chair and puts his hands behind his head, elbows pointed out. He stares up at Beatrice, waiting for her to identify his misstep. This is a new twist. Normally, Harry knows why he's in trouble.

"This courtroom adjourns at five-thirty, Mr. Madigan, not a moment sooner."

This is a woman with no plans for the evening. Her message is clear: She calls the shots now. We're not in Judge Leon Long's courtroom anymore.

"Call your next witness," she says.

Our next witness is Patty Hammond, but I had planned to call her in the morning. I don't want to call her now. I need to walk her through the testimony one more time before she takes the stand. Aside from Buck, she's our most important witness. She shouldn't be called so abruptly; she shouldn't be rattled.

Stanley wheels around in his chair and stares at me, a savage glee in his eyes. He knows I'm sweating.

I'm searching the recesses of my brain for a reason to delay, one old Beatrice will at least consider, when I feel a hand on my arm. It's Patty, on her feet and leaning over from the front row. "It's okay," she says, her eyes dry, her voice calm. "I'm ready."

CHAPTER 31

The room is silent while Patty Hammond makes the short trip from the front row to the witness box. She's wearing black slacks and heels, a white turtleneck and an oversized gray sweater. Small coral starfish rest on her earlobes and a pewter locket hangs from a chain around her neck. Her short hair is brushed back, away from her face. She has a fresh-scrubbed look—fair skin with a few freckles, no makeup.

Patty takes the oath, then perches on the edge of the witness seat, as if she doesn't plan to stay long. She faces the jurors and nods, then turns to me and folds her hands on her lap. Her gaze is steady. She looks sad, as always, but at ease. She really is ready.

We walk through the preliminaries smoothly. She is Patricia Lowell Hammond and she lives on Bayview

Road in South Chatham. She was born and raised here on the Cape. She is the wife of the accused and the mother of the deceased. The deceased child, that is. "Billy," she tells them, fingering her locket. "His name is Billy."

All of the women on the panel nod at Patty, then most of the men do too. The boy's name is important; he's real. They understand that. Finally, a genuine reaction.

I have always been of two minds about Patty Hammond's testimony. On the one hand, I want to prolong it, keep her on the stand as long as possible so the jurors can get to know her. I want them to witness her unassuming manner, to listen at length to her understated words. I want them to appreciate her gentle nature, still intact in spite of the grief. I want them to realize she owns the wisdom of those who have suffered too much.

In short, I want these jurors to care so deeply about Patty Hammond that they will be unable to subtract her husband from her world, a world already diminished.

On the other hand, I know that Patty's composure is fragile. And she needs to be clear when she tells the jury about the hours before and after the shooting. She needs to be certain about what Buck did—and didn't— say. She needs to be strong when she faces Stanley's cross-examination. And Stanley, though he'll undoubtedly handle her carefully, will be gunning for her.

Better to get to the heart of the matter.

"Let's start on Sunday, Patty, June twentieth, the day after Billy disappeared."

She nods.

"Where were you that Sunday evening?"

"Home," she says. "Sitting at the kitchen table. I'd been there since . . ." Patty swallows, groping for words. "Since it happened."

"Doing what?"

She shrugs. "Staring at the phone."

"And your husband?"

"Searching. He'd been searching for Billy since the police left the day before. They told him not to, but Buck couldn't bear the wait. He couldn't eat or sleep, couldn't even sit down. He had to go, had to try. He came home around nine on Sunday evening, for just a few minutes. Then he left again, to search some more."

"Did you hear from your husband later that night?"

Patty nods again. "Twice. He called first around midnight to ask if I'd heard from the police."

"Had you?"

She shakes her head. "No."

"He called again after that?"

"Yes," she says. "At one-thirty."

"One-thirty Monday morning?"

"Yes."

"You're certain of the time?"

"I am." Patty turns to the panel. "I looked at the clock as I picked up the phone. When I checked again, the minute hand had barely moved." She shakes her head at the jurors. "It seemed like hours had passed."

"What did Buck tell you during that call? The second one."

Patty swallows and cups each hand around the opposite elbow, pressing her arms against her stomach. These aren't the most difficult questions, but we're moving in that direction. She's bracing.

"He was at the station, the Chatham Police Station. He said he didn't want to keep searching blindly. There are so many desolate places here on the Cape, so many barren stretches where a man with a kidnapped child could avoid being seen. Buck said he was looking for direction, a lead. He'd driven back into town to ask the police for an update. He was hoping they'd unearthed some clue—anything. He said he needed to look someone in the eye, to ask his questions in person."

"Did he?"

"Yes. Well, no. I mean, he did go to the station, but he didn't ask any questions."

"Tell the jury why not."

Patty leans toward them and takes a deep breath. "Turns out the sergeant in charge was dialing our number when Buck walked up to the front desk. The sergeant assumed Buck was at home. They'd told him to stay there."

I nod to tell her to continue.

"The Chief had called in from the road. They'd found the body of a young boy near the bridge, behind the power plant. They thought it might be Billy." She looks down at her lap and shakes her head again. "The truth is, they were pretty confident that it was. The Chief wanted Buck at the county morgue as soon as he could get there."

"To identify the body?"

Patty bites her lower lip. "Yes."

I pause to fill a water glass and set it on the ledge in front of her. She mouths a silent thank-you.

"Did you know, at the time, how long it would take to drive from the station to the county morgue?"

She shrugs. "Forty minutes, maybe."

"Was Buck leaving the station as soon as he finished talking with you?"

Patty shakes her head. "He'd already left. He called from the truck phone. He was on the Mid-Cape Highway."

I walk toward the jury box and face the panel. "Patty, when was the next time you spoke to your husband?"

She takes a deep breath and falls silent for a moment. "He was in jail. They let me in around noon."

I pause so the jurors can do the math. "More than ten hours later?"

"That's right."

I turn to face her, but stay close to the box, my back to the panel. When Patty looks at me to answer these next few questions, she will necessarily face the jurors as well. And that's important.

"He didn't call in the interim?"

She's quiet for just a moment. "No."

"You've already told us he had a cell phone, a phone in the truck."

She nods.

"But he didn't call for more than ten hours?"

"He was arrested a little before five."

"But you didn't know that at the time."

Another nod. "That's right. I got a call from Chief Fitzpatrick at about ten-thirty. He'd just learned that Buck had refused to phone anyone. So he called to tell me what happened. He thought I should know, he said."

"Did you try to reach your husband between one-thirty and ten-thirty?"

She's perfectly still. "No."

"Nine hours. What did you do during that time?"

Patty blinks, looking as if she's never considered this question. "I'm not sure. I don't think I did anything. I don't think I moved."

I scan the faces in the jury box and lower my voice to just above a whisper. "Why didn't you call him?"

She blinks again and lowers her eyes to her lap. Her lips part, but no words emerge.

"Patty, your husband went to the county morgue to view the body of a little boy. You knew it might be Billy. You knew the cops thought it was. But you let nine hours go by without so much as a phone call." I pause until she looks up at me. "Why?"

Patty returns my stare for just a moment, her eyes brimming, then sets her jaw and shifts her gaze to the jurors. "Because I knew."

"Knew what?"

"I knew the little boy in the morgue was Billy."

"How did you know?"

Patty bites her lip again and fingers her locket. Her tears flow freely. "I don't know how I knew. But I did. I knew as soon as I hung up the phone at one-thirty. My heart ached. I knew."

I scan the panel. They're frozen.

Patty takes a deep breath. "I also knew time was running out."

"What time?"

"The time when it wasn't certain. The time when there was some part of me—a slice—that could pretend it wasn't Billy, could swear it hadn't happened. I clung to that." She raises a hand toward the jurors, then presses it against her forehead. She wants them to understand. Words, though, are inadequate.

"I knew that once I talked to Buck the uncertainty would be gone. And I clung to the uncertainty like a life ring; it was all I had. I knew it was temporary."

Patty drops her eyes to her lap and wipes her cheeks with the palms of her hands. "It was selfish, I know."

I scan the panel again. No visible reaction.

Stanley clears his throat. "Your Honor, please. This woman isn't on trial. Is counsel trying to prove that the defendant's wife was insane too? Is it contagious?"

I keep my back to Stanley, my eyes on the jurors. Their eyes move from Patty to Stanley, but their expressions don't change. Patty Hammond doesn't deserve Stanley's sarcasm. I hope they realize that.

The courtroom is quiet while Beatrice waits for me to respond to Stanley's objection. It takes a few moments for her to realize I won't.

"Counsel," she says, "move on."

Even Beatrice Nolan has enough common sense not to bully Patty Hammond in front of the panel.

"Patty, what did Buck say to you when you saw him in jail at noon?"

She looks up from her lap, eyes wide. "He didn't

say anything. We just looked at each other through the glass. We sat across from each other for a long time, staring, but neither one of us said anything." She shakes her head at the jurors. "There weren't words."

"When was the next time the two of you spoke?"

Patty tilts her head to the side. "A few days later. I visited every day, stayed as long as they'd let me, but a few days went by before we spoke."

"Thursday?"

She nods. "Probably."

"Did you speak about the reason your husband was in jail? Did you speak about his shooting Hector Monteros?"

She winces at the mention of the name. "Yes," she says. "We did."

"Did you ask your husband why he shot Monteros?"

Stanley gets to his feet.

Patty considers the question for a moment. "No," she says. "I didn't have to."

"Your Honor . . ." Stanley wants to shut this down. The judge does too, apparently. She has her gavel in hand.

I nod at Patty, hoping she'll finish her thought. She turns to the panel, her eyes wide, but says nothing.

"You didn't have to?"

"No. Of course not. I knew why." Patty's expression changes while she looks at the jurors, as if she just realized something important. "My husband isn't a murderer."

"Your Honor!" Stanley's forehead erupts.

The gavel descends, but I ignore it. Last time I

checked, "Your Honor!" was not a valid evidentiary objection.

The jurors seem to ignore it too. They're zeroed in on Patty. She stares back and speaks directly to them, as if no one else is in the room. "Buck had to do it. Don't you see?"

More than a few heads shake in the box. Maybe they find it all too hard to take in. Or maybe they don't see.

"Your Honor!" Stanley's holding both hands up, palms toward Patty, like a traffic cop. He's ordering her words to halt. She doesn't look at him.

"He didn't have a choice," she says, speaking to the jurors as if Stanley doesn't exist. "He had to help Billy. Had to try."

The gavel descends again, on the edge of the bench closest to the witness box.

Patty jumps. Her eyes leave the jury and she turns to look up at the judge. The jurors do too.

Beatrice isn't facing Patty or the jury, though. Her gavel pounds again, near the top of Patty's head, but she's glaring at me. "Ms. Nickerson," she says, almost spitting the words, "this examination is over."

She's right, of course. We're finished. I couldn't have scripted better testimony to end the day. Better, though, to let Beatrice think it's her idea. I force a resigned smile. "Whatever you say, Judge. You're the boss."

CHAPTER 32

The holiday shoppers, Luke and Maggie, were in the back row of the courtroom during all of Patty Hammond's direct testimony. It wasn't by design. When I asked them to be here at four o'clock—with the Thunderbird—I thought we'd all be ready to leave the courthouse by then. But that was this morning, when Judge Leon Long was in charge. Everything is different now.

Buck is gone, en route to his cell with the regular prison escorts. Harry and I will meet with him before we go home tonight, review his testimony one last time. We had planned to go back to our office first, to run through it a time or two without Buck. We wanted one last check for holes, one last search for an inconsistency Stanley might see before we do.

But Judge Nolan just left the bench and it's almost six o'clock. Harry and I will have to do our consistency check while we prepare Buck. We're running out of time.

Patty is at our table, seated in Buck's chair between Harry and me. The shouting match at the end of the trial day left her flustered. She looks dazed now, exhausted. Her cheeks are flushed.

Luke and Maggie wait in their seats while the stragglers in the crowd move through the back door. When the center aisle clears, they head up front to join us. They leave their parkas and hats piled on the back bench. They both look damp and windblown. Maggie's sweater droops down to her knees and the ends of her hair are wet. She's still wearing her scarf and mittens.

Geraldine strides through the back door and follows Luke and Maggie down the wide aisle, her eyes following the tracks left on the worn carpeting by their boots. She has her own coat in hand, her briefcase too. She drapes the coat over one arm and sets the briefcase on the edge of our table. "Good news," she says, "about the judge."

"She's stepping down?" Harry bolts from his chair, looking like he just won the lottery. "Early retirement?" He faces Geraldine and plasters an alarmed look on his face. "Not a health problem, I hope."

She frowns at him. "Not that judge. No, she's not stepping down. And no, there's no health problem." Geraldine's frown flips into a wicked smile. "But Judge Nolan would be touched if she knew you were so concerned."

Harry shrugs. "She's touched, all right."

Geraldine turns away from him and faces me, rolling her green eyes to the ceiling. Her expression says she hopes I, at least, will be reasonable.

"Judge Long," I prompt. "He's okay?"

"Looks like it. The surgeon says the procedure went as well as could be expected. They're moving him to the intensive care unit now. He'll be there for a few days, anyhow."

Patty leaves her chair and moves in front of our table to hug Maggie. Maggie hugs her back, hard. I'd almost forgotten—they're neighbors.

Geraldine watches them for a moment, then turns back toward Harry. She has his attention now. Harry has always thought highly of Judge Long; he's been worried about him all day. Besides, we represent the accused.

"The judge is listed in serious condition," she says.

Luke joins Patty and Maggie, all three of them facing our table, listening. Patty's arm is still tight around Maggie's skinny shoulders. Maggie leans into her, welcoming the support. The beleaguered consoling the beleaguered.

"But his vital signs are stable," Geraldine continues. "The doctors expect to move him to a regular surgical unit some time next week. He should make a full recovery."

Maggie and Luke exchange puzzled glances. They don't know what we're talking about. Neither one asks, though. Patty leans over to whisper. They stare up at the bench while she talks and their eyes grow wide. She's filling them in.

"That's great," I tell Geraldine.

"He was stabbed twice," Geraldine continues. "The first wound was deep—it missed a kidney by little more than an inch. The surgeon says it needed extensive repair. That's what took so long in the operating room."

She rests her coat on the briefcase on our table and stares down at me again, her eyes troubled. "The second cut wasn't, though. It was superficial."

Geraldine's gaze moves to something behind me and her brows knit. I know that look. The information she's giving us bothers her somehow. Something doesn't add up.

"The surgeon says it looks like whoever attacked Judge Long was interrupted," she says, resting her chin in one hand. "Prevented from finishing the job."

Harry sits on the edge of the table and narrows his eyes at her. "And it's your theory that Nicky Patterson did it? That he stabbed the judge twice, stopped when Stanley arrived, then sat calmly in the front row until the rest of us found out?"

Geraldine doesn't let on she hears Harry's questions. "I'm headed to the hospital now," she tells us, lifting her briefcase and coat from the table.

"Is he awake?" I can't quite picture Geraldine keeping a silent vigil by Judge Leon Long's bedside.

"Not yet," she says. "But I want to ask him a few questions as soon as he is. Find out if he saw anything, heard anything."

"The nurses might not let you in, though."

Geraldine gives me her "Get a brain, Martha" look again. "The nurses and what army?"

She's right, of course.

Luke and Maggie head out as soon as Geraldine leaves. Patty does too. She'll follow them to Chatham, she says, in case Luke has trouble driving on the snowy highway. Or in case she does, she adds.

It will be at least a few hours before I can join Luke and Maggie at home. I plan to pay Sonia Baker another visit, see if we can't have a calmer discussion about Prudence Nelson. After that I'll meet with Harry and Buck to prepare for tomorrow's testimony. It feels as if this day will never end.

Snow falls steadily as Harry and I trudge through drifts in the parking lot, then climb the snow-clogged concrete steps to the Barnstable County House of Correction. Harry's arm around my shoulders is the best thing I've felt all day. When I lean into him, he rests his chin on the top of my head. If only I could spend this evening with Harry—alone.

But it's not in the cards. We part company at the top of the hill. Harry heads to the men's ward and I turn toward the women's. Harry will start the process with Buck while I spend some time with Sonia. I'll join them when I can.

Buck is my witness. I'll handle the direct as well as the objections during cross. Harry is with me tonight, preparing Buck, only because I insisted. I'm a good enough defense lawyer to know Buck Hammond deserves a better defense lawyer than I am.

CHAPTER 33

The decision to take the witness stand—or not—belongs solely to the accused. A good defense lawyer advises the client of the ramifications of each option: the damning admission of prior convictions if he takes the stand, the unavoidable suspicions of the jurors if he does not. A good defense lawyer also voices an opinion, usually a strong one, about which decision the client should make. But the final call rests squarely on the shoulders of the defendant. And rightly so.

Defense lawyers admit this truth only when the client testifies. "Mr. Smith has no obligation to take the stand," the lawyer will announce. "But he wants to. He insists. He plans to tell you people what *really* happened that night."

If Mr. Smith decides to keep quiet, though, his

attorney will lay claim to the decision. "The Commonwealth hasn't proved its case," the lawyer might say. "No client of mine will take the stand when the Commonwealth hasn't met its burden. I won't allow it. And the judge will instruct you that you're to draw no inference from Mr. Smith's silence. He's under no obligation to testify. He certainly has nothing to hide."

The truth, though, is that most criminal defendants, even those not guilty of the crimes charged, have something to hide. The neighborhood gang member accused of knocking over the local liquor store didn't necessarily do it. But if his alibi is that he was closing a crack deal at the time of the robbery, he probably shouldn't take the stand to say so.

Even a defendant with no priors runs a risk when he testifies. The stakes are highest when the crime charged is a violent one. If the accused is angry—and almost all of them are—then the prosecutor need only get under his skin, provoke an outburst. One flicker of rage from the defendant during trial and the Commonwealth is one giant step closer to a conviction.

In Buck Hammond's case, this is my greatest fear.

It's not that Buck is an angry man. He's not. His manner is calm, resigned. He rarely speaks unless asked a question. Even then, he pauses and thinks—often for an unnaturally long time—before he answers. When he does, his voice is always the same, low and steady.

I've spent dozens of difficult, tedious hours with Buck during the past six weeks. I've asked him questions he couldn't answer, a few that made his eyes fill. But I've never seen a trace of anger in him. Not even when he talks about Billy. And that, more than anything, is what worries me.

I'm afraid Buck has buried his rage, pushed it so deep into himself that no one—not even he—can see it. I'm worried that the stress of testifying, speaking publicly about all that happened to Billy, will be more than Buck can bear. I'm afraid that his fury has been pent up too long, that once it's tapped it will boil over into the courtroom. I'm scared as hell that Buck Hammond will erupt in the witness box.

Harry's not worried about buried rage, though. He's worried about Stanley.

"You can't let him get to you," Harry says as I join them. He and Buck are seated at an old, stained card table in the middle of a small meeting room. They both look comfortable, relaxed.

"Who? The little guy?" Buck arches his eyebrows. He's surprised to learn he should worry about the little guy.

Harry laughs. "Yeah. The little guy—the one with the big head and the mouth to match."

Buck looks up to see if I share Harry's concern. I nod silently as I hang my parka next to Harry's on the coatrack.

"Okay." Buck shrugs. "So I won't let him get to me."

Harry shakes his head. "It's not that simple. Stanley gets to everybody. Even people who aren't on the hot seat." Now it's Harry's turn to look my way. He wants backup.

I cross the small space between us and nod again.

Four metal folding chairs surround their rickety table. I wipe a layer of dust from one of the remaining two, then settle on it. "Harry's right, Buck. Stanley would like nothing better than for you to explode in front of the jury. He'll do everything he can to make that happen."

"Explode?" Buck's expression suggests he can't fathom such an event.

"Yes—explode."

I lean back in my chair and stare at Buck. He needs to take this to heart. "If you get mad, even for an instant, then Stanley has everything he needs for closing argument. You killed Monteros, Stanley will tell the jury, because you're out of control."

Buck shakes his head, but I keep talking. "You could kill again, Stanley will argue. You could take the law into your own hands yet again. You could become a vigilante. The jurors will worry about that."

Buck's eyes move from me to Harry, then down at his hands on the table. He's silent.

"Look," Harry says, "the bottom line is this: Stick to the script."

Buck looks up again. "The script?"

I'm glad he asked—so I don't have to.

"That's right, the cross-examination script."

Buck turns to me and I turn to Harry. I didn't know we had a cross-examination script. I wonder who wrote it.

Harry stays focused on Buck. "If Stanley's question calls for a yes or no answer, give him one. And give it loud and clear. If we don't like the way it sounds—the way Stanley phrased the particular question—we'll clean it up on redirect."

Harry points his pen at me when he says this, as if it's certain that I'll clean up whatever mess Stanley makes.

"But if Stanley gives you room to talk"—the pen moves from me to Buck—"you only know three topics."

"Three?" Buck looks as if this news makes him smarter than he thought he was.

"That's right," Harry says. "You know all about Billy before June nineteenth: the funny kid he was; how he was growing like a weed; the names of his best friends; how he loved fishing and the Red Sox."

Buck closes his eyes, sways from side to side on his folding chair.

"You know what happened to Billy on June nineteenth."

Buck stops swaying, but his eyes stay closed.

"And you know you had to stop Monteros—for Billy."

Buck opens his eyes and nods, but says nothing.

"If Stanley tries to get you to talk about anything else—I don't care what the hell it is—you steer the discussion right back to the script. Three topics. That's it. You know nothing about anything else."

Buck nods again, but Harry isn't satisfied. "In particular," he says, "you know nothing—less than nothing—about the insanity defense."

For a few moments all three of us are quiet. Finally, Buck breaks the silence. "I know it's a crock."

"Goddammit!" Harry slams both fists on the table

and an overloaded ashtray jumps into the air, three butts slipping over its sides. Its dark green beveled glass is chipped in about a half dozen places. This table has been slammed before.

Harry leans close enough to Buck to whisper, but he's almost shouting. "Do you think maybe that enlightened opinion of yours is something you shouldn't mention in the courtroom?"

Buck rubs his eyes, then leans forward on his elbows toward both of us. "I'm sorry. Really. I know you're trying to do your job. And I'm grateful. It's just . . ."

He swallows hard, drops his head and stares at the table. "I won't say that tomorrow. I swear."

"If you do, you'll regret it. Your wife needs you. Remember that." Harry waits until Buck looks up at him, then leans forward and lowers his voice. "Maybe—just maybe—these jurors want to let you walk. And maybe they see the temporary insanity defense as the only way they can do that. Take it away from them, pal, and you might throw out your only shot."

Unlike me, Harry has always thought the temporary insanity plea was Buck's best bet. True jury nullification, he says, is rare. And he's right. For our jurors to return an outright acquittal, they'll have to be willing to say that the law in this particular case is just plain wrong. Rare is the juror willing to adopt that notion. Rarer yet is the juror willing to say so. The odds of an entire panel taking that route are slim. Even I have to admit that.

If the jurors accept the temporary insanity plea, on

the other hand, they can have it both ways. They can send Buck home, spare him an eternity at Walpole, even though they acknowledge he committed the crime. They know he's not innocent, but they can find him not guilty—the law allows that.

There is an important distinction between the word *innocent* and the phrase *not guilty*. *Innocent* means they've got the wrong guy; the accused didn't do it. *Not guilty* is broader than that. It may mean the accused did it but has a legally recognizable excuse. Despite the media's insistence to the contrary, there is no such verdict as *innocent by reason of insanity*. *Not guilty* is as good as it gets.

"I understand," Buck says, dropping his hands to his sides. "Honest to God. I do." He leans back in his chair, looks exhausted. "Are we finished?"

"No," Harry says, "but almost. There's one more thing I want to talk about."

"What's that?" Buck looks as if he can't believe there's a topic we haven't covered.

"Your hunting rifle," Harry says.

Buck nods. "The rifle . . ."

Harry jumps up from his chair, both hands held out toward Buck to silence him. "I said *I* want to talk about it."

Buck looks surprised. I'm not. I know exactly what Harry's doing.

"I want to tell you about a client of mine," Harry says.

Buck turns to me, question marks in his eyes.

"Listen," I tell him. "This is important."

And it is. There are probably a hundred reasons

why I wanted Harry here tonight, a hundred points Harry knows how to cover that I don't. This one, by far, is the most important.

"My client," Harry says, walking toward the wall, "is a two-bit hood. He's got a record his mother isn't proud of, but it's all pretty low-level stuff."

Harry turns and pauses to make sure Buck's listening. He is.

"Then one night he shoots a guy—kills him. Says it was self-defense. Swears it was. The guy came out of nowhere, he says, with a knife. Mad as hell about a woman. Tried to slit my client's throat."

Harry walks slowly toward our table again, hands thrust into his pants pockets. Buck watches, his expression blank.

"The Commonwealth—in the person of Attorney Geraldine Schilling—doesn't buy it. My client's no stranger to the system, don't forget. She doesn't buy much of what he says. So she charges him with first-degree. Premeditated.

"The arresting officers take him to the station and book him, then lead him to the interview room. The cop asking the questions wants to know about the handgun, where it came from.

"What my guy should do is keep quiet. He shouldn't say a word until I get there. But he's not the sharpest knife in the drawer. He talks. He tells them he had the gun in his pocket, in the inside pocket of his jacket."

Harry pulls his chair out from the table and flips it backward before he sits.

"The next question the cop asks is important.

Everybody in the room—except my guy—knows how important it is."

Buck shifts in his seat and looks my way for a moment before turning back to Harry. He's wondering what any of this has to do with him, I'm sure.

"The question the cop asks is: *Do you always carry the handgun? Or did you just happen to have it with you on that particular night?*

"Remember," Harry says, "I know this guy. He probably isn't a murderer, but he's a hell of a good liar. He thinks it over. He decides the cops—not to mention the judge and jury—probably don't like guys who carry guns. Especially guys who aren't licensed. So he tells them he almost never carries it. It was a fluke. He just happened to have it in his jacket pocket that night."

Buck shrugs. "So?"

"So," Harry says, "the Commonwealth's case just got a hell of a lot easier. My two-bit hood just handed them premeditation."

Buck's gaze lingers a moment on Harry, then moves to me. He's still, silent.

"So," Harry continues, "I thought you might find that interesting."

Buck's eyes leave mine and return to Harry. He nods, slowly. He gets it.

"On June twenty-first, where did the hunting rifle come from? Where did you get it?"

Buck shakes his head. "Do you think . . . ?"

"I don't think anything." Harry leans over the seat back, his eyes holding Buck's. "I'm asking a question."

For a moment, no one speaks. The room is still.

"From my rack," Buck says. "I have a rack in the truck. I keep it there." He leans back on two legs of the chair. "Always."

Harry stands and bangs on the metal door. "You're ready," he says. "Get out of here. Go to sleep. You need to be clearheaded tomorrow."

The guard appears instantly and ushers Buck out the door, leaving it open for Harry and me.

I lean in the doorway and watch them walk down the brightly lit corridor while Harry packs up his old schoolbag. The guard's head is turned upward toward Buck, the two of them exchanging comments as if they're buddies, on their way to a ball game, maybe.

Harry and I have known from the beginning that Buck should testify. In this particular case, it's critical that the jury hear from him. If he had opted to keep quiet, we would have done our level best to change his mind. But that wasn't necessary. From day one, Buck insisted he would take the stand, insisted he would tell the jurors what happened that morning, from where he stood in the shadow of the airport hangar. And he never wavered from that decision, never needed a push from us.

I'm glad. Glad it's Buck's decision. Glad he's so sure about it. It's Buck, after all, who will live with the outcome.

CHAPTER 34

It's almost ten o'clock by the time Harry and I reach Cape Cod Hospital. Neither one of us has had dinner, and we're both soaking wet. Snow melts on our hair and eyelashes and trickles like little rivers down our faces as soon as we enter the building. We stomp our feet and bang our briefcases on the inside mat, hoping to leave at least some of the slush and snow in the lobby.

Two security guards eye us from the front desk, then exchange wary glances. It's plain from their expressions that they don't like what they see. And I don't blame them.

Harry looks like an unusually well-fed refugee. Shin-high work boots and an old tan coat hide his suit. A day's worth of salt-and-pepper stubble covers his cheeks and chin, and dark half-moons underline his bloodshot eyes. He's either a man on a mission or he's a nut.

I don't need a mirror to tell me I look every bit as bedraggled as Harry does. Even my soul is tired.

One of the uniformed guards listens to Harry tell our story and checks both our IDs. The other one rides the elevator with us to the third floor, clutching a two-way radio. He faces his reflection in the elevator doors throughout the ride. He doesn't look at us, doesn't speak.

Geraldine sits in the small waiting area outside the intensive care unit, writing in a notepad. It's a rare sight, Geraldine in a chair. She looks no different now than she did at nine o'clock this morning. Her dark gray suit and starched white blouse are unwrinkled. Her black spiked heels and smoky nylons are flawless, relentless snowstorm or not. And every blond hair is in place. I don't know how she does it.

She stops writing as we approach, removes her glasses. Her arched eyebrows say she wasn't expecting company. "Good of you to drop in," she tells us. "But His Honor isn't receiving guests at the moment."

There are a dozen empty chairs in this antiseptic square, but Harry drops into the one next to Geraldine's and leans toward her over their shared armrest. "Is he awake?"

Harry's been doing this to Geraldine—invading her personal space whenever possible—for the past month. He's aspiring to greatness, he tells her, emulating her hand-selected protégé, Stanley.

Geraldine doesn't think it's funny. She growls at

him like an annoyed German shepherd, then gets to her feet. "No, he's not awake. But he was a couple of hours ago—for a few minutes."

"Did he say anything?" Harry pats Geraldine's vacant chair, inviting her to reclaim it.

She scowls at the invitation, directs her answer to me. "No, not a word. But he tried. He couldn't get anything out. His throat is bad."

Geraldine takes a pack of cigarettes from her jacket pocket and taps one out. I'm relieved, to say the least, when she doesn't light it. She twirls it around in her fingers instead. "His throat is sore from the tubes—or whatever the hell they put down there—during surgery. The poor guy's dying of thirst. He kept reaching toward the water pitcher, but the nurse"—she points her unlit cigarette at us for emphasis—"and *she's* a story for another day—anyway, she'd only give him ice chips."

Geraldine waits for a reaction but neither of us has one. "*Ice chips,*" she repeats, as if we must not have heard.

Still, Harry and I are silent.

Geraldine shrugs, gives up on us. She puts the unlit cigarette between her lips, turns away, and starts pacing. "So he went back to sleep."

At the wall she pivots to face us, cigarette in hand again. "I'd go to sleep, too," she says, "if all the world could offer me was ice chips." She points her cigarette at me, her expression suggesting she's shifting gears. "The lab work," she says. "It's back."

Harry straightens in his chair. I take a few steps toward Geraldine. "The blood?"

"All Sonia Baker's," she says.

Harry arches his eyebrows at me. This is good news.

I turn my attention back to Geraldine. "And the prints?"

She smiles. "All Sonia Baker's."

This news is not so good.

A sheet of white fills the small entry to the waiting area, and Geraldine lights up like a hundred-watt bulb. "Ah, Nurse Wilkes," she says. "May I call you Annie?"

The large woman in white folds her arms beneath her substantial bosom and frowns. She's apparently not a Stephen King fan. She points to her name tag: Alice Barrymore, RN.

"The judge is awake again," she says in a full baritone. "But I'm not taking a crowd in there."

Geraldine stares up at her newfound friend, who has a good six inches on her. "Crowd? What crowd?"

Nurse Wilkes keeps her eyes fixed on Geraldine but tips her gray bouffant toward Harry and me. Her undersized nurse's cap doesn't budge.

Geraldine looks over her shoulder at us as if she hadn't realized we were in the room. "Oh, them." She flicks one hand at the giant nurse, directing her out of the doorway. "They won't say a word. They promise."

For reasons I've never been able to articulate, people obey Geraldine. Annie Wilkes is no exception. She steps aside, then follows as Geraldine leads the way down the brightly lit corridor. Harry and I bring up the rear.

Annie takes charge again, though, when we reach the doorless entry to Judge Long's cubicle. "Hold on now. Stop right there." She issues her command to Geraldine's back. And, surprisingly enough, Geraldine complies.

The nurse steps in front of her and blocks the entry to the cubicle. "Put it away," she says.

"Put what away?" Geraldine looks around the corridor as if the nurse might be speaking to someone else. Her scowl says she already took one order; surely she can't be expected to take another.

"That." Nurse Wilkes points at the unlit cigarette.

"Oh, for Christ's sake." Geraldine taps the butt into its pack and drops the pack in her pocket, shaking her head.

Annie Wilkes turns her back, then, her authority reestablished, and leads all three of us into Judge Long's small compartment.

It's high noon in here. Fluorescent tubes beam down from above, exaggerating the glow of silver equipment and white linens. Machines hiss and beep from every direction. A brightly lit monitor displays four lines of constantly changing graphics. And it must be eighty degrees. It's hard to imagine anyone—even a postsurgical patient—sleeping here.

Judge Long lies perfectly still on his hospital bed, his head and shoulders somewhat elevated, a thin white blanket pulled up to his chest. Two IV bags drip from a pole at his bedside. One delivers blood to his left arm, the other a clear solution to his right. He turns his face toward us as we approach, his eyes open and pleading. He lifts his left hand just an inch, toward the opposite side of his bed, toward the water pitcher.

Nurse Wilkes stations herself between the bed and the bedside tray, blocking Judge Long's view of the pitcher. "No water," she says. "Not yet." She takes a small paper cup from the tray and scoops a plastic spoonful of ice chips between her patient's parched lips.

"The guy just wants a sip," Geraldine argues. "He's not asking for a goddamned martini."

The nurse shakes her head.

"You're an angel of mercy," Geraldine tells her.

Annie Wilkes glares.

Geraldine turns her attention to the judge, all business. "Try," she says. "Try to tell us what you know."

Judge Long makes a guttural sound. It sounds like "Ndt."

It's Geraldine's turn to shake her head. The nurse delivers more ice. And the judge tries again. This time it sounds like "Hndt."

Harry moves to the head of the bed and squats, so his face is level with Judge Long's, and the judge gives it another shot. It sounds no different to me, but it's clear at once that Harry gets it. He nods at the judge, then turns toward Geraldine and me.

"Hand," he says. "He saw a hand."

Judge Long nods, then lifts his head an inch from the pillow. "Mnz."

"A man's hand," Harry translates.

The judge nods again.

"White."

We all got that.

With considerable effort, the judge raises one arm and presses his hand against his shoulder, forcing his upper body further down on the pillow. His assailant must have braced him from behind with one hand, stabbed with the other.

"Anything else?" Geraldine has her notebook open, pen poised, but so far there's not much to write.

We all stare at Judge Long. "Tis," he says.

"I always thought you were Irish," Harry says. "Now I know for sure."

A smile spreads across Judge Long's lips. It's faint, but it's there. He points to the bottom of his bed, wiggles his foot.

"Shoes?" Harry asks. "You saw his shoes?"

The judge nods.

Geraldine clicks the pen, tucks it in her pocket, and rolls her green eyes to the ceiling. "So we're looking for a white guy with shoes."

"That narrows it down." Harry grins at her. "And I'm glad to hear you're looking."

Geraldine smirks at him as if he's an annoying child, but she knows he caught her. She slipped. She's still holding Nicky Patterson in custody, but she doesn't think he did it. And she just admitted as much to the firm representing him. A rare mistake on her part.

Harry's beaming now. He turns back toward Judge Long, leans on the bed's guardrail. "Attorney Schilling has Nicky Patterson in custody."

The judge's eyebrows arch.

"The deadbeat dad," Harry tells him. "The guy who ordered the special at Zeke's."

Judge Long closes his eyes and frowns. He remembers.

"Attorney Schilling thinks he's the perp," Harry says.

The judge squints at Geraldine, shakes his head.

"At least that's what she tells us," Harry adds.

"Nicky Patterson was there," Geraldine answers. "He's a white male. And I'm pretty sure he was wearing shoes. I haven't heard anything here tonight that rules him out."

The judge shakes his head again, but I'm the only one who notices. Geraldine and Harry are facing off.

"Come on," Harry says, "you don't have anything to rule him in. And you know it."

"Keep your voices down." Annie Wilkes sets her paper cup of ice chips back on the tray and hurries around the bed. She intends to usher us out.

"Everything rules him in." Geraldine hisses.

"Shut up. All of you." The three of them turn my way.

Harry and Geraldine are surprised. Nurse Wilkes looks stunned. I don't imagine she's told to shut up very often.

Their eyes follow my index finger to Judge Long. He's silent, but his eyes aren't. He shakes his head at Geraldine, mouths "No."

"Never argue with opposing counsel," I tell Harry, "if the judge will do it for you."

Late as it is when I get back to the cottage, I am unable to resist the allure of Mr. Justice Paxson. Once more, I center his words under my desk lamp, the only light on in the house. I flip ahead in the opinion, past the remaining evaluation of expert witnesses, and turn to his discussion of the defendant.

> Orfila has said that the mind is always greatly troubled when it is agitated by anger, . . . overcome by despair, haunted by terror, or corrupted by an unconquerable desire for vengeance.
>
> Then, as is commonly said, a man is no longer master of himself; his reason is affected, his ideas are in disorder, he is like a madman.
>
> But in all these cases a man does not lose his knowledge of the real relations of things; . . . his misfortune is real, and if it carry him to commit a criminal act, this act is perfectly well motivated.

And in the near-darkness of my bedroom, I realize that this is precisely my concern. One truth about Buck Hammond is beyond debate. His misfortune is real, and if it carry him to commit a criminal act, this act is perfectly well motivated.

CHAPTER 35

Friday, December 24

It's not a dream, not a nightmare. I bolt upright, my heart racing. My adrenaline pump switches on, an instant cold sweat seeping from every pore in my body. I will my breath silent, my eyes open.

The darkness is complete but for the glowing red numbers of the alarm clock. It's two A.M. And the noise—the one I thought I imagined in my sleep—it's real.

Scratching. Something—or someone—is scratching, digging maybe. But not outside; it's not a fox or a coyote. The sound is here. In this room.

I decide against the light, swing my legs out of bed, and grab the telephone from the nightstand. The scratching stops, though, abruptly, and I freeze. A split second later, something lands on my feet and I jump up. My heartbeat halts. The phone falls to the floor.

My attacker whimpers. It's Charles. I forgot about him. He lifts a pudgy front paw and runs it down the shins of my red flannel pajamas until I pick him up. He licks my chin as I flip on the lamp. Dog breath.

It was after midnight by the time I got home. Luke had left the outside floodlight on for me, illuminating the back stairs and deck. And the aroma in the driveway told me the woodstove was still burning. Otherwise, though, the cottage was dark. Luke and Maggie were asleep. Half an hour later, I was too. Charles never crossed my mind.

I put the phone back in its spot on the nightstand and examine the leg of my headboard. Sure enough, little dog scratches at the base.

Charles's tail wags against the inside of my arm when I scoop him up. He looks up at me hopefully, mouth open, long tongue hanging over one side again. He really does have dog breath. And he's hungry.

Danny Boy snores in his bed, oblivious to his adopted son's needs. Every mother hen deserves a helper, I believe, so Charles and I head for the kitchen. It's been a long time since I've done a two A.M. feeding, but I remember the drill. Feed him till you're wide awake, then he'll fall sound asleep.

One heaping bowl of puppy chow later, Charles is tucked back in with Danny Boy and the cottage is quiet. I'm not, though. I'm on edge.

I stoke up the woodstove, then head upstairs to check on Luke. This is not something I normally do in the middle of the night. But tonight doesn't feel normal. I crack open Luke's bedroom door without making a sound and listen. He's deep in the abyss of teenage slumber.

I head back down to the first floor, where Maggie's steady breathing from the sofa bed tells me she's out cold. I wish I were too. But I'm on edge, and the knot in my stomach is growing. It's not every day that one happens upon a judge in his own chambers with a knife in his back. It's the memory of finding Judge Leon Long that has me rattled, I tell myself as I climb back into bed. After all, it hasn't even been twenty-four hours.

But that's not it. I'm up again in an instant, circling my bedroom on cold feet. We're missing something—all of us. That suspicion grows steadily into a near-certainty as I pace. It nags at me as I force myself to sit, to use my brain instead of my stomach. My brain is cluttered, though. Minutes pass while I struggle to sort out my thoughts. If I'm right—if we are missing something—I can't name it.

And then I can.

My cold sweat begins again as I reach for the phone. Geraldine's number is unlisted, but I've called her a thousand times in the past decade; I know it by heart. I punch it in and listen to the rings. She'll be furious with me for waking her—and I'll never hear the end of it—if she's all right.

But I'm afraid she might not be.

The surgeon told Geraldine that Judge Long's attacker was interrupted, prevented from finishing the job. If he's right, then the assailant would have stabbed the judge again if he could have. Maybe again after that. Maybe eleven agains.

A parole officer and a judge in the same week. Both on their jobs about two decades. Coincidence perhaps. But if not, then revenge is at work here. And the prosecutor is almost certainly on the short list.

There's only one living person who's prosecuted more cases in Barnstable County than I have. And she's been on the job just shy of two decades.

I hold the receiver away from my ear as a loud screech follows the fourth ring and a recorded message kicks in: "The number you have dialed"—an automaton takes an excruciatingly long time to recite each digit—"is temporarily out of service."

CHAPTER 36

I grab my parka and a pair of boots. Together they hide all but the knees of my red flannel pajamas. I pull on an old ski cap, tuck my hair inside, and avoid looking at the mirror. I'm out the kitchen door, careful to lock it behind me. I don't normally lock the cottage doors, but I don't often go for a spin at two-thirty in the morning either.

The roads are slick but empty, and within minutes I'm doing eighty along Route 28, a two-lane road that snakes around the dark shoreline of Pleasant Bay. There is no moon tonight and snow falls steadily as I cross the Chatham line into East Harwich and speed toward Orleans, Geraldine's hometown.

In no time, I approach the ENTERING ORLEANS sign, a plain square placard I've probably passed thousands of times in my life. INCORPORATED 1797, it says. Funny the things you notice doing eighty in the middle of the night.

The flashing blue lights are just about in my backseat before I notice them, though. Damn. At this particular moment, there is probably one police officer on all of Cape Cod who's not in an all-night doughnut shop. And here he is.

The cop takes forever to leave his car so I jump out of mine. He's surprised to find me standing in the road—in the falling snow—when he opens the cruiser door. His eyes come to a grinding halt at my knees as he emerges. I wish I'd changed.

The cop shakes his head, then straightens up and faces me, pretending he's seen nothing out of the ordinary. He looks like a tall version of Opie from *Mayberry R.F.D.* And he doesn't look much older than Luke.

"Ma'am," he says, polite as a Boy Scout, "I'm afraid you'll have to wait in your car . . ."

"Officer, listen, I'm an attorney. A former ADA."

He shakes his head and raises gloved hands to shut me up. "We don't make the deals, ma'am. The lawyers do that."

I have an overwhelming urge to smack Opie into silence.

"Please, ma'am, wait in your car. It's dangerous in the middle of the road."

I restrain the smack impulse and use my angry mother voice instead. "Listen to me."

Opie's head jerks back and his eyes grow wide. His mouth opens, but no words emerge. The angry mother voice is better than a smack any day.

"I'm not looking for a deal. I'm on my way to a colleague's house—"

He nods knowingly. "And at the rate you were going, you'd have gotten there yesterday."

"—to make sure she's all right. I have reason to fear she may not be. Her phone's been disconnected—it's out of service, anyway—and I—"

Opie raises his hands yet again, then points to the Thunderbird, ordering me back to it. I'm just a routine middle-of-the-night stop, another speedster with a sob story. Well, I can fix that.

"The colleague I'm worried about is Geraldine Schilling."

His hand freezes, still pointing at my old car. "Geraldine Schilling? You mean the new DA?"

"Yes. That's the one." I wonder how many Geraldine Schillings he thinks there are in Orleans. "She lives—"

"We know where she lives." He opens the cruiser door, reaches for the radio.

"What are you doing?"

"Calling it in."

"But I don't know for sure that anything's wrong." The truth is, though, I'm relieved that he's calling. Geraldine's house is a stone's throw from the Orleans station. They'll be there long before I will.

"Doesn't matter. You think she's in trouble and her phone's out. She's the DA. That's enough."

He gets back into his car and again directs me to mine. "You should head home, ma'am." He points his radio at me. "*Slow*. We'll take it from here."

Fat chance.

Opie pulls out first, lights still flashing, siren newly activated, but the old Thunderbird is riding his tail in seconds. It's too bad that the streets are empty, that no one's around to witness this scene. It's not every day you see a middle-aged woman in an old car chasing a young cop in a screaming cruiser.

CHAPTER 37

Maybe she's not home. Maybe her place is locked up tight and she's spending the night with friends. Better yet, maybe she's off on a romantic rendezvous, stealing some time with a long-kept-secret lover, away from the public eye, unwittingly avoiding the ex-con with the short list.

But no. Geraldine's navy blue Buick is in the driveway, washed in a sea of blinding beams. An empty cruiser is parked behind it, roof lights flashing. Four more squad cars form a semicircle on the lawn, all pointed at the front door, bulbs ablaze but sirens mute. They're empty too. At least two more marked cars light up the backyard, covering the rear of the house. I can't tell if they're occupied.

Neighbors with boots and coats thrown over pajamas and bathrobes huddle on the opposite side of the street. I seem to have started a fashion trend.

Opie and I emerge from our cars at the same time. He's not happy to see me. "I thought I told you to go home," he grumbles.

"You did." Never pass up an opportunity to agree with a cop.

"Then why are you here?" He draws his weapon and releases the safety.

That's a good idea. I pull the Lady Smith from my inside pocket and join him against the wall on the porch. "I told you. She's a colleague. I'm worried."

Opie does a double-take when he sees the Lady Smith in my hand. I can't really blame him. A woman in red flannel pajamas and a ski cap wielding a loaded weapon in the middle of the night would raise concerns in most people.

"It's okay," I assure him. "I know how to use it."

He looks skeptical.

"Geraldine Schilling trained me personally."

He still looks skeptical.

We can see Geraldine's living room through the porch windows. It's empty but for her sleek furnishings and modern art collection. The room is undisturbed; even the magazines are lined up neatly on the coffee table.

My reluctant partner reaches for the front doorknob and turns it easily. This isn't good. Geraldine always locks her doors, always lectures me about not locking mine. She also has an elaborate security system. It's apparently disarmed. Where are all those cops from the squad cars?

We enter without making a sound. Like the living room, the foyer is in impeccable order, coatrack and telephone table tidy, oak floor spotless. The stairway to the second story is empty. No sound from above.

We're halfway down the first-floor hallway—crouched against the wall—when we hear the voices.

And the laughter.

Opie stands up straight and takes a deep breath. He blows it out slowly, glaring down at me, and tucks his weapon back in its holster.

I put mine away too, as I straighten, then grimace my apology to him. Call me Barney Fife.

They're in the kitchen. Ten cops, including the Orleans Chief, standing around Geraldine's polished cherry table having coffee. She's in the midst of them, pouring and laughing, elegant in a black silk dressing gown. She's more than a little surprised to see me enter the room, but Geraldine always recovers quickly.

"Martha," she says. "Do tell. What brings you to our little gathering?"

"I thought you might be in trouble."

"You? You're the anonymous tip?"

I consider myself neither anonymous nor a tip. "Look, Geraldine, it just hit me—Howard Davis, then Judge Long—this could be a revenge thing. And if it is, you're almost certainly a target."

Geraldine shakes her head and her blond bangs fall into her eyes. She turns to the Chief. "Is there a way to ban her from movie theaters?"

They all laugh and resume their conversation. It seems the first poor cop to arrive on the scene found himself staring down the barrel of a 9mm Walther PPK. Geraldine's. She knew he was an Orleans cop—knew his name even—but held him at gunpoint anyway, until the others arrived. Just in case he was a good apple gone bad, she told him.

There don't seem to be any hard feelings. The mood around the table is downright jovial. Even Opie's enjoying himself, a steaming ceramic mug soon cradled in his hands.

Geraldine turns back to me. "Coffee? It's decaf."

I shake my head. "Your phone is out."

"Yes, it is," she says, smiling. "It'll be fixed by morning. The nice man from the telephone company promised."

The Chief drains his mug, puts it in the sink, then heads for the back door. "We'll leave you alone now. You'll call if you need anything?"

"I will," Geraldine says. "I've got my cell."

Her cell. Damn.

The other cops take the Chief's cue. They abandon mugs in the sink and on the counter, then zip up jackets and reposition winter hats. They file out the back door, thanking Geraldine for her hospitality.

"Anytime," she tells them, eyeing the wall clock. It's three A.M.

Opie is the last to leave. I put a hand out to stop him as he passes and fish a business card from my wallet. "Mail me a ticket."

He stares down at me a moment, then tucks the card in his shirt pocket and nods. "I might."

Geraldine waits until he's out the door, then lights a cigarette. "Martha," she says, "your concern for my welfare is touching—truly. But you've got to stop imagining serial killers around every corner. Maybe you should see somebody, you know, a therapist or something."

Geraldine says the word *therapist* as if it's profane.

"I'm not talking about a serial killer, Geraldine. I'm talking about a revenge killer. Someone who passed long days in prison plotting to do in the people who landed him there."

Serial killers and revenge killers are distinct creatures. A serial killer gets his thrills from the rituals of murder. His victims are chosen randomly, their identities unimportant. But for a revenge killer, the identity of each victim is critical. He has reasons for wanting a particular person—or group of persons—dead. To Geraldine, of course, this is a distinction that makes no difference.

"I'm serious, Martha. Maybe you should talk to a . . . a counselor."

Counselor is also a word to be avoided in mixed company.

I head for the kitchen door. "And maybe you should take a few extra precautions."

She follows me to the doorway and I pause on her deck. "A parole officer and a judge—both attacked with a knife in the space of four days. I'm not imagining that."

She takes a long drag, then blows smoke into the cold air. "But you're forgetting that the parole officer's assailant is already in jail."

Silence. I'm not taking that bait.

Geraldine laughs. "I'll walk on eggshells. Promise."

She doesn't mean it, of course, but there's no point in arguing with Geraldine. I give up and head down the wooden staircase.

"Oh, and Martha . . ."

I pause on the bottom step and turn back toward her, heavy snowflakes coating my ski cap and eyelashes. The orange tip of her cigarette glows as she inhales. She takes it from her mouth and points it at the bunched red flannel protruding from my boots.

"Your ensemble," she says. "Fetching."

CHAPTER 38

Sonia Baker is no dope. She refused, last night, ever to speak with Prudence Nelson again. But by this morning, Sonia had reconsidered. She phoned the office at seven-thirty and caught me before I left for the courthouse. If the lady shrink can help, then go ahead and send her back, Sonia said. I assured her she was doing the right thing, whereupon she reiterated her assessment of Prudence as a condescending bitch. I didn't argue.

J. Stanley Edgarton the Third is no dope either. He opened his cross-examination of Patty Hammond with condolences. "Mrs. Hammond," he said, "let me tell you at the outset that I am sorry—we are all so very sorry—for your loss."

Stanley swept his arms across the courtroom as he

delivered those words, as if he'd been appointed to speak for the entire population of Barnstable County. He approached the witness box and Patty confidently, pity plain on his face.

Patty thanked him, then looked away.

Stanley's cross-examination, so far, has been matter-of-fact. Patty readily agreed that she is not a mental health professional, not competent to comment on psychiatric questions. She admitted that she had no contact with her husband between the moment he viewed their son's body and the moment he shot Hector Monteros. She acknowledged that she didn't see Buck during that time, didn't speak to him, didn't even know where he was during the later hours.

Stanley should leave it at that. He has all he needs to tell the jurors to disregard Patty's direct testimony. He has all he needs to argue that her testimony—every word of it—is irrelevant. He has all he needs to accuse me of calling her to the witness stand only to rouse their sympathy. And, as Beatrice Nolan will certainly instruct them, sympathy is an emotion that should play no role in their deliberations.

Stanley doesn't seem satisfied, though. He wants more. He paces the front of the courtroom, hands clasped behind his back, his blue forehead vein throbbing. He's apparently framing another question.

"So you have no personal knowledge, do you, Mrs. Hammond, regarding your husband's state of mind during those early-morning hours?"

Patty stares at him as if English must be his second—or perhaps third—language, as if he couldn't possibly mean what he just said. "Oh, but I do," she says, turning to the jurors. "I may be the only person who does."

"Objection!" Stanley's outburst is so loud Patty jumps in the witness box. She presses a fist to her mouth.

I'm up. "To what? Your own question?"

Stanley turns toward the bench, his back to the jurors. Too bad; the pulse of his forehead vein is picking up speed and his pasty complexion is sprouting red, Rorschach-like designs.

"Nonresponsive!" He raises an index finger in the air, as if beginning a war cry, then points it at Patty. "The witness's answer is nonresponsive! Move to strike!"

Beatrice nods.

"Motion opposed." I stay planted behind the counsel table, facing the judge but keeping the jurors in my peripheral vision. "Counsel asked a question and the witness answered. He doesn't get to strike her response because he doesn't like it."

The jurors look from me to the judge, their faces blank.

The truth is, I don't give a damn whether Beatrice strikes the answer or not. Patty's response can't be un-uttered. It's one more bell that can't be unrung. But the longer we argue about it, the louder her words will echo. That's what I hope, anyway.

Beatrice fixes her gaze on me. Her thoughts are apparent. I'm not as bad as Harry Madigan, but I'm a certified pain in the ass.

"The motion is granted, Counsel. Your witness's answer was indeed nonresponsive."

"Let's have it read back—the question and the answer." I direct my suggestion to the court reporter, a pale, pencil-thin man who has worked in this dreary courtroom for decades, showing up each day in a black suit, white shirt, and string tie. He leans forward, dons frameless spectacles, and lifts the narrow strip of encoded white paper snaking from the front of his machine.

"We'll do no such thing!" Beatrice bangs her gavel, her grackle eyes darting from me to String Tie and back again. She's unsure—for just a second—which of us to skewer. Me for suggesting such a dastardly deed or the old man for daring to comply.

She's settled on me. Imagine that.

"Ms. Nickerson, whose courtroom is this?" Beatrice is using her special diction for the dull-witted child.

Judge Nolan seems to enjoy spitting out sarcastic questions. I hope she likes listening to honest answers. This is a fact I don't mind pointing out to the jury. A reminder. An important one.

"This courtroom, Judge, belongs to the citizens of the Commonwealth of Massachusetts."

Beatrice sprouts a few Rorschach blotches of her own.

"Who is *in charge* in this courtroom, Ms. Nickerson?"

"Oh." I smile up at her. "That would be you."

CHAPTER 39

Judge Nolan was so pleased with having put me in my place, she called a fifteen-minute recess. To savor the victory, Harry told me. She's back now, though, erect in her seat. She doesn't say a word until the jurors settle in their chairs.

"Let me remind you again, Ms. Nickerson. *I* give instructions in this courtroom. *You* do not."

We all know her reminder was for the jury's benefit.

She swivels her chair completely around to face the jury box. Apparently my read-back suggestion is rejected. And I'm dismissed.

"Ladies and gentlemen, you will disregard the witness's last answer."

The jurors stare at the judge, their expressions still

unreadable. The retired schoolteacher, though, sets her jaw and shakes her head at me. Damn. She thinks I've misbehaved.

Judge Nolan turns toward the daredevil stenographer and points at his narrow white paper. "The court reporter will strike the response from the record."

String Tie leans over his machine again and makes a check mark next to the offending testimony, then keeps his eyes lowered and sighs. A working life spent with Beatrice Nolan would try any man's soul.

Finally, the judge's eyes rest on Patty. "Henceforth, the witness will confine her answers to respond to the questions posed. No extraneous comments."

Patty stares up at the judge, blinking, a puzzled look on her face. It's an expression I've seen her wear before. It's a bewilderment, I think, particular to those who grieve, an inability to comprehend a person worked up over something trivial.

Judge Nolan takes a deep breath, her eyes still locked with Patty's. "Do you understand me, Mrs. Hammond?"

The judge's tone is harsh; she's misread Patty's expression. Beatrice thinks it's her words that aren't getting through.

Patty shakes her head, still staring up at the judge. "I guess not," she says.

Judge Beatrice Nolan doesn't like that answer. She clamps her lips together and leans toward the witness box, eyes protruding, nostrils flaring.

Patty actually recoils.

Beatrice opens her mouth to speak—or perhaps to breathe fire—but Stanley intervenes. "Your Honor," he says, "I have no further questions for this witness."

I'm sure he doesn't. Badgering Patty Hammond in front of the panel would be a big mistake. Stanley doesn't want it happening on his watch, even if it's the judge doing the badgering.

Beatrice straightens in her chair and looks at me, her eyebrows knitted into one.

I return her stare. "No further questions from us, Judge. Patty Hammond said it all."

Beatrice fires a threatening look in my direction before announcing yet another morning recess. I'll pay for that editorial comment, it says. I wonder if Beatrice is having stomach problems. She never calls breaks so close together. She's off the bench even before the bailiff tells us to rise.

Harry's on the move as soon as Beatrice leaves the room. He saunters the length of our table, tapping his pen against his temple, as if coaxing a thought from his brain. He stops when he reaches my chair and points his pen at the bench.

I roll my eyes at him. I have a pretty good idea what's coming.

"I could be wrong again," he says, shaking his head, "but I think you're headed for the cell block."

Chapter 40

It doesn't appear that the back-to-back breaks did anything good for Beatrice Nolan's disposition. She ascends to the bench wearing a sour expression, eyes narrowed, lips in a thin straight line. She swivels her chair toward the empty jury box and studies the wall behind it as the jurors file in and take their seats. Old Beatrice should have dropped a lump or two of sugar in her midmorning coffee.

At least she's not staring at us. Buck is sitting up straight, composed, hands folded and steady on the defense table. He's ready to testify. He doesn't need any last-minute eye contact with our ill-tempered judge.

"Ladies and gentlemen of the jury . . ." Beatrice leans back in her chair, one hand on an armrest, the other fingering her gavel, just in case. "It's now time for the attorneys to deliver their closing arguments."

Harry and I jump up as if choreographed. For a split second we're both speechless.

Harry recovers first. "Whoa," he says.

It's not much of a recovery. "Whoa" isn't a word normally bandied about in the courtroom.

Beatrice bolts forward, her eyes no longer narrowed. "Whoa?" She lifts her gavel from the bench and holds it midair, like a tomahawk she might hurl at any moment. "Did you say *whoa*, Mr. Madigan?"

Harry winces. "I'm afraid I did, Judge. But that's not what I meant."

Beatrice lowers the gavel slightly, cupping its head in her hand. "I'm glad to hear that, Mr. Madigan." She stares down at the small hammer, examining its veneer, then glares up at Harry. "Enlighten us, Counsel. What *did* you mean?"

"What I meant to say was: Excuse me, Your Honor, but the defense didn't rest."

"Didn't rest?"

"We're not finished."

"Not finished?" Beatrice looks at me as if I'm Harry's mother and I ought to control him better.

Harry takes a step toward the bench. "We have one more witness, Judge. Mr. Hammond. He's our last witness."

"Mr. Hammond?" Beatrice looks like she's just been told a potted plant will testify.

"The defendant." Harry points at Buck and Buck raises his hand, as if the judge might not know who he is.

Beatrice grimaces. "Counsel, approach."

Stanley and Harry get to the bench before I do, but Judge Nolan doesn't feel compelled to wait. It doesn't matter. She's loud enough to be heard in the far corners of the small courtroom. It's becoming pretty clear that Beatrice calls these sidebars to keep her comments off the record, not to conduct any sort of private discussion.

"What's going on here, Counsel?"

The question, of course, is directed at Harry.

"What's going *on* here?" Harry leans one hand on the bench, runs the other through his thick, tangled hair. He looks mystified. "The defendant is ready to take the stand. That's what's going *on* here."

Beatrice's nostrils flare again. "What does he plan to say?" She's bellowing now, not even pretending this is a real sidebar.

"You can't ask me that." Harry's steaming.

"I most certainly can. I'm the judge."

"I don't give a damn who you are."

Uh-oh.

"I'm the defense lawyer." Harry is booming now. He points a thumb over his shoulder at Buck. "And he's the defendant. That means he has a right to testify on his own behalf without giving a sneak preview to the prosecutor."

Harry's thumb moves from Buck to Stanley and Stanley backs away, as if he thinks it might be loaded.

Beatrice leans forward, suggesting she plans to whisper, but she doesn't. She's as loud as ever. "He has no right to commit perjury."

"Perjury?" The word escapes Harry and me simultaneously.

"And you people have no right to suborn it."

"You people?" Again, we're in unison.

"Did you explain the penalties for perjury to your client, Counsel?" Beatrice's eyes shift from Harry to me. She wants to be sure I realize I'm included in her accusation.

Harry's about to explode, his ruddy complexion as dark red as it gets. I put my hand up to stop him, then turn to face the judge. I wait until her eyes lock with mine.

"Why would we do that, Judge?" I keep my voice markedly lower than hers and Harry's, barely loud enough for the jurors to hear.

Beatrice stands, leans completely over her bench, and pats the top of Stanley's television set. She holds my stare, her eyes fierce. "I've seen this videotape, Counsel. Pictures don't lie. If your client plans to contradict the content of this film on the witness stand"— she points to the chair as if I'm unfamiliar with the layout of the courtroom—"then he plans to commit perjury. And I won't allow it."

She folds her arms, but doesn't wait for a response.

"And if he doesn't plan to contradict the content of the videotape, then his taking the witness stand is foolhardy. Have you so advised him?"

One might expect a pause here. But no.

"If you haven't advised against his taking the stand, you're incompetent. I'll remove you from this case."

"Remove . . . ?"

"If you have, and he's not listening, you're ineffective. I'll remove you from this case."

Beatrice has thought this through.

A hundred people are crammed into this room and not one of them moves. The only sound to be heard is Beatrice's labored breathing. She's still standing, her torso concave, folded arms pressed against her chest as if she's cold. Her eyes invite me—dare me—to fight.

On an ordinary day, Beatrice Nolan could outbitch me with little effort. But not today. Beatrice doesn't realize she's taken on a woman who got almost no sleep last night. Today I'm every inch the bitch that she is.

I turn away from her and walk toward old String Tie. His eyes meet mine for just a second—leave me out of this, they say—before he stares down at his machine.

"The defense calls Mr. William 'Buck' Hammond to the stand."

No one moves, not even String Tie. I stand still in front of his machine and point my pen at him. "You were supposed to type that."

He looks from me to the judge—uncertain—then drops his eyes again and starts tapping the keys. She may be the judge, but I'm close enough to hurt him.

"Ms. Nickerson, did you not hear my questions?"

My back is to Beatrice, but I'm certain she's still on her feet, sprouting icicles. "I did, Judge. I heard your questions and I heard your threats."

Beatrice takes an audible breath as I turn to face her. She sets her jaw, bracing to deal with the dull-witted child yet again. "There were no threats, Ms. Nickerson, but I'd like to hear answers to my questions, if that's not too much trouble."

I take my time walking back to the bench. "You just did."

She drops into her chair and leans forward, poised to lecture. "Counsel . . ."

"The defense calls William 'Buck' Hammond to the stand." I signal Buck to his feet and point toward the witness box before fixing my gaze on Beatrice. "That's our answer, Judge. That's our answer to all your questions."

Buck is halfway across the courtroom before Beatrice bellows again. "Just a minute, Mr. Hammond."

He pauses, looks at me; I tell him with my eyes to continue.

Beatrice bangs her gavel, her Rorschach blotches back in bloom, but Buck pays no attention. He finishes his trip and settles quietly in the box.

"Counsel, what are you doing?"

"I'm calling my client to the witness stand, Judge." She glares at me.

I move away and walk toward the jury. "You want to stop Mr. Hammond from taking the stand in his own defense, go ahead and do it." I lean against the jury box, my back to the panel, and fold my arms. "But I won't let you do it in a fictional sidebar."

I pause to check on String Tie, who's dutifully tapping away, then point at Buck in the witness box, my eyes still focused on Beatrice. "You want to shut this man down, Judge, you're damn well going to do it on the record."

Beatrice's mouth opens, but no sound emerges. If I weren't so mad I'd enjoy this. I move toward the bench and lower my voice again, still confident that the jurors—and String Tie—can hear. "And you'll be reversed before you call your next case."

Beatrice straightens in her chair and purses her lips. "It was never my intention to shut Mr. Hammond down, Counsel."

This is news. I turn and raise my eyebrows at the jurors, but they don't react. When I look back at the judge, she's waiting for me. Her bird eyes fix on mine and her lips arc downward at the corners. They barely move when she speaks.

"The courtroom clerk will swear the witness."

Beatrice's eyes don't move. They speak volumes. She'll give me this battle, they say, but the war is a hell of a long way from over.

CHAPTER 41

Everything about Buck Hammond says he has nothing left to lose. He's allowed to wear his own clothes during trial, but they don't fit anymore. His gray suit jacket hangs loosely, its cuffs too wide for his wrists. His black pants are baggy, as if he borrowed them from a much heavier man. He's not permitted a belt; no shoelaces or tie, either. He wears an old pair of scuffed loafers and a white, starched shirt, unbuttoned at the neck.

All male prisoners on trial are given the opportunity to shave each morning, but Buck hasn't bothered for the last couple of days. A dark shadow of stubble covers his cheeks, chin, and neck. His black hair is neatly parted and combed, but it's ragged at the edges, in need of a trim. His face is that of a man who has only a distant memory of a good night's sleep. Dark circles underline his eyes.

Buck could be a physically imposing presence—he's taller than Harry by a couple of inches and almost as broad—but his approach to other people is cautious, timid even. His shoulders, a match for any line-backer's, sag as if taxed by a burden the rest of us can't see. His light gray eyes, wide and moist, reveal little and ask less. It's not that he has no questions. It's that the questions—the few that still matter to Buck Hammond—have no answers.

He will ask to go home, though; of that I'm certain. Buck will ask these jurors, in his own muted way, to send him back to his South Chatham cottage, to spare him the void of a lifetime at Walpole. He'll make that request for Patty's sake, not his own, but he'll make it just the same. And it's my job to give him the opportunity.

The task is simple, really. We'll start with questions that allow Buck to describe his life before June 19. The jurors will hear about a solid family man who went to work every day and ate dinner with his wife and son every night. They'll hear about a man born and raised on Cape Cod who, until six months ago, never had a single encounter with the law. And then they'll hear how all of that changed.

Stanley, of course, is a problem. His forehead vein has been throbbing all morning. He's perched on the edge of his chair, prepared to pounce, and we're just getting started. He might object, it seems, before I ask my first question.

Judge Beatrice Nolan, of course, will be all too

eager to sustain Stanley's objections. She's another problem.

"Mr. Hammond, please state your full name for the record."

"William Francis Hammond. People call me Buck."

Stanley's chair creaks and he clears his throat. When I turn to look at him, he mouths the word *hearsay*.

He can't be serious.

Stanley flutters his fingers in the air and leans back in his chair, a small, tolerant smile spreading across his face as his gaze moves up to the judge, then over to the jurors. He'll let it slide, he's telling all of us. Just this once. He's a reasonable guy.

This could take a while.

When I turn away from Stanley and face the witness box again, Buck looks up from his lap, his expression calm. He's waiting patiently for my next question, oblivious to Stanley, unconcerned with his prosecutor's posturing.

It hits me so hard—the obvious truth—that I have to lean on the witness box for a moment. Buck is right. Stanley is irrelevant. His tiresome objections don't matter. His petty antics don't matter. And my preliminary questions don't matter either.

These jurors know who Buck Hammond is. They know where he lives; they've met his wife. They can pretty well guess his age and they don't give a damn how he makes his living. They know what he did to Hector Monteros. The only thing that matters now is why.

I head back to our table and take two photographs from my briefcase. Eight-by-ten laminated glossies of Billy. One before. One after.

Buck hasn't seen either one of these photos. He took the "before" shot, but was jailed before it was developed. He has no idea Patty gave it to me, no idea she kept it from him at my direction.

The "after" shot is one of a dozen taken during Billy Hammond's autopsy. Standard procedure.

Ordinarily, it's not a good idea to surprise your own witness on the stand. But this was no ordinary murder; it's no ordinary trial. The rules—most of them, anyway—don't apply here. We're in uncharted waters.

Harry sets up an easel where both Buck and the jurors can see it. I tuck the autopsy shot under my arm, careful that only its white backing is visible against my jacket. I set the other photo on the easel and pause so they can take it in: Billy on the beach, beaming, a glorious sunset behind him, streaks of violet against a pale pink sky. He holds a surf-casting rod in one hand, a three-foot-long, shimmering fish in the other.

"Can you identify this photograph?"

Stanley leaves his chair and marches toward the jury box, ostensibly to see Billy Hammond's picture, in reality to distract the panel. He's seen all of the photos before. He has his own copies.

Buck stares at the glossy and blinks repeatedly as his eyes fill. He says nothing. If I didn't know him better, I'd think he hadn't heard the question.

"Yes," he says finally. "That's my son. Billy."

"Who took the photo?"

"I did. We'd been fishing for stripers at Potter's Landing." Buck points toward the glistening fish. "Billy caught a few earlier in the season, but they weren't big enough. This one was his first keeper."

"When was that?"

"Saturday, June twelfth. A week before . . ." Buck stares at his lap again for a moment, then back at the panel. "A week before."

"Before what?"

"Your Honor."

Beatrice had her gavel in hand even before Stanley spoke.

"Before what, Buck?"

"Your Honor!"

The gavel descends.

I knew this would happen, but I thought it would take a little longer. I thought I'd get at least a half dozen questions out before the prosecutor-judge team began its power play. But I'm ready.

Maybe I'm overly defensive. Maybe I'm sleep-deprived. I don't give a damn. I've planned this moment. I intend to shut my opponents down. Both of them.

"Before what, Buck?"

"Your Honor!"

Beatrice leans toward me, but I don't turn. I fix my gaze on Buck, keep the judge in my peripheral vision. "Counsel," she barks, "there's an objection pending."

"I haven't heard one, Judge." Still I don't look at her. "Before what, Buck?"

Beatrice bangs her gavel and then points it at Buck. She sits up straight, apparently taken aback by my poor manners. "The witness will remain silent. Counsel, Mr. Edgarton has raised an objection."

She inhales audibly when I wheel around to face her. "No, he hasn't, Judge. You're interrupting my examination of the defendant and there's no objection pending."

I turn my back to her and point my pen at String Tie. His eyes grow wide, but his fingers keep tapping. "It seems *you* have an objection, though, Judge. So let's hear it."

When I face her again, her mouth is a perfect oval, as if she's about to begin an aria.

"Go ahead, Judge. Put your objection on the record. And we'll ask the Big Boys to rule on it."

My irreverent reference to the appellate panel is more than Beatrice can bear. "Now just a minute, Counsel."

"No, Judge. You don't get a minute now."

She's no longer taken aback. She's indignant.

"*Now* is my client's time to testify, Judge, my time to question him. And nobody interrupts—not even you—unless *this man*"—Stanley takes a step back when I aim my pen in his direction—"voices a coherent objection."

Now Stanley's mouth is circular. Maybe they plan a duet. "You're not the prosecutor, Judge. He is. It's his job to raise viable objections. 'Your Honor' doesn't cut it. Those words don't appear in the Rules of Evidence. If the prosecutor can't state a legal basis for his objection, then the judge can't rule on it."

The gavel pauses midair. Beatrice looks like she might reach out and pound it on the top of my head.

"And if you've got nothing to rule on, then *this*

man"—Buck stares into his lap again when my pen finds him—"keeps talking."

My face must be maroon by now. I'm winded. I lean against the witness box until Buck looks up, and then I turn to the jury. They're gaping at me.

"Buck Hammond sat in this courtroom all week without uttering a word. He listened to a parade of the Commonwealth's witnesses without making a sound. He's the man on trial; it's his fate we're deciding here. It's his turn to talk now."

Side-by-side men in the back row rub their chins and stare hard at me. The rest of them avoid my gaze. They look instead at the judge, at Buck, at the floor.

"Buck Hammond is entitled to his turn. The Constitution says so."

Still, almost no eye contact. The retired schoolteacher looks at me for just a second, then turns quickly away.

Stanley remains on his feet but says nothing. Beatrice sets her gavel on the bench and folds her hands into her sleeves.

I'll take that as a go.

"Let's get to the point, Buck"—I pause to glare at Stanley—"while we still can."

"Counsel, that's enough." Beatrice retrieves her gavel and pounds again. "One more editorial comment from you, Ms. Nickerson, and you'll take a break—a long one."

I block her out, block them all out. The judge. Stanley. String Tie. Even the spectators. What happens now is between Buck and the jurors. No one else.

"What did Hector Monteros do to Billy?"

In the silence that follows, I study the jurors. Their gazes move from Buck to the easel, then back to Buck again.

"Took him," he says, "took him from the beach."

"And?"

Buck grasps the arms of his chair, as if he just hit turbulence.

"And hurt him."

I pour a glass of water and set it on the railing of the witness box, but Buck shakes his head.

"How?"

Now a few of the jurors grasp the arms of their chairs too. They don't want to hear the details again. Once was more than enough. They don't want to hear the story again from anyone, but certainly not the boy's father. They needn't worry. Buck has never even been able to say the word.

"He . . . did terrible things, and then . . ." Buck changes his mind, takes a sip of water. "And then he killed Billy."

"How did he kill Billy?"

Buck lowers his head. For a few moments, he seems unable to lift it again.

"Your Honor," Stanley whines, "perhaps we should take a brief recess."

"It won't be any easier ten minutes from now, Judge."

Beatrice glares at me, her pursed lips arcing downward at the corners again. That's one of those editorial comments I'm not supposed to make. Next time I'll tell her ten years won't make much difference either.

"Take your time," I say to Buck, and I mean it. Every minute he spends on this witness stand should take us one step closer to a decent result. To me, his agony is apparent, his grief tangible. I can't tell, though, if the jurors feel it. Their faces reveal nothing.

When Buck lifts his brimming eyes, they settle on the photo tucked under my arm, the autopsy shot. He can see only its blank back, but the look on his face tells me he knows what it is. And he doesn't want it here. He turns to the jury, still clutching the arms of his chair.

We practiced this testimony. Not because we doctored the answer, but because Buck couldn't address the question at all, at first. He couldn't say it out loud. Even now, he has to say the words quickly, or he won't get through the answer.

"He bound Billy with metal cables . . ." Buck lets go of the chair arms and presses his wrists together. "At the wrists and ankles. And he smothered him."

Buck drops his hands to his lap. That's all he can say on that topic. He's reached his limit.

"And what did you do, Buck, to Hector Monteros?"

"Your Honor, please, these jurors watched the videotape, they heard from the Chief of Police. They know what the defendant did."

Stanley knows better. His objection is nothing more than a ploy, a manufactured opportunity to make a speech.

Beatrice stares at me—grimaces—when I look up. I'm tempted to smile. She won't dare prevent Buck Hammond from telling the jury what he did. There isn't an appellate panel in the country that would uphold that ruling. Stanley knows that. And Beatrice does too.

"Ladies and gentlemen," she says, "I remind you of the limiting instruction you were given on the first day of this trial. I caution you now—that instruction is still in full force and effect."

Funny, that's the only ruling of Judge Long's that Beatrice has acknowledged. The jurors nod, though, almost as one.

Stanley acts as if he isn't satisfied. He folds his arms across his chest and stamps one foot ever so slightly on the worn carpeting. Yet another temper tantrum, this one stifled.

"Buck, what did you do to Hector Monteros?"

"I tried to stop him." Buck shifts in his chair so he can face the jurors. "I shot him."

"Were you able to stop him?"

"No."

"Why not?"

He closes his eyes, still facing the panel. "I tried. But I failed. I was too late."

I move to the easel and set the photo—Billy beaming with his striped bass—to one side. Next to it I position the other one.

Buck keeps his face averted, toward the jury box, his eyes still closed. The jurors, though, look first at me, then at the easel. One by one, their gazes settle on the photo. The awful one.

It's a close-up of Billy, from the chest up, on the autopsy table. His arms are bent at the elbows, hands open, palms up, on either side of his head. His eyes are closed and his freckled face looks as if he might be sleeping. But on his wrists the ligature marks are plain.

Finally, Buck follows the jurors' gazes and stares at the autopsy shot. "You see?" he asks them through clenched teeth. "I couldn't stop him. I was too late."

CHAPTER 42

"Too late?" Stanley scrutinizes Buck Hammond as if he's a still life about to be auctioned.

Buck's expression is blank. Seated in the witness box, he's the same height as Stanley on his feet.

"That was your testimony, was it not, sir? That you were too late?"

Buck leans forward in his chair and nods. "Yes."

"You were too late long before you fired the shot that killed Hector Monteros, weren't you, Mr. Hammond?"

"I don't know what you mean." Buck shakes his head, but his expression doesn't change.

"Your boy was already dead, was he not, sir, when you pulled the trigger?"

Buck nods, agreeing. "He was."

"And you knew that to be the case, didn't you?"

"I know it now."

"And you knew it then!"

I'm tempted to get up, but I don't. Stanley shouldn't testify, shouldn't act like a witness. But I shouldn't act like Stanley, either. Besides, we've got a long way to go. Stanley's just getting started.

He waits for a response, but he won't get one. Buck and I went over this a thousand times in the past few weeks. If there's no question pending, Buck's not to say a word. And he's good at not saying a word.

A moment of silence. And then Stanley gets it. "You knew your son was dead, didn't you, Mr. Hammond, when you fired that fatal shot?"

"I'm not sure."

"Not sure?"

Stanley moves the easel to the wall, tosses the photos of Billy on our table. He walks toward the jury, hands clasped behind his back, a slight smile on his lips. For a moment, his footsteps are the only sounds in the room. A well-planned dramatic pause.

"You were in the courtroom, were you not, sir, when Chief Thomas Fitzpatrick testified?"

"Yes."

"And you *listened* to his testimony, I presume?"

"I did. Yes."

"You heard him tell us, then, that you identified your son's body at the morgue?"

"Yes."

"Do you remember doing that, sir?"

"Do I remember . . . ?"

"Identifying the body."

Buck looks as if he thinks Stanley might be temporarily insane. "Of course I do."

"No memory problems, then?"

Buck shakes his head. "No."

"And you did that, Mr. Hammond—identified your son's body—more than *two hours* before the chopper transporting Monteros reached Chatham. Isn't that correct?"

"I don't know."

"Did you hear Chief Fitzpatrick tell us exactly that?"

"I did."

"Is it your testimony, then, that Chief Fitzpatrick was lying?"

The question is improper, but it's not worth an objection. Cheap shots say more about the questioner than anyone else. And we anticipated a few from Stanley. Buck is as well prepared to deflect them as any witness can be.

"No," Buck says evenly, "that's not my testimony."

"You agree, then, that you identified the body more than two hours before killing Monteros?"

Buck takes a deep breath and answers the panel. "The Chief said more than two hours, so it must have been."

"But you don't have personal knowledge of that fact, is that your testimony, Mr. Hammond?"

Buck faces Stanley again. "Yes."

"You don't remember?"

"That's right."

Stanley lets out a short, sarcastic hiccup, not quite a laugh. He strides to the side wall, flips off the overhead lights, then makes a beeline for his star witness.

He holds the videotape in front of Buck for a moment—yet another dramatic pause—before popping it into the VCR. "Let's find out, Mr. Hammond, what you *do* remember."

Harry and I exchange surprised glances. We were certain Stanley would save his second run of the video for closing, certain he'd want the bloody runway to be the final scene emblazoned on the jurors' minds.

The glow from the TV screen illuminates Stanley's silhouette and Buck's profile. The rest of us sit in inky blackness. This is the advantage to a windowless courtroom: easy video viewing. It's the only plus, as far as I can tell.

Stanley retrieves a long wooden stick from his table. It has a white rubber tip, like the ones pointed at blackboards by teachers in elementary school. He waits patiently while the military chopper comes into view on screen. He watches silently as the chopper descends to the runway. Then he presses a controller, freezes the frame.

I leave my chair and walk quietly across the room to lean against the wall beside the jury box. I want to keep an eye on Stanley's pointer.

"You've seen this helicopter before, have you not, Mr. Hammond?"

Buck nods. "Yes. I've seen this tape."

"I'm not asking about the tape. I'm asking about the military helicopter, the real one. U.S. ARMY printed on its sides. You saw it on June twenty-first, did you not?"

There it is. A question I didn't ask. It never fails.

There's always a question I didn't ask. More than one, in most cases.

Buck tilts his head toward one shoulder, considering the prosecutor's query. "I'm not sure."

Stanley jumps back, as if surprised by the answer. He plasters an incredulous look on his dimly lit face, then turns it toward the jurors. "You're not sure?"

"I know I must have," Buck says. "But I don't remember actually looking at it then." He shrugs, shakes his head. "I don't know if I saw the words. I don't think I realized it was an army aircraft."

Stanley shakes his head too, and presses the controller again. "You don't remember," he mutters.

On screen, a uniformed marshal emerges from the chopper, his sidearm drawn. One step behind him is Monteros, handcuffed and shackled loosely, so he can negotiate the stairs. A second guard follows a few steps behind, his weapon pointed upward, as if he might fire into the air at any moment.

Stanley freezes the frame again. "Do you remember these men?" He moves his pointer from the first guard to the second, skipping over Monteros.

That's question number two I didn't ask.

"The guards?"

Stanley nods. "And I'm not asking you about the videotape. I'm asking about the morning of June twenty-first."

Buck frowns, as if even he doesn't like the answer he's about to give. "No," he says, "I don't."

Stanley smirks, presses his controller, and the action on-screen resumes. He stops it again as soon as Monteros's feet reach the runway.

"And I don't suppose you have any memory of this gentleman, either, Mr. Hammond." Stanley's pointer rests on Monteros. "Is that your testimony?"

This question I didn't overlook. I shift my position against the wall, so I can watch the jury as well as Buck.

He sits perfectly still in the witness box, his eyes on the white tip of Stanley's pointer. "No," he says. "That's not my testimony."

Stanley turns from the TV screen to the jurors, mock surprise on his face. "Do tell us," he says. "What do you remember about Mr. Monteros?"

Buck's eyes leave the screen and he turns toward the jury. "I remember everything," he says.

"Everything?" Stanley holds his stick in two hands at chest level, as if he might tap dance once the music begins. "Perhaps you could be more specific."

"The tattoo on his arm, the scar on his chin, the sneer on his face. I remember everything."

Stanley appears satisfied with this answer. He starts the tape again. "And tell us, Mr. Hammond . . ." Stanley presses his controller and points the tip of his stick at Buck on the screen, one step from the shadow of the hangar. "Who is this?"

"That's me."

"So it is." This time Stanley presses twice. I know what he's doing. Continuing the tape. And turning on the volume. It's been muted until now.

The shot thunders through the courtroom. Most of the jurors jump in their seats; a few cover their mouths. Buck doesn't move.

On screen, Monteros collapses and police officers

scatter. A pool of red seeps from Monteros's head onto the runway.

Stanley freezes the frame and moves so close to the witness box that Buck leans backward in his chair. "You fired that shot, Mr. Hammond?"

"I did."

"Whose rifle?"

"Mine."

"You hunt?"

"Yes."

"What for?"

"Deer."

Stanley turns his face toward the jury, but his body stays pressed against the witness box.

"Deer season in June?"

"No."

"Anytime in spring?"

"No."

"When?"

"Fall. November into December."

Finally, Stanley walks away from the witness box and Buck exhales. Stanley's pointer finds Monteros on-screen again, taps against him a few times. "You intended to kill this man, didn't you, Mr. Hammond?"

"I did."

"You sighted his temple and your shot was on target, correct?"

"Yes."

"Pretty good aim."

Buck says nothing.

"For a man who's insane."

Harry swivels his chair out from the table, meets my eyes, and shakes his head. He's afraid I might make the objection. He shouldn't be. I may be new to the defense bar, but I've tried a few cases in the past decade. Jurors don't like sarcasm—from either side of the aisle. We'll let Stanley's caustic comment stand.

Still, Buck says nothing.

Silence appears to unnerve Stanley. He hurries back toward the witness box, his pointer directed at Buck, the rubber tip almost touching his white shirt. "Is it your testimony, Mr. Hammond, that on the morning of June twenty-first, you drove your truck to the Chatham Municipal Airport, loaded your hunting rifle, took aim, fired a single shot, hit your target, all the while insane?"

So much for passing on objections. I leave my post against the wall and move toward the bench. "Just a minute, Judge. This witness isn't an expert."

Beatrice doesn't respond.

"Mr. Hammond offered no opinion on his own mental state during direct, Judge, and there's a reason for that. He's not qualified. The prosecutor already cross-examined our psychiatrist. He doesn't get to put the same questions to a lay witness."

"I'll allow it."

"You'll what?"

"You heard me, Counsel. I'll allow it."

"On what grounds?"

Beatrice bangs her gavel and leans forward on her bench. "I've ruled, Counsel. I don't intend to give you a table of authorities."

"But the Commonwealth called two experts on this

topic, Judge. How can it ask now for a lay opinion?"

"I've *ruled,* Counsel."

Harry's right. She doesn't like me.

Stanley inserts himself between me and the bench, flicking one hand in my direction, shooing me away. I stay put.

He moves past, sidles up to the witness box again, and leans over toward Buck. "So tell us, Mr. Hammond . . ." Stanley extends his pointer backward, toward the frozen scene on the television screen. "Your lawyers claim this was a moment of temporary insanity. Was it?"

Buck's eyes stay fixed on Stanley a few moments. He doesn't say a word, doesn't move a muscle. Stanley doesn't either.

Finally, Buck glances at me, takes a deep breath, then turns to the jurors. "I'm no expert," he says, shaking his head. "I've no business agreeing or disagreeing with the doctors who testified here."

He shifts in the chair and looks at me again, apology plain in his eyes. He takes another deep breath, then faces the panel. "But I do know one thing."

All fourteen jurors sit completely still, their eyes riveted to Buck. Those in the back row lean forward to listen.

For the first time today, Buck's voice cracks. His eyes fill as he points toward the TV, his arm parallel with Stanley's pointer. "If that man were alive today, I'd hunt him down and kill him."

CHAPTER 43

"Hunt him down and kill him," of course, was not in the cross-examination script. We passed on redirect. That way Stanley had no opportunity to recross, no chance to get Buck to repeat those words. Stanley will undoubtedly quote them a time or two during his closing. No need for Buck to help the Commonwealth again.

Stanley finished with Buck at two o'clock, whereupon Beatrice called a one-hour lunch break. Closing arguments would begin promptly at three, she promised the jury. She cast a pointed glance across the room in my direction as she spoke, as if certain I might otherwise linger over a lavish meal. I glared back at her until she looked away.

Harry looked from me to Beatrice as she left the

bench, then reiterated his belief that I'm destined for the cell block. He repositioned the rickety easel and the two photos of Billy Hammond as soon as Beatrice and the jurors were out of the room. We both donned jackets and boots, then, to brave the snowstorm. I went to see Sonia Baker, to reinforce her decision to try to cooperate with Prudence Nelson. Harry went in search of an open deli.

When I got back to the courthouse, Harry was waiting with two cardboard cups of lukewarm clam chowder and two turkey clubs. Each of us had a chowder. Harry ate the sandwiches. Now, as I stand to face the jurors, I wish he'd eaten both chowders as well.

The jurors look a little more relaxed after their lunch break. They're settled comfortably into their chairs, a few with notebooks and pens on their laps. Their eyes, and their attention, are all mine. Still, though, their emotions are well hidden. I stand before them, silent, and wait until the gallery is quiet.

"There are two sides to our judicial system: the civil and the criminal. And there are important distinctions between the two. Most are differences of degree.

"The burden of proof, for example. In a civil matter, the complaining party must prove his case by a preponderance of the evidence. But in a criminal proceeding, the burden of proof is far more steep. The complaining party, the Commonwealth, must prove its case—every element of it—beyond a reasonable doubt."

Widespread nods. They know this, of course. They read the paper; they watch TV.

"Punishment is another example. A losing defendant is penalized no matter which system he's in. On the civil side, we take his assets. But in the criminal justice system, we take something far more valuable, far more precious. We take his freedom."

More nods. They know this as well.

"There is, though, one difference between our civil system and our criminal system that is *not* a matter of degree. It's a matter of substance. And it's important. In Buck Hammond's case, it's critical."

A few of them straighten in their seats. Some pick up pens and open notebooks. I scan their faces as I walk to the jury box and lean on the railing. They're focused.

"In our civil system, it's incumbent upon the judge to direct a verdict when the evidence is uncontroverted. If the controlling facts of a civil suit are not in dispute, the judge must take the case away from the jury, decide it himself, as a matter of law.

"Not so in our criminal justice system. In fact, the opposite is true. In a criminal case, the defendant is *entitled* to a decision rendered by a panel of his peers. Our Constitution guarantees it. The jury has the final word in criminal trials. Always."

The jurors with notebooks and pens haven't written anything, haven't taken their eyes from me.

"Most of the important facts in this case aren't contested. The Commonwealth told you Buck Hammond shot and killed Hector Monteros. Buck Hammond took the witness stand and said the same thing. The Commonwealth told you he intended to kill Monteros. Again, Buck took the witness stand and said the same thing . . ."

I turn to the defense table for just a moment, arch my eyebrows at Buck before facing the panel again.

"More emphatically than Mr. Madigan and I would have liked."

Most of the jurors look toward the defense table, at Harry and Buck; a few almost smile. A couple of the men in the back row shake their heads, though. I don't know what that means.

I pause a moment before directing their attention to the easel. The few near-smiles disappear.

"Some of the evidence in this case was difficult to present. And I know it was difficult to receive. It was gut-wrenching to listen to Chief Fitzpatrick's testimony. It was awful to look at the two photographs of Billy Hammond.

"And it still is."

Their eyes remain on the easel, so I wait. They can stare at those photos until summer, as far as I'm concerned.

"We had trouble—all of us—listening to the details of Billy Hammond's unspeakable suffering, his unimaginable death. It's safe to say that those details made us angry, outraged even. And not one of us ever met Billy Hammond."

Their gazes stray from the easel. Some eyes rest on me; others stare across the room again toward Buck. The retired schoolteacher shakes her head in his direction; her face reveals nothing.

"If the details of Billy's ordeal—of his suffering and his death—made you and me angry, outraged, what did those details do to the child's father? To decide this case, you must answer that question."

Most jurors drop their gazes from me to their laps, considering the question, I hope. Two men in the back row, though, exchange troubled glances, shake their heads again. Maybe they can't imagine what the details would do to the boy's father. Or maybe they don't like their assignment.

"Dr. Simmons told you that Buck Hammond was in the midst of a psychotic episode—a break from reality—when he pulled the trigger of his hunting rifle on the morning of June twenty-first. Even the Commonwealth's expert psychiatrists agreed that Buck was in the throes of severe trauma at the time. Was he insane?"

I pause here, let the question hang for a moment.

"That's for you to decide."

I turn from the panel and point toward Buck. "Should he spend the rest of his life at Walpole—in the penitentiary—for what he did?"

Another pause.

"That's also for you to decide. And that—"

I wait until their eyes return to mine.

"—is as it should be.

"This, people, is what's *right* about our criminal justice system: you, twelve of Buck Hammond's peers, are the final arbiters of justice. You decide what happens next. You and your consciences."

Stanley drums his fingers on the prosecution table. I stare at him until he stops. He shakes his head at me; I'm an unreasonable opponent, it seems. I turn back to the jurors.

"This is my final opportunity to speak to you. When I'm finished, the prosecutor will address you. I have no way to know what he will say. I get no opportunity to respond. Those are the rules.

"My guess, though, is that he will spend at least some time discussing the need for you to send a message. He might tell you to convict so that our streets won't be overrun with men taking the law into their own hands. He might tell you to convict so that other would-be killers will think twice before slaying their victims. He might say your failure to convict will unravel the very fabric of our society.

"I tell you now, because it's my last chance to do so, don't buy it." I turn from them and cross the courtroom to stand beside Buck's chair.

"Your verdict is about one man and only one man. This one. You are seated in that jury box for one reason and one reason alone. Not to send a message to the masses. Not to predict the future of crime control. Not to theorize about the fabric of our society. You're here because you are Buck Hammond's peers.

"It's an awesome thing, people, to sit where he sits, to face the machinery of the Commonwealth as it moves systematically against you. This is his trial. He's entitled to it. Don't let the prosecutor convince you to make it about anyone—or anything—else."

Not one juror moves as I leave Buck's side and cross the silent courtroom toward them.

"In recent weeks I've spent more than a few evenings in the Hammonds' living room, talking with Buck's wife, Patty. We talked about Billy, and about Buck. We talked about Hector Monteros. And we talked, a lot, about this trial, about all that would happen in this courtroom.

"At the time, I thought I was preparing Patty Hammond for this ordeal, for this public rerun of her little boy's tragic end. But I see now that I was wrong. Patty was already prepared. She'd already been through much worse. She'd lived through the real thing. And she knew I hadn't. She was preparing me.

"One night about two weeks ago, just before I left their cottage, Patty asked a question she'd never raised before. It was a question I'm sure she'd thought about often during the past six months. But until two weeks ago, she'd never said the words—not out loud, anyway.

"Patty asked, that night, if I'd be able to send Buck home, if I could give them the opportunity to piece together the shards of their shattered lives. She asked if I could bring a close to this seemingly endless tragedy, if I'd be able to make at least this chapter of their pain-filled saga end the way it should.

"I was honest with Patty Hammond that night, people. I told her I couldn't do that.

"But you can."

Chapter 44

"Convenient, isn't it, this temporary insanity plea? Love it or hate it—believe it or not—you have to admit it's convenient." Stanley steps out from behind his table and shoves both hands in his pants pockets. He saunters across the front of the courtroom, head down, his back to the jury. When he reaches our table, he stops as if he hit a brick wall.

For a moment, he says nothing, stares at the tassels of his shiny black shoes. He looks sideways, then, and sneers at Buck before pivoting to face the jury. "It's not only convenient. It's clever."

He takes his hands from his pockets, folds his arms across his chest, and stands perfectly still in front of our table. "Yes, it's downright clever for this man to claim he was temporarily insane when he took a human life. Insane at that moment, mind you, but not now."

Stanley smiles at the jurors, as if they share a secret. "That's the part that's so clever—the temporary part. It's perfect. There's no need to commit him, you see, no need even for psychiatric care. Just send him home. As if it never happened."

Stanley shakes his head at the jurors, lets out another hiccup, another almost-laugh. "Don't fall for it."

He moves so close to our table that the hem of his suit coat brushes the edge. His gaze remains focused on the panel as he raises one arm and points into Buck's face. "Because if you fall for it, he gets away with murder."

Buck leans as far back in his chair as he can without tipping. Still, Stanley's index finger is only a few inches from Buck's chin. "Don't let him. Don't let him get away with murder."

Prosecutors point. I know this; I was a pointer too, in my day. Even so, I have a powerful urge to push Stanley's arm away, to get his hand out of our space, so we can breathe.

I don't have to, though; his visit to our table is mercifully brief. He hustles across the room toward the jury box, all the while pointing backward at Buck.

"Judge Nolan will instruct you that this man is guilty of first-degree murder if he acted with malice aforethought. And this—"

Stanley bangs the top of the TV and a few of the jurors jump yet again.

"—is malice aforethought."

He flips off the lights and simultaneously presses his remote control.

Harry and I both leap up in the dark.

"Hold on." My voice is so loud it startles me. My word choice is somewhat surprising as well. It wasn't *whoa*, but it wasn't much better. Even in the dark, I know Beatrice isn't happy.

"Hold on?" She's more than unhappy. Maybe *whoa* would have been better.

Harry's already at the bench, way ahead of me. The outline of his silhouette joins Stanley's in the glow from the screen. Mutt and Jeff.

"He's already run the videotape twice, Judge. He doesn't get a third shot." Harry flips off the TV set as he speaks. Now everyone's invisible.

"Says who?" Beatrice's voice booms from the blackness above the bench.

"This was decided during pretrial motions, Judge. There's an order."

"Whose order?"

"Judge Long's."

Silence.

"Judge Long no longer presides over this trial, Attorney Madigan. Perhaps you hadn't noticed." Beatrice's diction is its best yet when she utters Harry's name.

Stanley flips the TV back on.

Harry turns it off again. "It doesn't matter who presides over this trial, Judge."

"Doesn't matter?" Beatrice doesn't like being told she doesn't matter.

"No. This issue was decided on motion—before

trial. The defendant relied on the court's ruling. And he had every right to rely on it. It doesn't matter which judge signed the order."

"Tell me, Counsel, what difference does it make?"

I can't see Beatrice at all, but I'm confident she's enjoying this.

"What difference?" Harry's baffled.

"What would you have done differently, Counsel? Changed your strategy somehow?"

"That's not the point, Judge. The issue here is prejudicial impact. Probative value versus prejudicial impact."

"Your partner used photographs during her closing." Beatrice says the words *partner* and *her* as if both have lascivious connotations.

"But this videotape was the subject of a pretrial motion, Judge. There's an order."

"I'll vacate it."

"You'll what?"

"You heard me, Counsel. The order is vacated."

"You can't do that."

"I just did. The prosecutor is entitled to use demonstrative evidence during closing, Counsel. Just as your partner did."

Again, *partner* sounds lewd.

Stanley hits the button and the blue glow from the screen illuminates his satisfied smirk. He shoos Harry away.

Harry gives up, and he should. Fighting too long about this won't sit well with the jury. He returns to our table, drops into his chair, and shrugs an apology toward Buck.

"It doesn't matter," Buck whispers. "They've already seen it. They won't see anything this time they haven't seen before."

I hope he's right.

Stanley stops the videotape soon after it starts. Buck isn't even on-screen yet.

"One can only assume," Stanley says, "that Mr. Hammond was in the throes of what his lawyers now call temporary insanity at this point in time, a minute or so before he shot and killed Mr. Hector Monteros."

Stanley retrieves the long stick from his table and points its white rubber tip at the hangar's shadow. "And what was Mr. Hammond doing at this particular moment? Acting insane, perhaps? Ranting like a lunatic?"

Stanley's footsteps move toward the jury box. "Why no, not at all. He was hiding, lying in wait. Quietly. Patiently. Sound insane to you?"

Stanley hiccups again, just barely. "Sounds like a plan to me. A calculated plan. The plan of a man thinking clearly."

He presses the button and the screen comes back to life. He points his stick at the lower right corner and freezes the action again when Buck steps into view.

"And what have we here? Ah, it's Mr. Hammond. Acting insane yet? No, not at all. He's moving into position to take a clear shot, aligning himself—and his weapon—with his prey." Stanley's footsteps start up again, back toward the TV. "Sound insane to you?"

He hits the remote control, hits it again when Buck raises his hunting rifle. "And here's Mr. Hammond again, taking aim. Perfect aim, don't forget. See any sign of insanity here? I don't. Not a trace."

Stanley plants himself beside the TV, its screen frozen, and he faces the panel. It seems he intends to deliver his entire closing argument in the dark.

"Let's be candid, ladies and gentlemen. We're all horrified by what happened to this man's son. That murder was an ungodly act."

Stanley hits another button and the sound kicks in, the single shot heard 'round the Commonwealth.

"And so was this one."

No one moves—or breathes, for that matter—while Hector Monteros dies yet again. Stanley waits until a good-sized pool of blood collects on the runway, then he freezes the scene.

"What will happen, ladies and gentlemen, if you accept this man's temporary insanity claim? He'll go home, that's what. He'll be a free man."

Stanley moves slowly and deliberately toward the jury box. "And what will happen then?"

He stands still and waits, as if he expects one of them to volunteer. "I'll tell you what will happen. Someone else will set him off, send him into a rage. Maybe next week. Maybe next year. I can't tell you when. But I can tell you it will happen. I guarantee it."

Stanley turns on one heel and looks through the darkness in our direction. "And what then? Well, that's easy. Mr. Hammond told us himself. He told us exactly what will happen. He'll hunt down the person who enrages him. He'll hunt him down and kill him."

Stanley's footsteps tell me he's pacing slowly in

front of the jury box. I wish he'd turn on the damned lights.

"I must tell you," he continues, "I wondered about Mr. Hammond's mental state today. One has to wonder about a man who would utter those words in a court of law. But his mental state today isn't my concern. His mental state most days isn't my concern. It isn't yours either.

"Your concern is this moment." Stanley extends his pointer toward the bloody scene on TV.

"Frankly, I don't care if you think Mr. Hammond was insane on every other day of his life, today included. It doesn't matter."

He moves closer to the TV, taps his pointer on the glass. "Because this fragment of time is the only one that matters. And in this moment, Mr. Hammond was in control. At this moment, he was methodical. At this moment, he was purposeful."

Stanley bangs the tip of his pointer against the pool of Monteros's blood.

"We all know, ladies and gentlemen, that at this moment, William Francis Hammond was sane. Maybe—just maybe—it was a moment of temporary sanity."

CHAPTER 45

Beatrice's jury instructions were lengthy, but by the book. She glanced at Buck too many times when she defined *malice aforethought* and *premeditation,* but we couldn't do anything to stop her. Ugly looks from the judge don't normally form the basis of an appeal. In this case, though, we might give it a whirl.

Most members of the panel lost interest in the instructions, and their eyes glazed over about halfway through. I can't blame them; mine did too. Listening to the Commonwealth's Uniform Jury Instructions is like suffering through multiple bad sermons. Each one is more monotonous than the last, teeming with boilerplate directives and unqualified commands. The judge may as well read aloud from the phone book.

She's wrapping it up now, not a moment too soon.

It's almost seven o'clock. Most of the jurors slouch in their seats, their eyes half closed. Not the retired schoolteacher, though; her posture is perfect, her eyes alert.

"And that, Ladies and Gentlemen of the Jury, concludes my charge to you." Beatrice sets her glasses on the bench, folds her hands beside them.

The jurors look exhausted, but they rally when the judge tells them she's through. They shift in their seats, stretch their tight limbs. A few even rub their eyes, as if waking from a nap. Late as it is, they seem ready. Ready to get to work. Ready to take on *Commonwealth versus Hammond*. Ready to decide Buck's fate.

"At this point in time, ladies and gentlemen"—Beatrice covers her mouth, stifles a yawn—"it's my intention to dismiss you for the holiday."

Harry shoots up as if fired from a cannon. "Dismiss them?"

"That's right, Mr. Madigan. Dismiss them."

I'm up too. "But they're sequestered."

"Not tonight, they're not, Ms. Nickerson. It's late. And it's Christmas Eve."

"Christmas Eve?" Harry's at the bench in a flash. Stanley follows on Harry's heels, as if he thinks Beatrice might need assistance.

Harry points backward to our table, to Buck, and almost smacks Stanley's head in the process. "You think it's Christmas Eve for Mr. Hammond, Judge? You want him to go back to his cell and decorate a tree? Let visions of sugarplums dance in his head? His life is on the line here."

The judge doesn't care to look at Buck now. She doesn't acknowledge Harry's pointing at him. Her eyes don't move. She stares through Harry as if he's not there. "Spare us your poetry, Mr. Madigan. And your melodrama as well. The Commonwealth of Massachusetts doesn't impose the death penalty—not even in capital murder cases. No one's life is on the line here."

Beatrice shakes her head in the silence that follows her speech; she apparently finds it regrettable that death isn't an option.

For a split second, it seems no one in the courtroom breathes. Even Harry is speechless. He turns to me and blinks, momentarily unable to grasp what he just heard.

Beatrice faces the jury again. She's through with Harry. "We'll reconvene on Monday morning, December twenty-seventh, at nine o'clock."

"No. We won't." Harry's voice is low, controlled. I know that tone. This is war.

"Pardon me, Mr. Madigan?" Beatrice glowers at Harry, her gavel in hand.

"You heard me, Judge. We're not going to reconvene, because we're not going to unconvene."

"Unconvene?"

"You're not sending them home, Judge. Not until we have a verdict."

"Are you giving me an *order*, Mr. Madigan?"

"No. I'm not giving anybody an order." Harry turns to the jury, his voice still steady, restrained. "Judge Long gave the order. These jurors are sequestered until they reach a verdict. Quarantined with the evidence presented in this courtroom. Sheltered from the media blitz. That's been the standing order of this court since trial began."

Harry faces Beatrice again. "You can't change it now."

"I *can't?*"

"No. You can't." Harry's still addressing the panel, not Beatrice. "It's one more order Mr. Hammond relied upon. It's an order that guarantees him a trial by jury—this jury—not by the press. You can't take that away from him now. We won't let you."

"We?" Beatrice glares at the back of Harry's head.

The jurors look as if they might agree with Harry. One by one, they nod up at him, then check in with each other. More than a few look up at the judge, as if they'd like to be heard on the matter. Beatrice doesn't notice, though; she doesn't even look at them. Her eyes bore holes through Harry's back.

After a moment of paralysis, Beatrice straightens in her chair, still clutching her gavel. She sends a silent signal to one of her two court officers, a burly man with a red beard.

Big Red signals back—salutes, almost—then leaves his post beside the jury box and heads for the side door.

Harry and I both know where he's going. He's rounding up the troops, preparing for battle. Big Red has been involved in removing Harry from this courtroom before. It's not an easy task. If he and his partner need to do it this evening, and it looks as if they might, they'll need help.

Beatrice leans across her bench toward Harry and

takes a deep breath. "I'll instruct them to avoid the press, Counsel. They're perfectly capable of doing so. No TV. No radio. No newspapers. And no discussion of the case with anyone. Not family members. Not even each other, until they begin formal deliberations. This won't be the first jury to be so instructed. And it certainly won't be the last."

Harry turns to the packed gallery and lifts his arms toward the crowd as if he'll belt out a chorus or two as soon as someone strikes up the band. Simultaneously, TV camera lights focus on him and flashbulbs explode. He'll almost certainly be the top story on tonight's late news, the front-page photo on tomorrow morning's *Cape Cod Times*.

I can see the headline now: Defense Attorney Home for the Holidays—If Only in His Dreams.

"Avoid the press?" Harry laughs out loud. "How the hell are they supposed to do that? Spend the weekend in space, maybe?" His voice isn't restrained anymore.

Beatrice leans back in her chair, lips clamped, decision written on her face. The offer to instruct the jury was her final attempt at reasoning with Harry Madigan. She's had it. And everyone in the room, including Harry, knows that he's had it too.

"Once again, Mr. Madigan, you are in contempt of this court."

"You bet I am." Harry hustles across the courtroom, staring up at her. "This court is contemptible."

Beatrice pounds her gavel.

Harry keeps moving. When he reaches our table, he rests his hands on Buck's shoulders and faces the jury again. He's flushed, sweating. He's running out of time and he knows it.

"This man deserves your verdict before you leave this building, before you're bombarded with the opinions of those who *think* they know what happened here. No fair-minded person would say otherwise."

Harry steals a glance at Beatrice, in case she missed his drift.

She didn't. She fires eyeball missiles at him.

"You have a say in this," he tells the jurors.

Big Red is back. His reinforcements include Joey Kelsey, who looks as if he's been drafted for the front lines of the next world war. His cheat sheet apparently doesn't cover taking a lawyer into custody.

Big Red looks up at the bench, checks in with Beatrice, and she gives him the go-ahead.

They surround Harry—four court officers in all—but Harry keeps talking to the jury as if he doesn't notice.

"Don't let her railroad you. She doesn't get the final word. Tell her you want to stay, want to deliberate now, tonight. If she says no, we go straight to the Court of Appeals, Christmas Eve or not."

Two of the officers take Harry's arms and try to move him toward the door. He drops to his knees on the worn carpeting instead. It's pretty clear to all of us that *he* won't be going to the Court of Appeals tonight. Or anywhere else, for that matter.

I get to my feet. "Absolutely," I tell the jury. "We'll call in an appellate panel."

As if to confirm my promise, the Kydd emerges from the crowd and stands with me at the defense table. The jurors don't seem to notice him, though. Their eyes are glued to Harry and the struggling court officers. It's hard to move Harry when he's on his knees.

The retired schoolteacher turns to the man beside her, the restaurant owner, and whispers. He looks back at her and nods once, then again. Whatever it is she said, he agrees.

Big Red seems to be in charge of Operation Remove Harry; he's calling the shots. He slaps a handcuff on one of Harry's wrists but can't get hold of the other one. He orders Harry to stand.

Harry sits.

"Oh, for crying out loud," Big Red says.

A few jurors snicker.

"Enough!" Stanley's losing it. He backs away from the struggling guards, points at Harry. "This man is vile! Reprehensible! Get him out of here!"

All action stops, even the guards' efforts to restrain Harry, and all eyes move to Stanley. He's frozen in front of the jury box, still pointing at Harry.

The room is quiet until Harry starts laughing—howling, actually—and tosses his head toward his captors. "What the hell do you think they're *trying* to do, pal?"

"Your Honor!"

Stanley undoubtedly has been called many names in his lifetime, but "pal" apparently isn't among them.

The elderly schoolteacher twists around in her seat, whispers to the juror behind her. That juror, in turn, passes a message down the back row. The restaurant owner does the same in row one.

The guards have Harry in hand now—literally. Two grasp his shoulders while the other two hold him by the ankles. His wrists are cuffed behind his back. And he's still talking. "You're in charge," he tells the jurors. "Don't forget that."

This is one of the first things that impressed me about Harry Madigan. I noticed it years ago, before I knew anything else about him. When Harry gets carted off to jail, he goes out the courtroom door talking to the jury. Always.

With a good deal of effort, the court officers drag Harry, still talking, across the worn carpeting and through the side door. When it closes behind them, the room falls abruptly still, silent.

I lean toward the Kydd. "Follow them. See where they put him. Then get him the hell out."

The Kydd does a surprisingly good imitation of Big Red's salute, then heads for the door.

Our retired schoolteacher raises her hand, but Beatrice doesn't notice. The older woman clears her throat and gets to her feet. "Excuse me, Your Honor."

Beatrice looks startled.

"We've discussed it, you see."

"Discussed what?" Now Beatrice looks annoyed.

"We'd like to deliberate." She fingers her lapel, looks apologetic. "Now."

"Now?" Beatrice takes hold of her gavel again, as if she might use it on the elderly juror.

"Yes, Your Honor. No disrespect intended. We feel it's the right thing to do. It's what we all expected to do. And it's what Mr. Hammond expected of us. It was planned that way from the start, you see."

She gives the judge a slight bow, then sits again.

Beatrice turns away from the impudent juror and glares at me. She looks as if she's certain I orchestrated this. I'm flattered.

Big Red and Joey Kelsey return to the courtroom. The other two must have Harry under control. That means he's in a cell. And it's locked.

I pull my phone from my briefcase and place it in the center of the defense table, then drop into my chair and smile up at Beatrice.

She scowls at the phone, so I know she gets it. Either she allows these jurors to deliberate or I place a call to the Court of Appeals' emergency line. And the appellate panel won't like that. The judges on call won't appreciate being summoned on Christmas Eve. Far better that Beatrice work the holiday than the Big Boys.

"Oh, and Your Honor." Our schoolteacher is on her feet again.

Beatrice turns an angry face to her. "What now?"

"I just thought I should mention . . ." The older woman looks resolute, not a bit nervous. "We're in agreement on this. It's unanimous." She takes her seat once more.

Beatrice's face turns to stone. She signals Big Red again, and he strokes his beard. He tells the panel to stand and follow him, and they do. Just like that, they're gone. Deliberating. Beginning their draft of the final chapter.

Joey Kelsey looks relieved as he approaches our table to escort Buck Hammond back to the House of Correction. Compared to Prisoner Madigan, Prisoner

Hammond is a breeze. He surrenders to the handcuffs willingly, as he always does, then asks Joey Kelsey to give him a moment. Joey hesitates, then agrees.

Buck turns toward me. "Thank you. And thank Harry too." He smiles. "If you ever see him again."

I laugh. "Don't worry. We'll see him again. But don't thank us yet. It's too soon."

Joey gestures toward the door.

Buck leaves his seat, shakes his head. "It's not too soon," he says. "I mean it. No matter what happens. Thank you." He stares into the first row for a moment, at Patty, then allows Joey to lead him away.

Beatrice watches them exit, then looks from Stanley to me. "Well, Counsel, I trust you'll enjoy your evening. I'm going home."

"Home?" The word escapes before I realize I've thought it. Beatrice lives in Provincetown, a solid hour from here even without the snowstorm.

She leaves the bench, her footsteps decidedly heavy, and pauses at the chambers door. "That's right, Ms. Nickerson. Home. These jurors want to bring in their verdict on the holiday, they can damn well wait for me to get back."

CHAPTER 46

Santa Claus spends Christmas Eve—every Christmas Eve—in Chatham. He arrives at dusk, waving from the bow of the year's designated Coast Guard vessel, thigh-high oilskins protecting the legs of his cherry red suit. Coastguardsmen outline the masts of the chosen boat with twinkling white lights each year. The crew docks at the Fish Pier, where Santa disembarks and glad-hands his way through the wind-whipped, near-frozen assembly. He distributes candy canes as he makes his way through the crowd, ho-ho-ho-ing all the way.

On the street side of the pier, the Chatham Fire Chief waits in his official truck, heater running and red lights ablaze, to serve as Santa's surrogate chauffeur. The reindeer, we've always been told by town selectmen, are busy elsewhere. After all, they explain each year, some children don't live in Chatham. Someone has to deliver their toys.

Every year, Santa and the Fire Chief lead a caravan from the Fish Pier to the Main Street Elementary School, where the Cape Cod Carolers and the Chatham Band greet one and all with holiday music, home-baked cookies, and mulled cider. There, Santa sits ‑enthroned on the gymnasium stage, chatting leisurely with every good boy and girl in town. The naughty ones usually stop by for a few words as well.

When Luke was little, he worried about the rest of the world's children. Who visits them, he wondered, if Santa spends all of Christmas Eve—every Christmas Eve—with us? Helpers, I told him. Santa has thousands of helpers, and many of them look remarkably like him. The *real* Santa, I said, would just *rather* spend Christmas Eve in Chatham. That explanation made perfect sense to my son, for more years than he now cares to admit.

Luke and his friends still attend the Christmas Eve festivities each year. They stay until the last cookie is gone, then head out to a movie, an annual tradition of sorts. This year Maggie plans to join them. Luke actually invited her, she told me breathlessly this morning. When Luke got into the car, though, she acted as if the evening plans had all but slipped her mind. She's good, that Maggie.

She's not happy with me at the moment. She and Luke appeared in the courtroom's back row at five, expecting we'd all head to Chatham and the Fish Pier shortly thereafter. It didn't work out, of course. It's almost eight now. Santa and his entourage are well into the festivities at the elementary school. And the baked goods are almost certainly gone.

"Can we *please* get out of here?" Luke drapes one arm across his forehead, to show me how gravely he suffers, as he and Maggie approach the defense table.

My plan was to drive them to Chatham, then return to the courthouse to await the verdict or, more likely, the jurors' departure for their hotel rooms. That way I'd have the car. Luke and Maggie can hitch rides with any number of Luke's friends.

Inherent in my plan, though, was an expectation that Harry would sit here, at the defense table, while I was gone. It doesn't seem right to leave our table unmanned. Especially not with Stanley entrenched at his.

The Kydd returns to the courtroom grinning. I can't imagine what he finds funny. He crosses the front of the room, drops into the chair next to mine, and laughs. "He wants to stay."

"What?"

"Harry. He wants to stay."

"Stay where?"

"In lockup. He doesn't want us to get him out. Doesn't even want us to try."

Sometimes I think Harry's been ensconced in the underworld too long, needs a new set of friends, maybe.

"He says if this thing goes the wrong way, if Buck's convicted, the judge's bias will make a decent appealable issue. We'll argue ol' Beatrice had a conflict of

315

interest—a huge one—and she should have recused herself at the outset. With that argument in mind, he says, the longer he spends locked up, the better."

Sometimes I think Harry's pretty damn smart.

The Kydd laughs again. "He also says he's beat. He told me to get lost. Says he could use a few hours' sleep. And the county's accommodations are fine with him. There's no phone, it's quiet, and the cots are comfortable."

And sometimes I think Harry's certifiable.

"Can we *please* get out of here?" Luke repeats his plea, complete with arm drama.

"Go ahead," the Kydd says. "I'll stay."

"Are you sure?"

"Sure I'm sure. The Kydd taps the phone in his jacket pocket. "I'll call you if there's even a peep."

"Okay."

Luke and Maggie dash for the back door.

"I shouldn't be gone much more than an hour," I tell the Kydd as I zip up my parka. "I'll just drop them off."

"Take your time. I'm not going anywhere."

The gallery is all but empty as I head down the center aisle. Only one spectator remains: Patty Hammond. She traded her front-row seat for the back bench, where the lighting is dim. She looks concerned as I approach. Of course she is. One of Buck's lawyers is in jail. And the other one is leaving.

"I'll be back," I tell her.

She looks only slightly relieved.

"I'm taking Luke and Maggie to Chatham, to the elementary school."

Her face changes, collapses a little. Relief turns into a different emotion. Pain, maybe. Physical pain.

She stares into her lap for a moment, then looks back up at me, her eyes moist.

Physical pain it is. Billy should be at the elementary school tonight. No doubt he was there last year.

"Why don't you come with us?"

"To Chatham?" Patty looks as if our hometown might be somewhere on the West Coast.

"We'll be back in an hour. It'll probably take the jury that long to elect a foreperson."

She looks uncertain.

"Come on. Let's get some fresh air. You can keep me awake on the ride back."

"Okay," she says, reaching for her coat.

Waiting for a verdict in any case is nerve-racking. In a murder trial, it's an impossible combination of tedium and panic. The opportunity to do something useful with the time is irresistible. And I wasn't kidding. Patty can keep me awake on the ride back. I'm exhausted. It's been a long time since Opie and I visited Geraldine this morning.

The snow, it seems, will never end. Paths through the parking lot, apparently plowed out earlier in the day, are half filled again. Luke and Maggie wait by the locked Thunderbird, hoods up, their breath creating misty gray clouds amid the swirls of white snowflakes. Maggie dances by the back door to keep warm.

The old car starts without a problem, as it always does—a recurring miracle. In minutes, we're traveling the back roads toward Chatham, the defrost and the heat at full blast, the radio silent. Christmas carols don't feel quite right tonight, no matter what the calendar says. Again, there's no moon. Inky blackness envelops us.

Patty turns in the seat beside me to face Maggie. "How's your mom doing?"

That's a question I should have asked. Add guilt to the menu of emotions I'm carrying around tonight.

"She's okay." Maggie leans forward, between Patty and me, and the dashboard lights illuminate her face. "She says it's not too bad in there. She made a friend. One of the other ladies is real nice, Mom says. Her name is Cassie."

"That's good," Patty tells her. "She needs a friend. We all do."

"I want to go back tomorrow, see her on Christmas, if that's okay with you, Marty. The guard ladies say it's okay by them. And Luke says he'll drive me."

"Sounds like a plan." I'm fairly certain I'll be coming back myself, though, to pace the hallways and wait for Buck's verdict.

"I have a present for her. A necklace. I know she won't be allowed to wear it in there, but I want to show it to her anyhow."

Presents. Double the guilt. Most years, Luke's Christmas Eve schedule with his friends works out well for me and the presents problem. I shop until the last store locks its doors, then wrap till I drop. Not this year, though.

This year I have only a handful of packages for Luke. And half of those, the items that aren't strictly male, I'll cull out for Maggie. They're small things, for the most part, trinkets I purchased during early fall, when the weather was conducive to strolling through Chatham Center and I was unemployed. The good old days.

Lucky for me Luke's been saving for a pickup truck, a used one he spotted for sale at the local gas station. I'll write a check in the morning, one hefty enough to bump up the total in his passbook to almost match the asking price. I figured out the math during one of our breaks this morning. Working for a living is expensive.

I look into the rearview mirror, catch Luke's eye, and fire a silent reminder into the backseat. He nods back at me, then rolls his eyes to the Thunderbird's roof. Chill, he's telling me; he hasn't forgotten. His assignment, tonight, is to find out what Maggie's saving for. Let's hope it's not a condo on the Riviera.

"It's beautiful, Maggie." Patty holds a small white box in the dashboard lights, a glittering necklace dangling from its dark blue velvet lining.

"It is," I agree. And it is. "Where in the world did you get it?"

"Luke and I found it today. At Pedro's Pawn Shop. Have you ever been there?"

Patty and I both shake our heads.

"It's on Main Street in Hyannis," Luke volunteers. "You should check it out. Pedro cuts great deals."

Triple the guilt. My son cruises pawnshops while I'm working. Calls the owners by name. Cuts deals.

Patty snaps the box shut and returns it to Maggie. "Well, your mom is going to love it. What a nice present to have waiting when she comes home."

319

Silence. It's the coming home idea. It shuts us all down for a beat.

Patty recovers first. "He's pretty intense, isn't he, that prosecutor?"

I laugh. "J. Stanley Edgarton the Third? Intense? What gives you that idea?"

Patty laughs too. "Does he do all the murder cases?"

I shake my head. "Not yet. But eventually he will. He used to work in the New Bedford office; he was their lead homicide attorney. He's new to Barnstable County; he's only been here about a month."

She laughs again. "So for now he's specializing in Forest Beach, I guess."

I don't get it. "Forest Beach?"

"Buck and Sonia. Probably the only two Forest Beach people in history to be accused of murder."

I still don't get it. "And?"

"And the intense guy is prosecuting both of them. Seems like a specialty, doesn't it?" Patty smiles over at me.

I glance back at her, but I can't return the smile.

"I'm kidding," she says.

I know she's kidding. But my stomach isn't laughing. On some visceral level, her words unnerve me. "Why did you say that?"

My mind starts racing without a road map. My eyes alternate between Patty's face and the winding, snow-covered road.

"It was just a joke. Honest. I didn't mean anything by it." Patty looks at me as if I'm scaring her. I probably am. I'm scaring myself too.

I pull onto the shoulder, stop the Thunderbird under the ENTERING CHATHAM sign. INCORPORATED 1712, it says. A nearby streetlamp casts a glow on Patty's features. Luke and Maggie lean forward between us.

"Patty, listen to me. It's important."

Her eyes grow wide.

"Why did you say Stanley's prosecuting both of them?"

She shrugs. "Because he is."

"Sonia Baker?"

"Sure," she says. "I saw him there on Monday, shortly after"—she glances sideways at Maggie—"it all happened."

I have an enormous urge to grab her by the shoulders, but I resist. "You saw him where?"

"At the cottage."

"Whose cottage?"

Another glance at Maggie. "Sonia's."

"When?"

"Right around two. I know because the kindergarten school bus went by, the one Billy rode last year."

"Why were you at their cottage?"

Patty frowns and looks at Maggie again.

"Go ahead," Maggie says. "It's okay."

"I heard the commotion earlier, so I thought I'd check in. Make sure Sonia and Maggie were all right."

"Did you go inside?"

"No. I didn't dare. Sonia's car was gone and Howard's truck was in the driveway, so I figured he was in there alone. Lord knows I didn't want to deal with him."

Good instincts. "So how did you see Stanley?"

"I saw him leaving. I was glad. I thought Howard had been arrested, thought Sonia had finally turned him in. I had no idea about . . . you know."

"How did you know who he was?"

Patty shakes her head, looks at me as if she's worried about my well-being. "Stanley? I knew who he was. I attended pretrial motions, remember? On Friday?"

Of course she did.

The Thunderbird does a U-turn on its own and retraces its tire tracks in the snow. I flip open my phone, though I don't know why. I've no idea whom to call.

And then my stomach knots, and I do.

With almost no hassle, the hospital operator connects me to the nurses' station in the ICU. I will myself to ask for Alice Barrymore, not Annie Wilkes. The unit secretary tells me to hold, she'll put me through.

Annie Wilkes picks up at once and listens to only a few words of introduction. "I know who you are," she interrupts. "You're the sassy one."

Not how I'd hoped to present myself. I press on the accelerator.

"The one telling us all to shut up."

Oh, that. "Where are you, Nurse Barrymore? Are you in Judge Long's room?"

"Yes, I am, as a matter of fact. He's sitting up nicely, thank you, having a bit of broth. And there's no one here telling me to shut up, I might add."

"Listen, Ms. Barrymore, I need a favor."

"Oh, do you now?"

"Yes. Ask the judge, please, if he was trying to say the word *tassel* last night."

"Now *you* listen," she says, "you lawyers have got to leave this man alone—all of you."

"What?"

"The three of you in here carrying on late last night and then another one here before dawn. When is the judge supposed to rest?"

"Before dawn? Who was there before dawn?"

"An entirely new one. Short, balding fellow. Why don't you lawyers talk to each other?"

The knot in my stomach doubles. "Did he say what he wanted, the short balding fellow?"

"Certainly. The same thing you all want. He wanted to ask more questions. Marched into the room as if he were the chief of surgery, telling me he'd need a few moments alone with the judge."

Panic tightens my grip on the phone. "And?"

"And I told him he'd be spending more than a few moments alone with security if he didn't turn around and march right out again. The judge was sound asleep. I think that lawyer would have wakened him if I hadn't been there."

My gut tells me Annie Wilkes is wrong about that. Terribly wrong.

"Nurse Barrymore, please. One question. From you to the judge. It's important."

Silence on her end.

"Ask if he was trying to say the word *tassel* last night. Remember? We couldn't understand him. Harry made the Irish joke because it sounded like *'tis.*"

"Oh, for the love of Peter."

"Please."

Silence again. And then a rustling sound.

Annie Wilkes covers the mouthpiece, but I can still decipher her words. "Judge," she says, "it's the woman from last night, the younger one, the one telling us all to shut up. Damned if I understand it, but she wants to know if you were trying to tell them about a tassel of some sort . . ."

Annie's words trail off. "Oh, for the love of Peter," she says again, speaking to the receiver once more. "Listen, Miss, I enjoy a good word game as much as the next person . . ."

"What did he say?"

"Not a blessed thing. But his head's bobbing up and down like one of those little statues people put in the backs of their cars."

"Thank you, Annie. Thank you." I snap the phone shut. It takes a few seconds for me to wish I hadn't called her Annie.

I press harder on the accelerator, concentrate on negotiating the curves. My passengers remain silent, Luke and Maggie leaning so far forward they're almost in the front seat. Patty presses her hands against the dashboard as the Thunderbird tears through the black night.

When the pieces come together, I take a deep breath and open the phone again. Three more calls, I tell myself. One to the state dispatcher. One to the Barnstable Police Station. And one to the Kydd.

Howard Davis was a disgrace to the criminal justice system. J. Stanley Edgarton the Third said so. On a normal day, Stanley wouldn't have stood a chance against Davis. But on Monday, Davis was drinking himself into oblivion and Stanley knew it. He knew because I told him. I told him when I called from the hospital parking lot.

Judge Leon Long is despicable. Stanley said so. Nicky Patterson interrupted Stanley on Thursday morning. Not the other way around.

Harry Madigan is vile, reprehensible. Stanley said so just a few hours ago. And now Harry's asleep in a holding cell at the all-but-empty Barnstable County Superior Courthouse. Stanley's in the courthouse, too.

And Harry sleeps like a dead man.

CHAPTER 47

Swirling blue and white lights from a dozen police cruisers bathe the Superior Courthouse. The four granite pillars that frame the front entrance seem to sway as strobelike beams pulse over them. Uniforms pepper the courthouse steps and the hillside in front, most holding two-way radios close to their faces. Inside, the building is lit as if it's nine in the morning instead of nine at night.

The Thunderbird rolls silently down the snow-packed road, westbound, past the county complex and the courthouse. I pull over in the darkness on Historic Route 6A, under an ancient, leafless oak tree. There's no way I can get back into the county lot; the cops have blockades set up at both entrances. I'll have to go on foot from here.

Patty Hammond slides over to take the wheel. She'll keep Luke and Maggie in the car, she promises, won't bring them near the building until she's sure it's all clear. I motion for her to wait while I trudge through the snow to the trunk and retrieve the tire iron. Her eyes are wide in the side mirror as she pulls away.

I wave to Luke and Maggie, both still in the backseat, their faces pressed against the rear window, their breath making small side-by-side circles on its glass. When they're out of sight, I grab the Lady Smith from my jacket pocket, release the safety, and hurry across the street.

The cops have the north and east sides of the courthouse heavily covered because that's where the doors are. I approach from the west, avoiding the squad cars and the streetlamps, and run in the darkness of night up the steep hill to the courthouse. There, at the top of a grassy knoll on the west side of the building, is a window I can reach. I stop a few steps away from it, tuck the Lady Smith back into my pocket, and brace the tire iron with both hands.

With strength I don't ordinarily have, I hurl the heavy tool through the window and hear what I knew I would hear: the whoops and shrieks of the security system. I wonder, as I pull myself up on the outer sill and kick out more of the glass, if the alarm will unnerve Stanley, throw him off course somehow, make him slip just enough for Harry to react.

Inside, I find myself in a crowded storage area, a small room adjacent to Beatrice Nolan's makeshift courtroom. The air is stale, musty, and the room is lit only by the bulbs in the hallway. I retrieve the Lady Smith quickly, check all corners of the small room. No one's here.

No one's in the brightly lit corridor, either. I hurry next door, my Lady Smith leading the way, to check Beatrice's courtroom. Yet another uninhabited space. Our table—strewn with briefcases and legal pads—is abandoned.

So is Stanley's.

I hurry out to the hallway again, toward the stairway that leads down to the basement, to the holding cells. The uniform guarding the building's back door has it propped open and he's leaning against it, keeping an eye on the stairway as well. I force myself to wait until he's distracted. After what seems like an eternity, a fellow officer calls to him from the parking lot, the words indecipherable through the shrieks of the alarm. When the uniform walks outside, I head for the stairs.

He spots me, though, when I'm three steps down. "Stop right there," he orders. "Don't move."

I turn to face him, intending to explain, plead, threaten, if necessary. But I don't see him. I don't see anything. For a split second I can't think. Then I realize he can't see me either.

I take the remaining steps two at a time and lean against the wall at the bottom to catch my breath. And then I realize something else: the alarm has been silenced. The building is quiet. Quiet and dark. Someone flipped the main breaker. And I've little doubt who that someone is.

Down here, in the subterranean hallway that leads

to the four holding cells, it's not merely dark; it's black. Stanley wants it this way. I flash back to the closing argument he delivered just hours ago; he's at ease in the blackness.

A half dozen polka dots of white light erupt along the hallway, pressed against the outside cinder-block wall. The cops are already here, and they have pen-lights. The polka dots, and presumably the officers holding them, move steadily, silently, toward the cells. With all of my being, I will them to reach Harry before Stanley does. Harry's odds improve with each step they take. But if I can see their locations, their progress, then Stanley can too.

I press myself against the complete darkness of the inside wall and trail them, the Lady Smith pointed into the emptiness ahead. This wall is cinder block too, but it extends only half the length of the corridor; that's where the cells begin. The first three are empty. Harry is in the last one, at the very end. The Kydd said so.

A deep voice shatters the silence. The words, slow and deliberate, reverberate through a bullhorn. "Mr. Edgarton, this is Sergeant Briggs."

Sergeant Briggs has had quite a week.

"We can help you, Mr. Edgarton. Step into the hall-way. Drop any weapons you have on the floor in front of you. Kick them away, toward the staircase. Then put your hands behind your head. No one—I repeat, no one—will get hurt. We're here to help."

If nothing else, the Sergeant's announcement might wake Harry. Even with a knife, Stanley isn't likely to overpower Harry. Unless he's in his dead man's sleep.

My boot brushes against something as I reach the

bars of the first cell, just after Sergeant Briggs finishes his plea. I drop to my knees to find it. It's metal. A knife. Stanley already dropped one weapon, it seems. I wonder how many he has.

I hold my breath, run my fingers along both sides of the sharp blade. To hell with the rules of evidence collection. The blade is dry. Maybe it hasn't been used. Or maybe it's been wiped clean.

I drop it into my parka pocket and slip past the first two cells. They're empty, as promised. I inch halfway across the bars of the third cell, careful to stay a few steps behind the tiny dots of light, hoping that at least one of us will take Stanley by surprise.

We don't, though.

"Drop them, gentlemen." Stanley takes us by surprise instead. "Now."

There's a click, then a sudden shaft of bright light from Harry's cell.

First the penlights clatter to the concrete floor in front of me. Then the weapons—all of them. I almost drop my own. I swallow a gasp just before it escapes. The light from Harry's cell floods the hallway and illuminates the police officers' faces. There are a dozen of them; half weren't carrying lights. They stare into the cell—all of them—eyes wide, mouths open.

Sergeant Briggs, first in line, is the only one who moves. He lowers the bullhorn to his side, then squats and sets it quietly on the concrete floor. His eyes never leave the cell. He comes up with both hands in front of his chest, palms out. "Mr. Edgarton, what is it you want? Tell us. We'll do everything we can to meet your demands."

I can't see inside the cell. But the Sergeant's offer tells me the only two facts I need to know. Harry's alive. And that could change in a heartbeat.

Silence for a moment, then the scraping of metal against metal. It's a sound I recognize: a round being chambered in a semiautomatic weapon.

"A car." Stanley's voice sounds no different than it does on an ordinary day in the courtroom. "Unlock this door, and have the car outside, running."

Sergeant Briggs raises his hands again. "We'll have to get the key, Mr. Edgar—"

A hailstorm of bullets blows the padlock and chain off the fire exit at the end of the hallway. Stanley isn't willing to wait for the key, it seems. I jump backward and hit my head hard against the bars of the cell. The hailstorm moves upward, pelts the top of the door, then shatters the unlit exit sign above. The door swings halfway open, its top hinge decimated.

Cold wind carries snow into the corridor. Pieces of plaster and shards of the exit sign fall to the floor amid the flakes in a miniature avalanche. And then for a moment the wind's whistle is the only sound in the basement.

Sergeant Briggs turns to the officer beside him, the only woman in the lineup. "Go," he says. "Get a car. Radio when it's outside this door."

She takes off, almost slipping on the debris underfoot.

"Make sure it's an unmarked car," Stanley calls after her. "And no wires, either. No tricks. I'll know."

I know something too. Stanley emptied the chamber. And he didn't do it smoothly. He's used to knives, not guns. He can't fire again until he pulls the slide and resets. The process takes about thirty seconds. Not a lot of time, but it'll have to do.

I step out from the bars into the center of the hallway, both arms outstretched, the Lady Smith aimed into the cell at Stanley's eye level. Harry is on his knees, bent down toward the floor, hands clasped behind his head. Stanley holds a 9mm Stallard Arms semiautomatic handgun against Harry's left temple. A low-voltage work light sits on top of the disheveled cot, its beam aimed directly at Harry's head. For once, it seems Stanley wants to see what he's doing.

He doesn't see me, though. He's still facing the exit, keeping the line of cops in his peripheral vision. He presses his weapon harder against Harry's temple and lets out one of his hiccup-laughs. Then he lifts the handgun up to pull the slide. My hesitation is almost nonexistent. Almost.

In a millisecond I make the decision to lower the Lady Smith before I fire. Stanley howls, topples forward, and his handgun hits the floor just before he does. Police officers storm the cell. Harry drops to the floor and reaches out for Stanley's weapon. Stanley gropes for it too. And the cops, I realize, can't get there in time.

I raise the Lady Smith again. Harry's fingertips brush the handgun's barrel, push it slightly in the wrong direction, toward Stanley. Stanley's fingers reach the butt of the gun and—without hesitation—I aim at his head. But Harry lunges forward, into my line of fire.

Harry smacks the semiautomatic across the cell and

it clatters against the iron bars, out of Stanley's reach. One of the cops dives to retrieve it while the others surround Stanley and cuff him. He wails again and writhes like a wounded animal as they shackle his ankles. Instantly, it seems, an ambulance pulls up outside the bullet-riddled fire exit, and a team of paramedics rushes through the half-hinged door.

Harry gets to his knees again and stares as the cops disable their prisoner, then turns his ruddy, astonished face toward me.

Only then do I lower my gun.

I start toward Harry, but too many cops are in front of me. I can't get there. My knees give out. I fall against the wall and slide down the cinder blocks to sit on the concrete floor amid the rubble, still clutching the Lady Smith in both hands.

Geraldine appears out of nowhere, the Kydd right behind her. They stare at the ruins on the floor, then shift their gazes to the battle-scarred fire exit and the crowded cell. For a moment, it seems neither one of them can speak.

Geraldine recovers first, of course. She lights a cigarette, then shakes her blond head and looks down at me, blowing smoke toward Stanley. "You missed," she says.

I might strangle Geraldine.

The paramedics wheel the gurney out of the cell, Stanley strapped to it and still wailing, toward the open doorway. Harry emerges behind them. On hands and knees, he crosses the hallway and presses his face into my neck, breathing hard. Minutes pass, it seems, and neither one of us moves. Then Harry lifts his face up to mine. "Told you you'd end up on the cell block," he says.

I might strangle Harry, too.

Joey Kelsey appears in the hallway and walks toward us, looking like a man on his way to the electric chair. He stops dead in his tracks before he reaches us, though, dumbstruck as he surveys the battlefield. After a moment, he shakes his head as if to clear it. It seems to work. "I'm sorry to bother you . . ."

Joey addresses Geraldine as if the rest of us aren't here. It's pretty clear she's the only one he's sorry to bother.

"But those jurors . . ." Joey shifts from one foot to the other. "The ones who wouldn't leave?" He points at the ceiling, so Geraldine will remember where they are. "They're done now."

CHAPTER 48

Saturday, December 25

Joey Kelsey doesn't normally work in Judge Beatrice Nolan's courtroom. And that's a good thing for Joey. Beatrice doesn't have a positive impact on anyone's nervous system. But Joey's seems more fragile than most.

When it became clear that some unlucky bailiff would spend Christmas Eve tending our jury, though, Joey automatically got stuck. He's the new guy, the rookie. Big Red wasn't about to volunteer.

It's eight A.M. When Joey called Beatrice at midnight to tell her the jury was ready, she informed him that she was not. Snow or no snow, she said, Judge Beatrice Nolan doesn't drive in the dark. She'd leave her house at daybreak, she told him. Not a minute sooner.

Joey didn't seem to remember that Beatrice some-how managed to drive home in the dark, and I didn't mention it.

Beatrice's trip to the courthouse will take at least an hour, and it's been light only forty-five minutes or so. But Joey is watching the door to her chambers any-way, fingering his cheat sheet into tatters. After spend-ing the night trying to justify the delay to our jurors, he's a wreck. They're all exhausted, he reports. And they're mad as hell. Joey may never be fit for trial again.

Harry and I spent the wee hours in Geraldine's of-fice, the three of us drafting the tedious documents necessary to secure Sonia Baker's release. By four o'clock, the papers were ready and Geraldine left the complex with them to track down the required signa-tures. She was back by six, mission accomplished, whereupon Harry and I hand-delivered Sonia Baker's freedom to the Barnstable County House of Correc-tion.

The jail has its own formal exit rituals and paper-work, of course, but Sonia Baker should be out soon. And in a rare accommodating gesture—explainable, perhaps, by the spirit of the season—one of the ma-trons offered to bring her to our courtroom when she's ready. Maggie is twisted around in her front-row seat between Patty Hammond and Luke, watching the back door with all the anticipation of a child on Christmas morning. Which, of course, she is.

The Kydd went home as soon as he heard about Beatrice's aversion to night driving. He's back now, though, looking thoroughly refreshed. It's obvious he's had a few hours' sleep and a hot shower. I feel a twinge of envy. He grins at Harry and me, then slips into the aisle seat of the front bench, next to Patty.

Reporters and photographers roam the courtroom in search of a scoop. Most of them were hanging around the hallways waiting for the verdict when the police evacuated the building. For the moment, at least, Buck Hammond's fate is not their chief concern. They want to know what happened in the Superior Court holding cells.

The cops won't let them anywhere near the scene, of course. The elevator is shut down, and the staircase leading to the basement is roped off and guarded. But they all heard the gunfire from the parking lot and they all saw the ambulance leave the county complex. They also see that Harry and I are disheveled, to put it mildly. And, with the reading of the verdict imminent, more and more of them are questioning the whereabouts of J. Stanley Edgarton the Third.

The steady rumble from the gallery rises a notch when Geraldine Schilling arrives. The reporters pelt her with questions about Stanley. Has he been taken ill? Called to another crime scene? Found to have a conflict?

If Geraldine were inclined to answer, she could say "all of the above." She's not, though. She ignores them with a thoroughness honed over almost two decades. They may as well hurl their questions at the walls.

Geraldine crosses the front of the courtroom and pauses at our table to scowl. More than ten years I've known Geraldine Schilling. She's never looked worse. "You're a lousy shot," she says.

"How can you say that? My shot took him down. I hit him."

"In the *thigh*," she fires back.

"That's where I wanted to hit him."

She rolls her green eyes at me.

"Geraldine, I wasn't trying to kill the man."

Another eye roll.

I turn to Harry. "She thinks I was trying to kill him."

Harry nods knowingly. "Would've been better that way," he says. "Now he'll probably enter an insanity plea."

Geraldine scowls again and starts toward her table. She stops for a moment, though, and turns back to me. "Oh, and Martha, good of you to drop by the other night. We should get together more often."

It wasn't the other night. It was yesterday morning—early. Better left unsaid.

Harry watches her leave, then arches his eyebrows at me. "Drop by? You dropped by?"

"Please," I beg, "don't ask."

The courtroom grows louder still when two prison guards arrive with Buck Hammond in tow. He waits patiently while one of them unlocks his cuffs and shackles, then sends a signal to Patty and settles into the chair between Harry and me. He eyes Harry with obvious concern. "You okay?" Buck asks.

"Me?" Harry turns toward him. "Of course I'm okay. You're the one we're worried about."

"Did you have to stay in jail very long?"

"No," Harry says. "Marty shot the place up and got me out."

Buck laughs.

The noise in the courtroom subsides when the chambers door opens and Judge Beatrice Nolan emerges. She climbs to the bench, her expression on this Christmas morning even more dour than usual. Joey speed-reads through his litany. He wants to get this over with.

Beatrice pauses before taking her seat and stares down at Geraldine. "Attorney Schilling," she says, "you're here for the Commonwealth?"

Geraldine stands. "That's right, Your Honor."

"And Mr. Edgarton," the judge asks, settling into her leather chair, "where might he be?"

Geraldine gazes over at our table as she searches for words. Harry leans forward and smiles at her. She frowns back. "Mr. Edgarton is indisposed at the moment, Your Honor."

"Yes," the judge replies idly, erect in her chair. "Aren't we all?"

With that, Beatrice nods at Joey and he scrambles through the side door as if the room is on fire. He returns moments later with the beleaguered jurors in a single line behind him, every one of them scrutinizing the courtroom floor.

In my peripheral vision, I spot Geraldine casting a satisfied glance over her shoulder at the press. My knees go weak. Popular wisdom among criminal law practitioners holds that jurors who've acquitted look the defendant in the eye when they return to the courtroom with their verdict. Those who've convicted don't. If that theory proves true, then Buck Hammond is headed for Walpole.

But I don't buy that particular tenet of popular wisdom. Murder trials are gut-wrenching. Deliberations are worse. Jurors returning with a verdict in a murder case are exhausted. Most of them don't look at anyone.

The jurors take their seats and everyone else does too. Everyone, that is, except Harry, Buck Hammond, and me. We stand side by side at our table, Buck in the middle, facing the panel. We're close enough to each other that I can feel Buck taking slow, deliberate breaths. This is a tense moment, but he's been through worse. Even so, I'm glad when Harry rests a steady hand on Buck's shoulder.

Judge Nolan swivels in her chair to face the jurors. "Ladies and Gentlemen of the Jury," she says, glaring at them. "Have you reached a verdict?"

Juror number five, the fifty-something restaurant owner, stands in the front row, and I feel a small wave of disappointment. He wasn't high on my list of candidates for foreman. He's seated next to the retired schoolteacher and she's had his ear throughout this trial. I haven't been able to read her—or him, for that matter—at all. She looks up at him now and nods.

"We have, Your Honor." The foreman's voice is a deep baritone; his eyes are fixed on the judge.

Judge Nolan turns to Joey Kelsey. He stares back at her, blank. Beatrice sighs and grimaces—you can't get good help these days, her face says—then tosses her head at the foreman. He's waiting, verdict slip in hand.

Joey freezes for a moment, then recovers and scurries to the jury box. He fetches the verdict slip like a golden retriever and almost runs to the bench with it. Judge Nolan reads, expressionless, then returns the slip to Joey, who ferries it back across the courtroom to the foreman.

The judge doesn't glance in our direction. Her eyes rest on Geraldine's for the briefest of moments before she turns to the panel again. If she telegraphed a message, I missed it.

Geraldine's eyes linger on Judge Nolan a while longer. She missed the message too, it seems, if there was one.

"Mr. Foreman, what say you?"

Trials, by nature, are unpredictable. But certain aspects of them are not. The delivery of the verdict, for instance, follows a pattern, especially in murder cases. The juror announcing the fate of the accused always stares at the verdict slip and reads. And it's not because he forgets what's written there.

The verdict slip is a crutch. It allows the foreperson to avoid eye contact with the defendant. In a courtroom pregnant with anxiety, even the most stalwart juror needs a mechanism to control his emotions, his voice. The verdict slip provides it.

But our middle-aged restaurateur defies the pattern. He folds the verdict slip in half and palms it, lowering his hands to his sides. He shifts in the jury box and faces our table, looking neither at me nor at Harry. He stares at Buck.

Most trial lawyers can predict the verdict from the foreperson's body language. But for me, at least, this is a first. I've never seen a foreperson look directly at the defendant. I don't know what it means.

"We, the jury . . . ," the foreman begins.

My mouth goes desperately dry.

". . . in the matter of *Commonwealth versus Hammond* . . ."

Buck isn't breathing anymore. I guess I'm not either.

". . . on the charge of murder in the first degree of one Hector Monteros . . ."

The foreman pauses to swallow, and it takes a moment for me to realize he's choked up. This could mean just about anything. Maybe he's sorry for what happened to little Billy Hammond, for all that Patty and Buck have suffered. But maybe he's sorry about the verdict, about the eternal turmoil that lies ahead for Buck at Walpole.

". . . do find this defendant, William Francis Hammond . . ."

Buck takes a deep breath and holds it. He grasps the edge of our table with both hands and leans into it until his fingertips turn white. His eyes remain on the foreman, though. The two men seem unable to move, frozen in this moment of judgment.

Beatrice Nolan leans back, gavel in hand. This is her courtroom, after all. Face-to-face dialogue doesn't often happen here. She apparently finds it unsettling. She's poised to put a stop to it.

Finally, the foreman blinks and shakes his head. "Mr. Hammond," he says.

This is unheard of. No foreperson addresses the defendant by name.

"The truth is . . ."

The foreman's voice breaks and Buck looks sympathetic. He nods repeatedly, encouraging the weary restaurant owner to continue. I can take it, Buck's eyes say. Whatever it is you have to tell me, I can take it.

He's right, of course. He's taken worse.

"We agree with Attorney Edgarton."

Eleven heads nod in the jury box.

"We're disappointed," the foreman continues, "that Mr. Edgarton isn't here. We wanted to tell him—face-to-face—that we agree with him."

I've practiced law for more than a decade, tried more than a hundred cases. I've lost before. More than once, the reading of a verdict made my eyes fill, left my vision blurry.

But not this time. This time my eyes are dry. And I'm going to be sick. I sink to my chair. I can't help it; my knees are about to quit again.

"What Mr. Edgarton said was true, Mr. Hammond."

I find it hard to believe that the foreman is still speaking directly to Buck.

"When you shot Hector Monteros, it was, in fact, a moment of temporary sanity."

A low rumble emanates from the crowd.

The foreman looks at his verdict slip for the first time. "We find that the defendant, William Buck Hammond, knew exactly what he was doing when he shot Hector Monteros. He was *not* insane then, and he's *not* insane now."

I tell myself to take deep breaths, to focus on the appeal. The appeal of a capital murder conviction is automatic. We'll farm it out. An experienced appellate attorney can argue ineffective assistance of counsel.

I've got ineffective assistance written all over me. I never even gave an opening statement, for God's sake.

The foreman straightens his shoulders and pauses again. His eyes don't budge from Buck's.

Without making a sound, the gray-haired schoolteacher gets to her feet in the front row. Then the young pharmacist rises behind her. So does the construction worker. And the juror next to him. And the one next to her. The rest of the panel stands too, then, in unison.

For a split second, I don't get it. I look up at Harry and Buck. Buck's face is unchanged. Harry's mouth is open, his expression a question mark; he's not sure what's happening either. But his hand starts thumping Buck's shoulder.

The foreman pauses to look at each of his fellow jurors, gratitude plain on his face. Their show of solidarity spurs him on. He turns back to Buck and takes a deep breath. "We also find Mr. Hammond . . ."

He shakes his head, his eyes again locked with Buck's.

No one breathes.

"Not guilty."

Silence.

CHAPTER 49

The stunned courtroom stands mute for a full ten seconds. And then Joey Kelsey begins to clap.

Beatrice bangs her gavel and Joey pauses, but now Harry and the Kydd are clapping too. Buck's prison escorts join in, and Joey watches them before staring back at Beatrice and resuming his applause. Then the whole room explodes. A spontaneous, thunderous standing ovation.

The Kydd takes Patty Hammond by the hand and leads her through the crowd to our table. Buck and Patty stand at arm's length for a beat, both seemingly unable to move in the enormity of the moment. They melt into each other, then, and the rest of the Hammonds rush forward and embrace them as one.

Luke and Maggie jump to their feet in the front

row, whooping out loud and pounding their palms together over their heads. Maggie twists around toward the back door, lets out a shriek, and pushes her way into the center aisle. "Mom!" she shouts, fighting against the tide of humanity moving against her. "Let me through. Please. It's my mom!"

The crowd actually parts down the middle to let Maggie pass, even the press. Sonia Baker stands just inside the back door, waiflike in street clothes undoubtedly borrowed from the Barnstable County House of Correction. Her eyes grow wide as she surveys the unruly mob in the courtroom, then fill as she spots Maggie hurtling toward her. She bends to embrace her daughter, but Maggie seems to have other plans.

Maggie allows her mother only the briefest of hugs, then pulls away and presents the small white box from Pedro's Pawn Shop. Sonia hesitates, so Maggie opens it for her and stands on tiptoes to clasp the glittering necklace at the back of her mother's neck.

It's Patty who begins the applause this time. Patty, then Buck, then the rest of us. The TV camera lights and flashbulbs shift to the back of the room. Sonia looks confused, embarrassed. Maggie takes a bow.

Harry appears at my side and I reach up to brush my fingertips over his left temple. A light blue bruise is taking shape there, the result of pressure from Stanley's Stallard Arms. All at once, I realize how close I came to losing Harry and I'm overwhelmed by the thought of it. Words fail me, though; hot tears slide down my cheeks instead.

Harry leans over and cups my face in his hands,

brushing my tears away with his thumbs. "Oh, no you don't," he says, pressing his forehead against mine. "You don't get to fall apart yet."

He's right, of course. We'll both fall apart later. When we can.

"Break it up, you two"—it's Geraldine—"or I'll have you taken into protective custody." She pauses at our table on her way out of the courtroom and takes me aside. "Stanley confessed," she says, "before going into surgery."

"Confessed to what?"

"All of it: Howard Davis, Judge Long." She tilts her head back toward Harry. "Him."

I nod, but say nothing, and she leans closer. "He told me he didn't have a choice. He'd been sworn to uphold and protect the system. And they were destroying it, one case at a time. He said he knew I'd understand."

"Sounds like a vigilante, Geraldine. Better put his case on a fast track."

She frowns and tosses her head at the Kydd. "Tell the Georgia Peach I'll have Dominic Patterson out by noon."

"He'll be glad to hear it."

She starts to leave, but apparently thinks better of it and turns back to me, her green eyes intense. "Next time you shoot someone, Martha, for Christ's sake do it right."

Once again, I'm speechless.

Geraldine heads for the side door and as I watch her exit, I realize the bench is empty. I catch Joey Kelsey's eye. "Where's the judge?"

"Gone," he says, smiling.

"Did she call a recess?"

"Nope. She just got up and left." Joey's smile expands, as if the judge's departure is exactly what he wanted for Christmas.

So Beatrice Nolan just got up and left. She didn't bother to tell us we're adjourned, didn't bother to tell Buck Hammond he's free to go. She didn't thank the jurors for their dedicated service. She didn't even wish them a happy holiday.

We did.

If by moral insanity it be understood only a disordered or perverted state of the affections or moral powers of the mind, it cannot be too soon discarded as affording any shield from punishment for crime; if it can be truly said that one who indulges in violent emotions, such as remorse, anger, shame, grief, and the like, is afflicted with homicidal insanity, it will be difficult, yes, impossible, to say where sanity ends, and insanity begins . . .

We say to you, as the result of our reflections on this branch of the subject, that if the prisoner was actuated by an irresistible inclination to kill, and was utterly unable to control his will or subjugate his intellect . . . he is entitled to an acquittal.

Mr. Justice Paxson
88 PA 291
January 20, 1879

SCRIBNER
PROUDLY PRESENTS

MAXIMUM SECURITY

Rose Connors

Now available in hardcover
from Scribner

Turn the page for a preview of
Maximum Security. . . .

ONE

▥

Thursday, October 12

An old friend. That's what Harry called her when he broached the subject just moments ago. Would I agree to represent an old friend of his who's in a bit of a jam?

"Of course I would," I told him. "But why don't you represent your old friend yourself?"

I knew his answer before I finished my question.

Harry Madigan is uncommonly good at many things, but he'd die of starvation if he had to earn his living playing poker.

He leans forward in his chair by my desk and laughs, knowing I know. "All right," he says, raising his hands in mock surrender. "She's an old girlfriend. And I don't think I should represent her. Not in this case."

"You want me to represent your girlfriend?" I laugh too, fully expecting him to deliver a punch line.

He frowns. "As you happen to know," he says, "she's not my girlfriend. But she was twenty-five years ago. We were law school classmates."

He must be joking. Just in case, though, I turn to the bookshelf behind my desk and tap a pen against the red spine of the Massachusetts Lawyers Directory. "What? Is there a sudden shortage of attorneys in the Commonwealth, Harry?"

"Come on, Marty, we're not sixteen. We both have pasts. And we've both had other relationships."

I take off my frameless glasses, drop them on top of a file on the cluttered desk, then rub my tired eyes and roll them at him.

Harry gets to his feet, feigns deep concentration, and starts pacing around my small office. He's six feet tall and built like a linebacker; the room always seems crowded when he stands. His shoulders are broad, his arms muscular, and his hands enormous. His charcoal hair, thick, unruly, and always too long, has gone a paler gray at the temples. Harry can pace all night as far as I'm concerned; I'll watch.

He stops abruptly, glances sideways at me, and taps an index finger against his forehead, as if coaxing a memory to the surface. "Speaking of relationships," he says, "if I recall correctly, Attorney Nickerson, you even managed to squeeze in a husband."

"True. And if Ralph ever needs a lawyer, I'll be sure to send him straight to you."

My ex-husband is Ralph Ellis, a nationally acclaimed forensic psychiatrist. He tends to show up in high-profile trials and Harry has seen him many times on TV. The two have never actually met, though. And it's no secret between Harry and me that he's not looking forward to the occasion.

He walks to the darkened window, leans against the sill and sighs. "Please," he says. "She needs a good lawyer. She's in trouble."

"You're serious."

He bites his lower lip and nods. "I am."

"What's her name?"

"Louisa Rawlings."

Of course it is. Harry's old girlfriend wouldn't be a

Mary or a Peggy or a Sally. She'd be a Louisa. I'm sorry I asked.

"Rawlings is her married name," he adds. "She was Coleman when I knew her."

"How long were you and Louisa Coleman an item?"

"Through law school," he says.

"All of it?"

"Yep."

"What happened?"

Harry leaves the windowsill, drops back into the chair by my desk and falls quiet, drumming his fingers on the armrests. It's pretty clear that whatever happened wasn't his idea. "The public defender thing," he says at last. "It didn't appeal to her."

"She didn't want you doing the dirty work of a public defender?"

He laughs. "It wasn't the dirty work that bothered her. It was the puny paycheck."

"But didn't she know all along that you planned to become a public defender?" It's always seemed obvious to me that Harry was born with that plan.

"She did," he says. "But I think she assumed I'd change my mind—come to my senses—by the time we finished law school." He shrugs. "I didn't."

"So she dumped you and married Mr. Rawlings?"

"Nope. She dumped me and married Mr. Powers. She dumped *him* and married Mr. Rawlings."

"Oh."

"And I'm the one who introduced her to Glen Powers." Harry looks away from me and winces, the memory apparently still chafing a sore spot. "He was a friend of mine; graduated a class ahead of Louisa and me."

"But your friend had the good sense to pursue a more lucrative career?"

"Bingo," Harry says. "Trusts and estates."

"And Mr. Rawlings?"

"Cha-ching. Corporate mergers and acquisitions."

I try to stifle my laughter, but I can't. "All lawyers? All three of you?"

"What do you mean—all three of us? We weren't a men's club, for God's sake. She married the two of them. She wouldn't marry me."

I'm silent for a few seconds, while the implication of his words sinks in. "You asked."

Harry looks down at his hands and then back at me. "Yeah," he says, "I did."

I take the red directory from the bookcase and push it across the desk to him.

"Come on, Marty. That was another lifetime. And she needs help."

"She's a lawyer, Harry. Surely someone from her own firm can hook her up with whatever help she needs."

"She's never practiced."

"Never practiced? The woman graduated from Yale Law School and she's never practiced? What does she do?"

He looks up at the ceiling, as if searching for words. "She marries well," he says.

Well of course she does. Why didn't I think of that?

"Harry, I'm sorry your old flame is in trouble. Really I am. But I've been in court all day. It's late and I'm starving. Are we going to dinner?"

He jumps up from his chair, hustles to the back of mine, and makes a production of holding my suit coat for me. "Mais oui, Madame." His French accent is tortured, reminiscent of Pepé Le Pew. "Name zee establishment of your choice."

I look over my shoulder and roll my eyes at him again. We both know we'll end up at Vinnie's. The booths are private, the lights are dim, and the food's the best Italian on Cape Cod. Most important, though, the portions are big enough to keep even Harry happy.

"I'll tell you more about it while we eat," he says, pausing to massage my neck and shoulders through my jacket. I close my eyes and lean backward into his big hands. I'd have fallen for Harry even if he weren't a compulsive masseur. But I'll never tell him that.

"Why is this your project, Harry? You just said she marries well. Let her husband find her a good lawyer."

"He can't."

"Of course he can. If he's with a firm large enough to do mergers and acquisitions, he's well connected."

Harry turns me around to face him, still holding on to my shoulders. "Herb Rawlings is dead, Marty. He's somewhere on the ocean floor."

"Oh."

"And Louisa's in a bit of a jam."

TWO

"A jam? The woman's husband sleeps with the fishes, his life insurance company smells a rat, the police think she's involved somehow, and you tell me she's in a bit of a *jam?*"

Harry leans back on his side of the booth, drains his glass of Chianti, and pours another. "Poor word choice?" he asks. "A pickle? Would that be better?"

"Harry, this is serious."

He sets the glass down, leans across the table, and holds my eyes with his. "I know it is, Marty. If it weren't, I wouldn't ask you to get involved."

"How did *you* get involved? Where did this thing come from?"

"Louisa called the office this morning," he says. "The cops want her to come in for questioning. She told them she'll cooperate, but not without a lawyer. They agreed to give her a few days to find one."

"She's not in custody?"

"Nope." Harry's been attacking his chicken Parmesan as if the restaurant manager allotted him only five minutes to finish. "Right now they've got nothing on her," he says. "Just a mountain of suspicion."

"And the goal is to keep it that way."

He points his fork at me. "Bingo."

One of the many things I love about eating at Vinnie's with Harry is that I can order a whole cheese pizza—undercooked, the cheese barely melted, the way I like it—knowing not a morsel will go to waste. I slide a steaming slice onto my plate from the platter at the end of our table and wait until he looks up from his food. "Have you two been in touch all this time?"

Harry shakes his head. "I hear about Louisa every once in a while from mutual friends. But I haven't spoken to her in twenty-five years. Until this morning."

"How did she find you?"

He laughs and puts his fork down, and I brace myself. When Harry stops eating to tell me something, it's almost always a bombshell. He plants an elbow on the table, chin on his hand. "You're not going to believe this," he says, "but she lives in Chatham."

"Your ex-fiancée lives in Chatham?"

"She's not my ex-fiancée."

"No thanks to you."

Harry sighs and closes his eyes. I know what he's doing; he's counting to ten. When he's done, he retrieves his fork and digs in again. "She and her husband have only lived here about a month. They've been vacationing on the Cape each summer, though, since they got married twenty years ago."

He pauses, his knife and fork still for a moment, a thought apparently dawning. "She didn't keep Glen Powers around for long," he says. "I remember talking with him in my office shortly after their divorce. He said Louisa had been up front with him about it. Herb Rawlings could offer her more, she'd told Glen. A bigger house, a more lavish lifestyle, and an even more secure future. Glen was appalled that Louisa would actually admit those were her reasons."

Harry looks up from his empty fork and arches his bushy eyebrows at me. "He didn't get a hell of a lot of sympathy from me."

I return Harry's stare and, I hope, his sentiment.

He laughs and goes back to his meal. "Herb Rawlings was older than Louisa, by fifteen years or so. When he retired from New York City practice, they sold their house in Greenwich and bought a place on Pleasant Bay. Louisa noticed our sign the day they moved in."

"So she knew you were here a month ago, but you didn't know she was in town until this morning?"

He shrugs and mops up his red sauce with the last of the garlic bread. "She changed her name," he says. "I didn't."

"But Chatham isn't exactly a sprawling metropolis. You never ran into her around town?"

He shakes his head again. "I don't think Louisa and I travel in the same circles."

"Seems like that's about to change."

He takes a slice of pizza from the platter and drops it onto his otherwise clean plate, then leans back against the booth and sighs. "Marty, Louisa is someone I once cared about—a lot. She's in trouble. And she's scared; I heard it in her voice. When I told her I'd have to refer her case to another lawyer, she begged me to find the best one I could. That's why I came to you."

Time to roll my eyes again.

Harry reaches across the table with the wine bottle and tops off my glass. "Tell me the truth," he says, his hazel eyes searching mine. "Does it really bother you that I loved someone twenty-five years ago?"

I lift my glass and shake my head. "Of course not. I'm glad you loved someone twenty-five years ago. Louisa Coleman in the past doesn't trouble me at all. I'm just not sure how I feel about Louisa Rawlings in the present."

Harry pushes the dishes aside, leans across the table, and takes my hands in his. "You're my present," he says, his eyes still locked with mine. "You're my present and my future. If you have any doubt about that, tell me now, and we'll drop this whole damned thing. I'll never mention Louisa Coleman Powers Rawlings again."

He laughs when he recites all the names, but we both know his question is serious. And he wants a real answer. Knowing I need to give him one, I lean back against the booth and sip my Chianti. He leans back with his glass, too, swirls his wine around a few times, and waits.

Harry and I were cautious when we began spending time together. I bore the scars of a failed marriage and the hard-learned lessons of a few relationships that either went south or went nowhere at all. Harry's heart, too, had been wounded more than once. And both of us knew from the start, I think, that what we had found together was worth protecting.

In the early days, unwilling to acknowledge our feelings too soon, we manufactured reasons to touch each other. When we walked on the beach, Harry always wrapped his sweatshirt around my shoulders and pulled me close, as if I might otherwise get swept away by the ocean wind. We slow-danced a lot, sometimes without music. And then we progressed. We kissed through our dances.

Last winter, the night after Christmas, my son Luke went to Boston to spend a few days with his father, and I went to Harry's place for dinner. Harry and I were exhausted, having just finished a particularly difficult murder trial, and after we ate we curled up on the couch to watch *The Big Chill* on video. We argued, later, about who fell asleep first, but we agreed that neither one of us lasted long enough to see Glenn Close give her husband away.

When I awoke, the first hint of a gray dawn semilit the windows of Harry's second-floor apartment and large snowflakes drifted down in slow motion outside. The TV screen was black and the logs in the fireplace had burned to embers. I was as warm as I'd ever been, though, tucked between Harry and the soft cushions of the couch, my head nestled in the crook of his shoulder. His arms enclosed me, one hand cradling my hip, the other resting on my waist.

Without thinking, I reached up and ran my fingertips along his jawline and down his neck. I leaned over him, spread the open collar of his flannel shirt, and undid a few more buttons so I could breathe in his scent and press my hand and face against the warmth of his broad chest. He tightened his grip on me then and when I looked up, his eyes were open.

"I'm sorry," I whispered, "I didn't mean to wake you."

Harry fished my hand out from under his shirt, brought it to his mouth, and kissed each finger before he looked at me. "Yes, you did," he said.

His answer caught me off guard. I propped myself up on one elbow so I could see into his eyes. And in that moment I knew one thing for sure. He was right.

Harry introduced me to his brand of passion then, a passion so tender it melted my heart. I realized, that morning, what it takes to open up again, after love gone wrong has done its damage and left its wreckage behind. It takes a tender passion. And a heart willing to break one more time.

Harry covers my hand with one of his when I set my wineglass down. He reaches across the table with the other, brushes the bangs from my eyes, and then cups the side of my face in his palm the way he always does now. "Well," he says, half-smiling in the candlelight, "any doubts about me?"

I shake my head against his warm hand. "None."

"You'll meet with Louisa?"

"Okay," I tell him. "I will."

"You know," he says, his expression thoughtful, "you might find that you like her."

I lean back against the booth again and retrieve my wineglass. "I'll meet with her, Harry. But don't push it."

Visit
❖ **Pocket Books** ❖
online at

www.SimonSays.com

Keep up on the latest new
releases from your favorite
authors, as well as author
appearances, news, chats,
special offers and more.